COURIER 13

COURIER 13

Pete Docherty

Copyright © 2010 by Pete Docherty.

ISBN: Softcover   978-1-4500-0722-1
          Ebook   978-1-4500-0723-8

All rights reserved. No part of this book may be reproduced or transmitted in any form or by any means, electronic or mechanical, including photocopying, recording, or by any information storage and retrieval system, without permission in writing from the copyright owner.

This is a work of fiction. Names, characters, places and incidents either are the product of the author's imagination or are used fictitiously, and any resemblance to any actual persons, living or dead, events, or locales is entirely coincidental.

This book was printed in the United States of America.

To order additional copies of this book, contact:
Xlibris Corporation
1-888-795-4274
www.Xlibris.com
Orders@Xlibris.com
71696

CONTENTS

Prologue	June, 1989 Beijing, China	7
Chapter One	April, 1989 JFK Airport, New York	12
Chapter Two	Cia Headquarters Langley, Virginia	17
Chapter Three	Cia Headquarters	20
Chapter Four	Cia Headquarters	27
Chapter Five	Cia Headquarters	33
Chapter Six	Cia Headquarters	37
Chapter Seven	Cia Headquarters	43
Chapter Eight	Cia Headquarters	45
Chapter Nine	Minneapolis, Minnesota	51
Chapter Ten	Washington, D.C.	56
Chapter Eleven	London, England	62
Chapter Twelve	Paris, France	65
Chapter Thirteen	JFK Airport, New York	68
Chapter Fourteen	Rio De Janeiro, Brazil	70
Chapter Fifteen	Rio De Janeiro, Brazil	77
Chapter Sixteen	Rio De Janeiro, Brazil	82
Chapter Seventeen	Rio De Janeiro, Brazil	86
Chapter Eighteen	JFK Airport, New York	98
Chapter Nineteen	Minneapolis, Minnesota	100
Chapter Twenty	JFK Airport, New York	103
Chapter Twenty-One	Cairo, Egypt	106
Chapter Twenty-Two	Cairo, Egypt	111
Chapter Twenty-Three	Cia Headquarters Langley, Virginia	124
Chapter Twenty-Four	Cairo, Egypt	131
Chapter Twenty-Five	Cairo, Egypt	136
Chapter Twenty-Six	Minneapolis, Minnesota	140
Chapter Twenty-Seven	Los Angeles, California	144
Chapter Twenty-Eight	Beijing, China	148
Chapter Twenty-Nine	Beijing, China	155

Chapter Thirty	British Crown Colony Of Hong Kong	159
Chapter Thirty-One	San Francisco, California	161
Chapter Thirty-Two	British Crown Colony Of Hong Kong	164
Chapter Thirty-Three	Minneapolis, Minnesota	169
Chapter Thirty-Four	San Francisco, California	172
Chapter Thirty-Five	Beijing, China	178
Chapter Thirty-Six	Beijing, China	190
Chapter Thirty-Seven	Beijing, China	196
Chapter Thirty-Eight	Beijing, China	202
Chapter Thirty-Nine	Beijing, China	204
Chapter Forty	San Francisco, California	216
Chapter Forty-One	Minneapolis, Minnesota	219

PROLOGUE

JUNE, 1989

BEIJING, CHINA

The excitement caused beads of sweat to roll down Wu Feng's face as he stood atop a make-shift platform in Tiananmen Square. A hot, searing sun added to his discomfort, but he hardly noticed as he shouted in a hoarse voice that hurt his aching throat and lungs.

Hundreds of young men and women had gathered around him, listening to his strident pleas for democracy and showing their support by brandishing their fists in the air. The youths carried no weapons and were not unruly, but their vociferous outpourings in response to their leader's diatribes gradually drew the attention of other visitors to the Square, developing quickly into an enormous crowd.

The young man interspersed his oratory with pro-democracy slogans. When he shouted: "Democracy for China; Freedom for the People", a petite and strikingly attractive young woman, slim with long black hair that reached all the way down her back, moved her arms in a 'come-on' way to urge the assembly to join him. She stood by Wu Feng's side, encouraging him and giving him inflammatory suggestions to communicate to the crowd.

When his voice tired, she would take up the chant to give him a brief respite. And when she spoke her powerful slogans, the crowd roared its approval by joining in. Her name was Xiao Shiying.

With the passage of each minute, the assembly grew even larger until soon there were more than 10,000 people in the huge square picking up and screaming Shiying's chants.

At the south end of the Square, the customary long line of Chinese waiting to enter the mausoleum where the preserved body of Mao Tse Tung lay in state, now measured almost a quarter-of-a-mile. Those in line watched intently as the crowd around the young firebrand swelled to almost 20,000 people, with that number rapidly increasing as students coming from the Avenue of Heavenly Peace and the South Gate poured into the Square.

Suddenly, the waiting line for the mausoleum disintegrated as scores then hundreds of people deserted and ran to join their brothers and sisters who were clamoring for the right to be free.

What had started as a simple action by a student to plead with his government to let the people of China have freedom, to have democracy, had caught fire. Now the crowd covered more than half of the Square.

In the beginning, Wu Feng was surrounded by more than thirty of his close friends, fellow students from Beijing University. As he spoke, he watched other students and workers, the middle aged and the elderly approach to hear his message more clearly. At first, small groups of fours and sixes drew close, now they were coming in droves.

There was no disagreement; everyone chanted their approval as defiant fists continued to punch the air and the roar swelled in a deafening cascade of dissension.

The assembly was illegal. No one was allowed to hold public meetings to discuss any subject let alone harangue the government and criticize its policies.

The police stood nearby and watched the gathering storm. They did not know how to silence or disperse so large a crowd. They had not been trained in such tactics because there had never been a need for them.

A policeman of higher rank ran to the nearby Peking Hotel, approached the reception desk and demanded a telephone. He spoke to his superiors requesting help and warning that the act of civil disobedience he had just witnessed would soon explode into an unmanageable situation if it were not squelched immediately.

Less than an hour after his call, a column of six tanks clanked its way along the Avenue of Heavenly Peace. The lead tank proceeded to the far corner of the Square than braked its right track to turn and face the crowd. The other tanks, each separated from the one in front by about a hundred feet, also turned towards the Square and pointed their cannons ominously at the crowd.

A few minutes later, a platoon of soldiers in ill-fitting uniforms appeared and filled the spaces between the tanks. They stood rigidly at attention, their rifles with fixed bayonets by their sides.

The commander of the lead tank appeared in the turret of his vehicle and used a bullhorn to speak to the gathering, but his words could not be heard above the din of the enormous crowd which continued to shout: "Democracy for China; Freedom for the People."

He disappeared inside the tank and a few moments later, the monster's cannon was raised to its ultimate height to fire harmlessly into the air and over the heads of the crowd. There was a blast that shook the Square, and flames and a plume of thick, white smoke emerged from the gun's nozzle as it recoiled. The volley was a blank and intended to shock the crowd and make them disperse.

There was pandemonium as the crowd rushed to escape from what they thought was an impending move by the tanks to crush the people. Many of the elderly fell and were trampled to death as the huge mass of humanity dashed in every direction to flee the anticipated massacre.

The hatch of the lead tank opened with a harsh, metallic noise and the commander reappeared again, bullhorn in hand. "Comrades, listen to me. No harm will come to you. Listen to me." But his amplified words still could not be heard above the noise of the people who were screaming as they rushed to the safety of side streets.

But not everyone ran. While the ranks thinned considerably, there were still more than several thousand people gathered around the young student openly defying the laws of China, pleading for democracy.

The tanks formed a single parallel line and moved towards those who had chosen to remain. As the massive machines reached the perimeter of the crowd, they stopped and once again the hatch of the lead tank swung open. This time, the commander emerged completely and stood on its roof.

He raised the bullhorn and denounced the students' attempts to create anarchy. "You are violating the law and I warn you that unless you leave peaceably and refrain from such stupidity, you will be arrested. Disperse now. Do you hear me?"

As he spoke, more soldiers were being transported from their barracks on the outskirts of the city and taking up positions all around the Square, blocking any escape routes.

Wu Feng was still standing on his platform. He raised his fist and shouted "Democracy for China. Freedom for the People." Shiying repeated it and soon the chants were taken up once more as the crowd of students joined in and raised the slogans to a crescendo.

More than 100 soldiers advanced into Tiananmen, the largest square in the world, capable of holding over a million people, and lined up side by side. They raised their rifles into the air and fired aimlessly as a warning.

The chants continued as the majority of the students retreated before the tanks and regrouped in front of the Great Hall of the People, facing the Square. They surmised that the tanks would not fire for fear of damaging the magnificent edifice where China's leaders hold top-level meetings and entertain visiting dignitaries from around the world.

The commander returned to his tank and slipped inside, slamming the hatch behind him. He ordered the others to follow him as he deliberately maneuvered his tank toward the Great Hall.

A hundred yards separated the tanks from those students still in the Square who then backed away to a place of safety on the steps of the Great Hall.

One young man remained. He stood his ground as the tanks continued to approach. He refused to leave, failing to heed the pleas of his fellow students as they shouted to him to join them on the steps.

A hundred feet . . . sixty feet . . . . thirty feet . . . . ten feet. The tanks moved inexorably forward. The young man glared at the lead tank, reflecting a defiance born of hatred and discontent; he showed no signs of retreating.

The students pleaded with him. "You'll be crushed under the treads. Come join us," they implored. But he ignored their cries.

The lead tank stopped only five feet from the student. There was silence for ten seconds before Shiying and seven other students ran toward the young man and pulled him away from the certain fate he faced if the tanks rolled forward. The young man had won. He had faced down the might of the Chinese army and shown them what determination in the cause of justice and freedom can make ordinary people do.

By now, the other soldiers had moved from the edges of the Square and advanced towards the students gathered around the steps of the Great Hall of the People.

The chants were revived, softly at first then growing in volume as the soldiers approached.

The crack of a rifle was heard and a student fell, bleeding profusely from a chest wound. Panic set in and the students quickly dispersed. Rocks and sticks were thrown at the soldiers while a barrage of rifle fire rent the air.

The students ran, seeking ways to escape the military, and many were gunned down as they fled in several directions.

The skirmish was over within minutes. Bodies lay grotesquely twisted on the steps at the base of the buildings' columns and just inside the huge doors of the Great Hall of the People.

Pools of blood spread quickly on the ground and began to drip down the steps, splashing on the boots of the soldiers as they surged forward in pursuit of the students.

There was panic and confusion as bullets pock-marked the buildings or were stopped by bodies that dropped as they were struck. Many of the students were able to escape by rolling over the soldiers whose volleys could not stop the fleeing mass. Now it was the crowd that was crushing the soldiers in their terrified attempts to get away.

Wu Feng and 36 of the students were caught and made to stay close together. They were guarded by a dozen soldiers who pointed their rifles at them to insure they would not try to escape.

"Where is Shiying?" Feng asked one of the students. "Did you see what happened to her?"

"There is no sign of her," the student replied. "She must have got away."

"I hope so," Feng replied. "We are finished here, but Shiying will help our struggle to continue."

An officer walked up to Wu Feng and stared into his eyes. He shouted a command to the soldiers who withdrew clubs from inside their tunics. He issued another command and the soldiers began to slam the thick instruments against the heads of the students until rivulets of blood streamed down their faces. As they fell, they were handcuffed and carried to nearby trucks that sped quickly away.

The students' heroic attempts to seek democracy had been quelled. The voices that roared for freedom were stilled.

Squads of cleaners were brought in to wash away the blood and clean up the debris while other workers hastily patched the bullet holes in the columns and repaired the damage to the Great Hall of the People.

Tomorrow, there would again be a long, snaking line of peasants outside Mao Tse Tung's Mausoleum. The Chinese would wait patiently for hours for a chance to glimpse briefly at the glass-encased corpse of the man who had introduced Communism to China.

CHAPTER ONE

APRIL, 1989

JFK AIRPORT, NEW YORK

No matter how many times Drew Cummins had gone overseas, he never got used to traveling across time zones without feeling tired and listless for a few days. His business took him across the world; in fact, travel was his business. One week he might be in Hong Kong, the next in London. Two weeks later, it could be Australia or South America or the Soviet Union.

Tall and slim with dark, wavy hair, he had a pleasant, amiable personality, one that enabled him to engage facilely in conversation with people. He had a handsome, open face that attracted women with little difficulty and a little black book replete with names and 'phone numbers of women in most of the major cities of the world.

Drew knew intimately the most popular metropolises around the globe and was acquainted with their best hotels and restaurants. He had accompanied countless tours and heard so many guides give lively commentaries that they had conferred on him a comprehensive knowledge of the lay-outs and histories of cities around the world as well as the details of their attractions and monuments.

He could talk at length on the Taj Mahal or the Tower of London; he could discourse on Lisbon's Alfama district, Rome's Trastevere or Prague's Old Town. He knew well the world's most famous museums including the Louvre in Paris, the Rijk in Amsterdam, the Prado in Madrid and the Hermitage in Leningrad.

But travel never failed to exact its toll. Every time he returned home from a foreign trip, he got that same out-of-sorts, fatigued feeling and was always lethargic for a couple of days.

Drew had heard many of his co-workers say they were seldom bothered by 'jet lag'. Some said that only occasionally did they suffer that dragged-out weariness. "Take a sleeping pill on the 'plane and another before you go to bed when you arrive home," they had said. 'That'll put you right."

I guess one never really gets used to it, he mused as he waited for his luggage at the Pan Am carousel. He spotted his garment bag, picked it up and threw the strap over his shoulder. He collected his other small, soft-sided case in his left hand and, with his briefcase in his right, strode toward the green channel of Customs.

He had filled out his declaration form on the 'plane and presented it to the Customs officer who carefully studied his list of purchases before asking: "Is this everything?"

"That's it, all 13 dollars and 50 cents of it," Drew replied. "I wasn't over there on vacation, it was business. I didn't have time to shop"

"My, you're a big spender, aren't you? I've seen you come through here before, haven't I?"

"Most likely. I come through Kennedy several times each year. I know I've seen you before, too."

"What kind of business are you in?"

"Sales incentives," Drew replied. "We create marketing programs for clients to motivate their distributors, dealers and salesmen. We take their winners on trips around the world or they may choose gifts from our merchandise catalog."

"Oh, yeah, we get a lot of your people coming through here. It must be a good business 'cuz there seem to be more and more of 'em every year. And you've nothing else to declare?"

"No, that's everything, just like I said."

As Drew spoke, his face wore a disarming smile that was noted by the Customs officer. "If you found me telling one lie, even a little one, you would put a flag against my name in the computer and that means each time I come through U.S. Customs, you'd examine every piece of my luggage and then do a strip search. Oh, no, I don't need that kind of hassling, particularly as I always have a connecting flight to catch."

The Customs officer almost grinned as he looked over the declaration form. "You're from Minneapolis, I see."

"Well, beautiful Minneapolis 'cuz that's what the Chamber of Commerce requires us to say," he said, with a beguiling smile on his face. "Which also means that I have another flight ahead of me."

"Wouldn't know if it's beautiful or not. I've never been to Minneapolis," the officer said as he put a code on the form and returned it to him. "But I have heard it's a beautiful city. OK, present that to the officer before exiting Customs, and welcome home."

Drew put his arm through the strap of his garment bag and hoisted it on to his shoulder, picked up his other bags and looked for a Northwest Airlines representative.

"Hi Drew," said a voice behind him. He turned to see a petite redhead with piercing blue eyes and dressed in an airline uniform. 'Good trip?' she asked as she looked at his bags to see if they were properly tagged to Minneapolis.

"Well, if it isn't Airport Annie," he said, a smile beaming across his face. 'It sure is nice to be welcomed back with those beautiful blue eyes of yours."

"You must have been to Ireland again 'cuz the blarney's coming through loud and clear."

"No, Annie, it was Paris and even those gorgeous French mam'selles don't look half as good as you. And none of them has red hair or blue eyes like yours."

"Yeah, yeah, yeah. Well, it looks like your bags are all set, so just put them on the carousel over there and they'll be sent over to the Northwest terminal and put on our flight 463 for Minneapolis."

Drew thanked her and headed for the exit door where he gave the seated Customs official his declaration form. The officer looked at the form to find which code had been written by the first officer, and noted that it carried the one indicating that no search was necessary.

"Okay, you're all set," he said as he motioned Drew to pass through.

There were almost three hours to kill before his connecting flight, so he headed for the World Club, Northwest's private airline lounge, of which he was a member. He looked forward to relaxing with a cup of coffee, reading a newspaper and catching up on the news. But first, he had to follow company procedure and call the office to give a brief recap of the trip.

He dialed the 800 number of his office and heard the friendly voice of Marlene, the receptionist. "Hello, my little flowerpot, how are you?"

"Hi, Drew, how was your trip? Did you bring me something nice from Paris, like one of those French hunks?"

"Great to the first and 'of course' to the second. Put me through to Cole, will you, and I'll see you in a couple of days."

"Nice to have you back, Drew. Hold on and I'll ring Tennant's office."

"Tennant," said the gruff voice on the other end of the 'phone.

"Cole, it's Drew, back from a triumphant trip to the City of Light where I worked my ass off and didn't get laid."

"You're not supposed to get laid and you're supposed to work hard. That's why we pay you that astronomical salary. I take it that everything went well?"

"Yeah, it was a good trip. The client was happy, the people were happy and even Bitchy Bob was ecstatic."

Bitchy Bob was Bob Brennan, the account executive on the program. In the sales incentive business, the salesmen and saleswomen are never called salespeople, they are known as account executives or AEs. It sounds superior, more official, more grandiose. The AE is the one who sells motivational programs to companies to increase their sales and profits and usually travels with the group.

Fastidious and contentious, Brennan was not the travel staff's favorite AE. Although his role on the trip was to serve as an intermediary between the sponsoring company's VIPs and the travel staff, Brennan often poked his nose into areas where he shouldn't and more than once got into shouting arguments with the travel staff. He could be a real son-of-a-bitch, and frequently was.

"Well, it's good to know you survived another one," said Tennant. "When will you be in the office?"

"Day after tomorrow. I want to sleep for 24 hours with no alarm to interrupt my salacious dreams."

"OK, but be prepared for another trip in about a week. Millar's got the 'flu and he may not be able to go to Bangkok on the Danner Electronics program. Rest up well, 'cuz you may need it. See you Thursday."

'Dammit,' Drew thought as he replaced the receiver, 'I was hoping for at least three weeks in the office before having to go out again. Millar gets sick oftener than anyone in the whole damn company. I don't think he can take a steady diet of overseas trips. The time changes and different climates definitely affect him more than anyone else I've ever met in this business, including me. I wonder if he really has the 'flu.'

He knew Laurie, the receptionist in the World Club, from his frequent visits to the lounge and asked her if she would make sure he was awake when it was boarding time for his flight. "I'm sure I won't sleep, but just in case," he told her.

Laurie chuckled to herself. "You've got to be kidding, Drew. Every time you come in here, you pass out, and that's against club rules. Don't you know that you're not supposed to sleep in these sumptuous surroundings? Go ahead, I'll make sure you don't miss your flight."

He picked up a USA TODAY, settled into a comfortable chair and glanced at the headlines of a story on the front page that immediately caught his eye.

BULGARIANS CLAIM U.S. SPY SHOT BY POLICE

SOFIA, BULGARIA. An American businessman was shot earlier today in a street in the city's Old Town as he tried to elude police, according to Delo, the official Bulgarian News Agency. Delo reported that the businessman, identified as Henry Andrews from Wichita, Kansas, was observed receiving a package from an unidentified Bulgarian Defense Department official.

Andrews was arrested by police but managed to escape through the narrow streets of the Old Town.

Sofia police allege that in the chase they fired at Andrews after he drew something from his pocket and aimed at them. There was no mention of whether a weapon was found on the American who was taken to a hospital for treatment.

A spokesman at the hospital disclosed that Andrews underwent surgery to remove two bullets from his stomach and left leg. He is listed in critical but stable condition.

Andrews became the fourth American to be accused of "improper behavior" in the last three months, and the first to be shot by the increasingly aggressive police in the Eastern bloc countries.

State Department official Steve Curran said that . . . .

* * *

"Drew, time to wake up if you don't want to miss your flight." Laurie was shaking him gently. He had fallen sound asleep

"Here's a cup of coffee for you; it'll help shake off the cobwebs. Make it quick, 'cuz you should head for the gate in a couple of minutes."

CHAPTER TWO

CIA HEADQUARTERS
LANGLEY, VIRGINIA

Chase Barron hadn't slept well the night before and wasn't in the mood for bad news. He had been appointed head of a special department of the CIA only two months before and it seemed the world was turning itself upside down just to torment him and test his endurance in his new position.

The special responsibilities of Barron's department included the recruiting, training and management of couriers who were used for the delivery or pick-up of "packages" to or from contacts in countries around the world.

"Everything seems to be happening all at once," he told key members of his staff at a meeting in his office. "The Russkies never had a run of success like this when Pryce headed up this department. Are they mad at me or something?

"Are we recruiting the wrong people? Is there something wrong with our training? Those KGB bastards have knocked over four of our couriers in the past three months. It isn't the local police or the Bulgarian Security Service that caught Andrews, it was the KGB, and those SOBs are getting better at their job as the months go by. Or are we slipping? No matter what the country, the local authorities are KGB-trained."

One of his staff, Brendon McShane, shifted in his seat, sipped his coffee then cleared his throat. "Chief, I know we're trying to use the most unlikely individuals as couriers, but we need to come up with a less obvious type, people who do not easily arouse suspicion. Businessmen are great in business, journalists are great in journalism, but they just don't have the anonymity we need. They just seem to draw attention like a magnet draws iron.

"When these guys visit a country, the KGB or its surrogates watch them like hawks. They know that we're using non-spy types to carry information or packages. Maybe we should be looking for a different kind of person, someone who wouldn't draw attention. We give them the best of training, but most of them just don't have that singular talent that's a pre-requisite for this kind of business.

"And maybe that's the point; maybe we give them too much training; maybe we shouldn't give them any training beyond the most basic. I'm not kidding. Maybe we need more naivete."

Barron's eyes were slits and he appeared ready to doze off. "You know, I shouldn't eat pizza, especially pizza with a meat topping. It gives me hellish indigestion and I have one helluva time trying to sleep at night. Anyway, do you have any suggestions as to how we can start turning the score around? I'd like to have us win one or two for a change.

"Tell you what, McShane, since you think we should be recruiting a different type of courier why don't you and the rest of the guys come up a few ideas or suggestions. Think about it and all let's have another meeting in a week. Maybe then I'll feel better. Sure as hell I won't eat pizza the night before."

The staff rose to leave the office as Barron let out a noisy yawn and complained some more about pizza and meat toppings.

* * *

"You heard what I said at the chief's meeting. What do you think? Do we need to look for people in other professions? Do we need to revise our training methods or are we just having a stretch of lousy luck?"

McShane had picked three staffers to help him profile the right type of individual who would be able to elude the attention of the KGB, yet had the street smarts and all-round savvy to get the job done.

George Hollis, one of the latest recruits to the department, who had served with the FBI for almost eight years before applying for a position with the CIA, rubbed his bearded chin as though looking for the right words. "No, I think you're right, Brendon, but what type of individual should we be looking for? Let's see, among our couriers we have businessmen, journalists, airline employees, sports personalities and merchant seamen. How many more categories are there?

"The other side is using the same kinds except they don't have as many categories to choose from. They have fewer airline employees, journalists, etc. and what they do have don't travel as much as our people do. We have the best of the pickings and yet here we are, stymied and puzzled. Should we be looking for one-eyed or one-limbed jocks who will evoke sympathy rather than curiosity?"

Everyone laughed and someone shouted: "How about one ball?"

"No, that wouldn't work. It doesn't show, at least not most of the time."

The conversation continued for another half-hour, but it was obvious that no new worthwhile considerations were forthcoming.

"I think we need a little more time," Hollis said, punctuating an embarrassing few moments of silence. 'My mind is cluttered with so many other things I'm working on right now that the juices just aren't flowing. This is one of those things that'll pop into my brain if I see or hear something. You know, one of those situations where one thing triggers another."

"Why not let us have a few days to ruminate, and maybe in that time fortuitous circumstances will occur that will suggest the people we're looking for?"

"Okay," McShane agreed. "Next meeting will be Tuesday at two o'clock in my office. And I hope you all experience lots of those fortuitous circumstances 'cuz we're sure gonna need them."

CHAPTER THREE

CIA HEADQUARTERS

A half-filled cup of cold coffee stood next to a yellow-lined pad replete with ideas that had occurred to McShane after the meeting as well as numerous bold red scratches on the pages indicating ideas once considered but now rejected.

He cupped his chin in both hands, staring at the pad, unable to come up with anything really solid. Glancing at the clock on the wall, he murmured to himself: 'Let's see, now, the big hand is on the seven and the small hand is on the six. That means it's time I got the hell out of here.'

He pressed his CIA identification card into the door slot and headed for the elevator. Before exiting the building, he pressed his hand into a mechanism on the wall. His departure time was now recorded.

"Goodnight, Will," he said to the guard in the reception area as he headed toward the parking lot and his newly-acquired Oldsmobile Delta 88;. He turned the key in the ignition and the motor fired immediately. He was not a car fanatic. All he wanted was a reliable car, one that started without any trouble and could transport him comfortably and safely around town. He had considered buying a smaller car but the appearance and performance of the Olds in a test drive convinced him that this was the automobile he should have.

He recalled a conversation over lunch a couple of days ago. One of the newer members of the Agency, Tom Seehof was boasting about his new Toyota. 'Greatest car in the world, I swear," the rookie had said. He rattled off a lot of statistics about the Japanese building better automobiles that offered better styling and improved mileage.

"Yeah, and what happens when we all buy Japanese cars?" Jim Thomas from the Accounting Department asked. "Where does that put the American automobile business?"

"Yeah, and what happens when we have thousands of workers with no jobs? Who's going to pay for the welfare?" Chris Sorenson, an analyst from the Printed Materials Department chimed in.

Seehof retorted that more Japanese companies were building auto plants in the U.S. and hiring thousands of U.S. workers.

"I read in one of the magazines," Jimmy Smith, a photography analyst said, "that if U.S. automotive companies had built the plants that the Japanese had constructed, they would employ 36,000 more workers. Something to do with the Japanese using more automation, you know, robotics and technology, things like that."

"And, remember, Thomas continued, "that billions of dollars of profit are still going to Japan and that's one country that doesn't need our money. Did you know that our trade deficit with Japan in 1986 was $55 billion? Did you hear that BILLION? That figure increased to $56 billion in 1987. That's more than the Gross National Products of most countries in the world. That's not helping our substantial trade imbalance you know"

Brendon smiled as he remembered the arguments going back and forth and the rookie finally rising to leave and saying: "Gee, maybe I should mention this to my wife; she's thinking of buying a Nissan."

'Ah, the joys of free enterprise,' he thought to himself and smiled before changing to a frown as he pondered once more the assignment he had been given: Find people who won't attract the KGB's attention so easily. 'There have to be people who can get in and out of the country without being quite so noticeable.'

In the distance he made out the Keller Inn. 'Maybe I'll stop in and have a beer.' It had been a long and frustrating day; a beer might lubricate his thought processes and make an answer slide right into his mind. 'One of those fortuitous circumstances', he smiled, recalling Hollis's comment.

'Funny,' he thought, 'before the accident, I would never have dreamed of having a beer on my way home.'

It was difficult for him to think of that night, of his wife's battered and broken body as he pulled her from the car, but the thoughts kept recurring. A drunk had crossed the median and collided head-on as he and Mary were returning from a weekend with some friends in Baltimore. Mary was driving while he dozed. He had his seatbelt fastened, but she always made light of his constant nagging about using a seatbelt and seldom bothered to secure it.

She died on the way to the hospital, too far gone for the miracles of modern medicine to help. He had been more fortunate; he had cuts and bruises, but nothing broken or badly damaged. The State troopers had told him his seatbelt had saved his life and had prevented serious injury.

Stopping at a bar on the way home had never really interested him. There was always a martini waiting for him at home to help him relax while Mary put the finishing touches to dinner. A martini and a glance at the headlines of the evening newspaper. Simple, but real pleasures.

He pulled into the parking lot of the Inn, locked the Olds and walked into the bar. It was busy and full of smoke from a crowd of young people who were engaged in light-hearted conversation. Peals of laughter rent the air.

McShane looked around for a place to enjoy a beer but all the stools at the bar were taken and he couldn't see any vacant seats at the tables. Looks like I'll be having a stand-up drink, he thought, when suddenly he heard someone shout his name. "Brendon, over here." From one of the tables, he saw an arm waving to him.

It was Joe Bass, one of the Customs officers stationed at Dulles International Airport near Washington D.C. He was seated at a table for four with two other men. There was one empty chair at the table. "Come on over, there's one open."

"Hey, it's good to see you," Bass said as McShane seated himself in the empty chair. "Meet Bill Grogan and Sam Chayefsky. They work with me over at Dulles. Good guys to know if you want to smuggle anything through Customs," he added with a laugh as the others joined in.

They shook hands and asked McShane what he was drinking. "Oh, a beer would be fine if we can get somebody to take the order."

"That's easy for regulars like us," Grogan said as he waved his hand to catch the eye of a pretty, blonde-haired waitress who was delivering drinks at a nearby table.

"Hey, Gail, how about a beer for a thirsty man over here?"

"Coming right up," she shot back as McShane shook his head, grinning. "It sure does pay to have friends in the Customs Department."

"What branch of government are you in, Brendon?" Chayefsky asked as he pulled on a cigar.

"What makes you think I'm in government service?"

Grogan started to laugh and broke in. "That reminds me of the American tourist in Ireland who asked a local: 'Why do all Irishmen answer a question with a question?' and the local asked: "Who told you that?"

Everyone laughed as McShane said "Good guess. I am in government service. I work for the Internal Revenue Service. I, too, am a good man to know especially if you have questions on your income tax."

"What do you and Sam do for Customs? Do you pack a piece and chase smugglers or are you employed in a more mundane capacity?"

"They work alongside me, Brendon" said Bass, "checking incoming tourists and returning residents, making sure they haven't exceeded their exemptions, checking that they're not bringing illegal goods or live plants into the country."

"I'm sure that drug smuggling keeps you guys busiest. There must be literally dozens of means the smugglers use to get past you."

"More like hundreds,' Grogan chimed in. 'Every month, you learn of something new, something grotesque, something so horrible that you wonder about the minds of the people who conceive it."

Bass took over the conversation and pointed out that drug-smuggling was only a small part of their business. 'Drug smugglers use other means much more than carrying it on—or in—their persons. Most of that dirty work is carried out by others, in private 'planes, boats and so on. No, our work is mostly taken up with looking for those who cheat on their declaration forms, who've exceeded their tax-free limits or are bringing in harmful foods or plant products."

Suddenly McShane was jolted. 'A fortuitous circumstance' had just recalled his immediate assignment: Find someone whose job and persona would make him as invisible as possible to the KGB.

"I'm sure you have profiles that help you in your job, but you must have an instinct, too, some sort of intuition that triggers a reaction when you see someone presenting their baggage for inspection."

"Yeah, when you've been in the business as long as we have, you develop the instincts that make you wonder about someone a little more than another person. I can't put a finger on it, but it's there, and strangely, we're usually right."

"I'm sure your profiles are confidential, or certainly you don't want to make them too public, so I won't ask, but do you have a mental profile of the person who will get least hassle from you?"

Grogan squashed the butt of his cigar in an ashtray. "Yes, someone who looks normal, no long hair, no earring, no blue jeans with holes in them or wearing clothing that looked like it had been slept in for weeks. Someone clean-cut, neatly dressed. I don't necessarily mean that someone of obvious wealth, immaculately tailored and a snooty air would be automatically removed from any kind of inspection. I mean a regular kind of All-American look. And he could be wearing blue jeans as long as he had that neat, wholesome look."

"And a nice, genuine smile doesn't hurt, does it," Bass added. "You're inclined to be more receptive to people who have a nice, honest look on their face. Call it personality, if you like, but we're human, too, and we react to pleasant attitudes in a positive way just as we react to smart-alecky, hoodlum-looking types in a negative way. We don't show any emotion. We always try to be fair and impartial, but you can't help being influenced just a little bit by a person's demeanor and appearance.

"I remember when I was stationed at JFK just before being assigned to Dulles. There was this young fellow who would come through fairly regularly. He was a courier or guide or whatever the hell they call themselves, for some sales incentive company in the Midwest. He frequently accompanied groups to Europe and I got to know him by sight."

He was always in his company's uniform, navy blue jacket and gray slacks, shirt and tie, so he was neatly dressed. But whenever I would ask him a question, he always answered politely without any hesitation and never without a smile on his face. For example, the last time I saw him, I thought I would question him on the low amount he had on his customs declaration form. It was something like $15 or $20 although he was allowed $400.

"Normally, I wouldn't question someone on something that low, but I figured I would on this particular occasion because I had seen him so often. He told me that he had been in Europe on business and that he didn't have the time to go around shopping. The $20 or so was what he had actually spent. Then, with a big smile on his face, he says to me: 'I can't afford to lie to you guys and get caught. You would put a big flag against my name in your computer and then I am in trouble whenever I come back into the country. You'd put me through the wringer every time, and I don't need that kind of worry.'

"After he left, I thought to myself, he got that right, and he's smart. It's not worth having your name flagged in the computer just to cheat your government out of a few bucks. But the point is that I didn't question him because I thought he might be guilty of something, it was just because I had seen him so many times before that I thought I would just let him know we weren't always going to let him go through without some sort of questioning. But he certainly was the all-American type that I would let go through time and again."

Grogan pulled another cigar from his pocket, clipped the edge and was about to strike a match when he pointed out that it was really refreshing to have a conversation with grown men without once having heard a reference to sex. 'I just hope that doesn't mean we're getting old. You don't think it does, do you?"

That was all that was needed to take the conversation on another tangent, and for the next hour, the topic focused on the wonders and indispensability of women interspersed with a few off-color jokes.

Chayefsky started the ball rolling with a joke and everyone at his table laughed so hard, Gail, the waitress, asked him to repeat it so she and others nearby could laugh, too.

"Gee, I don't know, Gail, after all you're a refined young woman." Louder laughter followed that remark and Gail got suddenly upset.

"I don't know if I like the way you said 'refined,' Sam. I am refined. Hell, I must be 'cuz I've never dated any of you bums and that's got to say something for my better judgment. Anyway, are you going to tell us the joke or not?"

Four men at the next table egged Sam on until he finally relented.

"Okay, guys. At an army base in England, a general called in his sergeant and told him to assemble the troops on the parade ground at 3 o'clock for a short-arm inspection."

"What's a short-arm inspection?" Gail asked.

"Just hold on, Gail, you'll understand soon enough. So, to continue then, the sergeant took off and at the appointed hour, he had the troops standing in three lines with only towels around their waists.

"Preceded by the general, the sergeant walked down the line barking 'Open your towel' to the first soldier. The general then looked at what had been displayed, said 'all right' and moved on down the line. Halfway down, they came to a thin little soldier. 'Open your towel' shouted the sergeant. The soldier pulled back his cover and revealed an enormous erection. The sergeant looked at it, and furiously embarrassed, ordered the soldier to leave the line.

"The general and the sergeant completed the first line without further incident and moved to the beginning of the second line.

"Sergeant," said the general, "bring back that young man."

"Private Smith," roared the sergeant, and the soldier quickly marched forward and stood smartly to attention. "Remove your towel" The soldier pulled back his garment and revealed that the erection was still there. "Step out of line until you're more presentable." roared the sergeant, and the soldier marched swiftly away.

"They completed the second line and everything was fine without any comments from the general. As they approached the third line, the general ordered the sergeant to bring back the disgraced soldier.

"'Private Smith" he yelled, and the soldier immediately appeared. "Open your towel." The soldier whipped away his cover and there was no change. The erection was still there in all its glory.

"The sergeant, greatly agitated, looked at it, then turned to the general and said: 'If you don't mind me saying so, sir, I think he's taken a liking to you.'"

Gail blushed while the four men howled with laughter As she walked away, Sam shouted: "See what I mean, Gail, you're refined."

After another round of beers and another session of randy jokes, they decided to call it quits. As they walked to their cars in the parking lot, McShane told Bass he would like to discuss something with him and would give him a call.

"Any time," he answered, and gave him his number."

McShane's mind was preoccupied as he drove home. 'Bingo' he murmured to himself, 'I think I've found the type of courier we're looking for.'

CHAPTER FOUR

CIA HEADQUARTERS

"Joe, this is Brendon McShane." He had just returned from lunch and picked up the 'phone to call his Customs friend. He had decided not to call Bass first thing in the morning in case he alerted Bass to thinking his call was something more sinister than the simple request he had made of it.

"I mentioned when we left the Keller Inn last night that I had something I wanted to discuss with you."

"Hey, it was great seeing you again, Brendon, after such a long lapse of time. Yeah, I remember you said you would give me a call. What can I do for you?"

He told Joe that he was working on a project that required some information on travel, particularly incentive travel, and would like to get in touch with the young fellow he had questioned returning home after an overseas trip. "It sounds like he would be the ideal man to talk to."

"I recall the conversation, yeah, and the fellow. I can check with our computer people and see if they can come up with his name. Why would the IRS be interested in a travel man? Some big doings going on, Brendon?"

"Well, specifically an incentive man," McShane pointed out, and assured him that he was only interested in having a conversation with the young man in the hope that he could help him with a project on which he was working.

"Don't worry, Joe, I'm not pulling him in for anything. I only want to have him give me his viewpoints on aspects of incentive travel as they relate to tax-deductible destinations. You may know that we have places such as Bermuda and Puerto Rico where companies can take their winners for programs and meetings and have their expenses written off if they have a certain number of business sessions during the visit.

"I'm working on a plan to have other islands in the Caribbean considered tax-deductible, but I'm facing some obstacles that an incentive travel expert can answer better than the travel agency types. And since these tax-deductions are mostly centered around incentive programs, I thought he might be a good man with whom to begin my conversations."

"Give me a day or two and I'll get back to you, Brendon."

* * *

The 'phone rang, interrupting his thoughts on how he would next proceed with the incentive travel man once he had his name and telephone number.

It was Chase Barron. "How're you coming with that project, the one to find a new type of courier?"

"Well, Chase, I think I may have a worthwhile idea, but I need another few days. I have something in the works right now and hope to have a solid recommendation for you shortly. Can we delay our meeting, say for another week to give me the time I need to get all my details?"

"Sure. Call me when you're ready and we'll set up another date."

* * *

Joe Bass wasn't fooled one bit. He had always suspected that McShane was something other than what he said. Why couldn't he have contacted someone locally with his questions on tax-deductible meeting places? Why did he specifically want someone in Detroit or wherever it was that the young man lived?

He recalled that the incentive man was from the Midwest because he had made mention of having to take a connecting flight to . . . . now, where was it, St. Louis? Chicago? Kansas City? No, he thought, it wasn't one of those, but it was definitely somewhere in the Midwest.

He left the office he shared with Sam Chayefsky, walked over to the elevator and pressed the Up button. He rubbed his chin as he tried to figure McShane's real job with the government. 'I wonder if he's with the FBI or maybe even the CIA? Sure seems strange. Well, who cares? Heck, he's such a nice guy I don't mind helping.

The elevator door opened, interrupting his reveries. He stepped inside, pushed 7 on the panel and the doors closed. He continued his musings. 'What if McShane really was with the IRS and had picked up something from the way I described how I handled this particular returning traveler? What if I had erred in the way I had questioned the young fellow.

'Was there something I had missed? Nah, I've done this thousands of times and I ask the same questions. There was nothing so different about the kid that required harsher handling.'

The door opened on the seventh floor and he strode along the corridor to the computer center.

A black man was bending over a machine as he entered. He sneaked up behind him and goosed him, causing the black man to straighten up with a start.

"Joe, my man, you missed. What've you been doing? Haven't seen you up here in months. Are you trying to improve your mind in your old age?"

"If I were, Charles, I wouldn't be visiting this sterile graveyard. Say, I've got a big request to make of you."

Charles Holm was entitled to a few idiosyncrasies as much as anyone else, and one of his was that he did not like to be called by anything but his proper and full first name. If anyone addressed him as Charlie, Chick or Chuck, he invariably responded with "Yes, Dickhead" or "Yo-Yo" or some other demeaning term.

"OK, shoot. What can I do for you, my man?"

Charles affected the argot of the black man, and was inclined to sprinkle his conversation with up-to-date and hip expressions. But, behind his laid-back, with-it style was a talent for computers that earned him high respect from his superiors in the Customs Service as well as from his co-workers.

There wasn't any kind of program he couldn't write or any problem with a computer that he couldn't solve. He was a whiz kid when it came to automation. Just as he could spice his talk with the black jive, he could display his high IQ in discourses with other computer geniuses or his superior intelligence with the hi-pots of any other department. Hi-pots was the term given to the up-and-coming executives and was an abbreviation of high-potential, which Charles had in abundance.

"A friend of mine with the IRS needs some help and it really falls in your area. He has . . ."

"Wait a minute, Joe," Charles interrupted. "The IRS has no friends. And if by some stretch of the imagination you think you have a friend there, take my word for it, don't breathe it or you'll lose all the other friends you have. Don't you know that the IRS is full of extraterrestrials? They ain't human. They live in a world all their own."

"Cut the crap, Charles. If you met my friend McShane, you'd be the first to tell me what a great guy he is. Anyway, he needs some help. About two years ago, I took a declaration form from a young man coming into Kennedy from abroad. Can't remember which country he was coming from. In fact, I can't remember much about him except that he came through our lines quite frequently. I do remember that he worked for a sales incentive company and was employed in the company's travel division. He accompanied groups around the world."

"Wow, there's nothing wrong with your memory, Joe, when you can remember someone after two years and when one considers the thousands of people you process in a year."

"Yeah, you're right, but maybe I remember these few details about him because I saw him every month or so. I don't know what else I can give you and I know that I haven't given you much, but maybe there are more questions you can ask me that will help you zero in on this particular fellow."

"What's this guy done? Has he been smuggling drugs into the country or what?"

"That's the funny thing, I really don't know. I have a feeling that my friend is not with the IRS but with the FBI or CIA or some secret organization. He's a nice guy, he really is, and I suppose they have to be secretive and protect their identity or it would affect their usefulness.

"Anyway, he told me that he wants to speak to this young man because he thinks he could help him in his research into the whys and wherefores of the tax-deductibility status of certain islands in the Caribbean and other places in the world as it all relates to the incentive business."

Charles picked up his mug and asked Joe if he wanted to join him in some coffee as there were definitely some more questions he wanted to ask him and it would take a little more time.

Steam was rising from the two cups Charles carried when he returned to his desk where Bass was seated.

"OK, my man, let's see what we can do to help the Martians who're not really Martians but Dick Tracys in disguise."

He took a pad from his desk drawer and picked up a pencil. 'Joe, you said the young man came through Kennedy several times. Can you remember when?"

"You mean year or month?"

"Yeah, both if you can."

"I remember the last time was in April of last year because I was in my last week at Kennedy and getting ready for my transfer to D.C. I can only guess, but it seemed that he came through Kennedy maybe every two months or so, maybe more."

Charles made some notes, picked up his coffee and took a swallow. "OK, can you remember which city he lived in?"

"No, I was trying to think of that just before I came up here. I know it was somewhere in the Midwest. It wasn't Chicago or St. Louis. Cleveland, maybe? No, it wasn't Cleveland either."

"Sorry, Charles, I just can't . . . wait a minute, it was Minneapolis. Now I remember. He said he was connecting to a flight to beautiful Minneapolis and mentioned, as a joke, that the Chamber of Commerce required its residents to say that. Yeah, it was definitely Minneapolis."

"That'll be a big help. You can't remember which airline he came in on, or where he was coming from, can you?"

"No. Hell, I thought I was doing good remembering Minneapolis."

"Yeah, we'll give you a prize later. This is a wild one, but can you remember how much he claimed on his declaration form? I don't mean the exact amount, but was it over his limit, was it a high amount or maybe a small amount? Did he have to pay duty?"

"Wait a minute, I think I can give you something. It was a small amount, maybe $20 or $30. I did question him on the amount because it was so small. Bingo, he was coming from Paris. Yes, that's it. He was coming from Paris and I thought it strange that he was claiming just a few dollars. That's when he told me he was a working stiff and didn't have the time to shop. It's amazing what one can remember when a genius like you is asking the right questions and spurring my thought processes. How're we doin' now? Do you think you have enough or are there more questions?"

"Give me an idea of how old he was. Thirtyish, fortyish?"

"I would guess he was in his late twenties or early thirties."

Charles wrote down this information, dropped his pencil on the pad and took the last gulp of coffee. "Let's see. I'm working on something just now that I have to finish by quitting time. I'll stay on and ask the computer a few questions and hopefully come up with your information. I'll call you in the morning."

'Charles, I thank you, the IRS thanks you and maybe the Secret Service thanks you. I'll wait for your call. Oh, ring me at Dulles, will you? I'll be working the lines tomorrow but I can be reached at 726-5523.

* * *

It was even easier than Charles thought it would be. He entered a few facts, pressed several buttons and narrowed the list down.

He created a few more questions, put them on the screen and the machine flashed more than a hundred names. A few more questions to the computer and the list was reduced to about 60.

Charles asked the machine to list only the names of those in Minneapolis who had claimed less than $50 on their declaration forms in April of last year.

Over a hundred names were now on the screen. 'OK,' Charles murmured to himself, 'how many made more than 10 trips abroad last year? The list dropped to seventy-two.

'Well,' he thought, 'here's the last or next-to-last question. Let's hope it can whittle the names down to one or two.'

He asked the machine how many of them were under 40?

Two names popped up: Drew Cummins, 15 Harlequin Place, Minneapolis, and Dirk Beauchamp, 1733 Courtland Street, Minneapolis.

He typed one more question: Were Cummins or Beauchamp in Paris last year?

Success. Only one name appeared on the screen: Drew Cummins.

* * *

"Joe's working the line just now," the voice at the other end of the 'phone said. We've got two international flights in at the moment, so all officers are clearing the passengers. I can have him call you in about 30 minutes. Is that OK?"

"Yes, that'll be fine. Ask him to call Charles at 333-5008, and thanks."

"OK, Chuck, I'll have him give you a buzz."

'Shithead,' Charles whispered as he replaced the receiver.

Twenty minutes later, Charles' 'phone rang. He picked it up and heard Joe's voice on the line.

"Joe, do da name Drew Cummins ring yoh chimes?"

"That's it, yeah, that's the guy. I'm, sure of it. Great work, Charles. You really are a genius. Do you have an address for him?"

"Sure do," he replied. "He lives at 15 Harlequin Place in Minneapolis."

"I owe you a drink, buddy, thanks much."

CHAPTER FIVE

CIA HEADQUARTERS

The CIA cafeteria was busier than usual when McShane pushed his tray along the rail towards the cashier. He paid the amount and looked for a table with some interesting conversationalists. There were few empty seats but he did notice a couple of vacancies that might prove worthwhile.

Tony Julius was obviously deep in discussions with a number of men and women at one of the 'bullshitters' tables', so-called because they were long and capable of seating about 14, thus creating more nonsensical conversation. Most of the tables in the cafeteria were designed to accommodate fours, sixes and eights. There were about a dozen of these 'BS' tables which were originally installed to accommodate those who were attending meetings and wanted to continue the discussions over lunch.

The other seating opportunity involved two men at a table for four. It took McShane only a few seconds to determine that Tony's table would be the one that would provide more animated conversation, and he felt like a good jaw-breaking session this morning. As he neared the table, the topic of discussion became audible to him.

" . . . and if we got a chance to interview him, we could find out a lot more information that would be helpful to us, too. After all, we might be the peons of the company, but if having such a guy for a day would help us, why not give us some time with him. Are the glory boys so occupied with their new toy that they can't give us a chance? We don't need him right away. Some time in the future would be fine, but by then, they've got him spirited away some place with a new identity so that nobody can find him."

"Room for a neutral here?" McShane asked as he dropped into one of the empty seats.

"Glad to have you, Brendon," Tony said. "We're talking about that Russian who defected."

'Who's that? I haven't seen the 'paper this morning. I was planning on reading it in my office after devouring these substitutes for real sausages and eggs."

"A KGB defector, Ilya Massimov, turned himself into our embassy in Turkey a couple of weeks ago. Says he's fed up with the mess that his country is in. No food, no clothing, no housing. That's a laugh because he probably had the best of everything being in the KGB, or maybe the guy has a heart and he really is concerned about his fellow Soviets."

"That'll be a novelty," one of the table companions said. 'I've never met any of the defectors who have come to us, but what I've read of them, they feather their own nests pretty well and to hell with the rest of the people."

"That's my point," said Tony, "we've never really met any of them. I think we should have an opportunity to talk to them and perhaps learn a few things that would be helpful in our areas of operation. I asked a couple of times to interview defectors, but was told that all the information worth gleaning has already been gotten. How'd you like that for a self-satisfying answer? I'm certainly not up there on the firing line or with the brass, but I know that a couple of hours with one of those Russkies could be very helpful to me in my work."

Tony Julius's department was responsible for clothing, disguises, foreign currency; customs anything relating to how Americans should dress and behave in foreign countries, particularly Eastern Europe. His job was to write reports on new styles, new fads, new cigarettes, new drinks, new entertainment, anything that an agent should have, know and do when entering another country. His information was taken from newspapers, magazines and any other periodicals that were forwarded to the CIA by U.S. embassies and consulates around the world.

"I'm not arguing the validity of your point, Tony," McShane said, "but maybe the boys upstairs feel that these defectors are mostly concerned with work outside their country and couldn't be particularly helpful on trends and styles within the Soviet bloc. And you know they don't trust the sons-of-bitches until they have iron-clad proof that they do want to foreswear the Communist system.

"I concede that may be so," Tony continued, 'but I could still find out worthwhile details about any of the Communist countries he's been in with just a few questions. I wouldn't ask anything pertaining to politics, only a query or two on the less important aspects of the cold war."

McShane sliced one of his sausages with his fork and put it in his mouth. "Maybe they should bring the defector down to our cafeteria. It would change his mind about our food and convince him to go back to Mother Russia."

"Oh, he's not complaining about the quality," another table companion laughed. "He's bitching about the quantity. After all, a dozen lousy sausages are better than no sausages at all."

"Is this Massimov in the U.S. now?" McShane asked.

"Probably. The newspaper report indicated that he had defected but as you know, they are already in the U.S. days before those announcements are made."

"Say, did any of you notice the story in the Post about that Romanian model who's burning up the runways in New York? She's supposedly the hottest thing in the modeling world. I always thought those Eastern European women did their modeling between the shafts of a cart, pulling it around their villages and towns while shouting 'turnips for sale.'"

Laughter followed the comment and there were references to the Eastern European beauties of yesterday who made it big in British and American films.

"This one in New York has great T&A. Slim, willowy."

"If you guys are gonna talk dirty, I'm leaving," McShane said as he rose. Thanks for the fun conversation. See ya."

Normally, he would have stayed longer and enjoyed a few laughs and camaraderie over a second cup of coffee, but the news of the Russian defector intrigued him and he wanted to learn more of Comrade Massimov. An idea was forming in his mind.

"Good morning, Brendon," his secretary Susan burbled as he passed her desk. "Want some coffee and a donut or did you eat downstairs?"

"Good morning to you, Susan, and yes to the two questions."

The newspaper was lying on his desk with a bunch of telephone messages. He seated himself in his comfortable executive chair, leaned back in it and put his feet up on the corner of his desk.

The story of the defection was on the front page. It was datelined Ankara, Turkey, and read: "A high KGB official with the Soviet embassy in Turkey has defected, it was confirmed today by a U.S. embassy spokesman here. The defector, Ilya Massimov, a colonel in the Russian Secret Service, entered the U.S. embassy three weeks ago seeking asylum.

"A spokesman for the embassy revealed that Massimov was being interviewed by the CIA 'somewhere outside Turkey' but would not comment on whether he was already in the U.S. or in Europe."

The story gave some background on Massimov who had been a member of the KGB for 16 years and had also served in Soviet embassies in Finland and Spain.

He picked up the 'phone and dialed Chase Barron's office. "Chase, this is McShane. Have you seen the morning 'paper?"

"About the defector?" asked Barron. "Yes, I saw it. We lose two or three couriers and we win a big defector. It evens out. This was our turn, I guess. Why do you ask?"

"Chase, I'd like to talk to the guy for about 10 minutes. Can you arrange it? The big boys must be through with their interrogations by now. Do you remember that courier idea I have been working on? I think I'm on to something worthwhile, but if I could have ten minutes with the Russkie, I know it would be of tremendous value to me in my research. Just ten minutes. Can you do it?"

"Brendon, it's not a matter of can I do it, it's more a matter of whether the brass want to keep him under wraps without any interference for a few months. You know the drill."

"There were a few seconds of silence before Barron continued. "Let me see what I can do and I'll get back to you."

McShane sifted through his 'phone messages and noticed one was from Joe Bass. It was buried in the pile, but became his first call. The call was to his direct line which circumvented the CIA switchboard, thus depriving the caller of knowing he was calling the CIA.

"Joe, it's Brendon. Got something for me?"

"Sure do, Brendon. Have I ever told you about Charles Holm, one of the managers in our computer area? He's a genius, I swear. The guy lives and breathes computers and I don't think there's anything he can't get them to do for him. I'm not sure that he doesn't fuck them occasionally. Anyway, Charles came up with the name of the kid we've been trying to locate for you. It's Drew Cummins and he resides at 15 Harlequin Place in Minneapolis. I leave the rest up to you."

"Joe, you're the greatest. I appreciate all the work that you did in finding Cummins. And thank Chuck for me, will you? I'll send him over a token of my appreciation. What does he drink, do you know?"

'Well, first of all, don't address it to Chuck. He gets himself all twisted out of shape when anybody calls him that. It's Charles, and he drinks scotch."

"Right, Joe, and I owe you a big one. Next time the IRS audits you, give me a call."

"Glad to help, Brendon. Speak to you soon."

'Drew Cummins,' McShane mused to himself. 'Nice all-American sounding name."

CHAPTER SIX

CIA HEADQUARTERS

McShane was enjoying a cup of coffee with several of his cohorts in George Hollis's office when someone shouted out his name and told him that Barron was looking for him. "He's been calling your office and no one is answering your 'phone. Did you give your secretary the day off?"

"No, she's entitled to a coffee break, too, now and then, you know. I'll call him."

"Chase, it's McShane. Have you been looking for me?"

"Yeah, come over to my office. I've got something for you."

McShane respectfully knocked lightly on Barron's office door before entering. "Do me a favor, McShane," Barron boomed at him. "Tell me where the hell your hiding spots are, would you? I can never find you when you're not in your office. You don't hide in the ladies' room, do you? Anyway, here's the scoop. You wanted to talk to that defector, and I've arranged it, but first you have to call Pierce Powell who's in charge of this project. He's on extension 5525."

"Who's Powell? I don't know him."

"Oh, I keep forgetting that you're just a little shit in this organization," Barron said with a sneer on his face. "He's with the department that handles, among other things, defectors. Give him a call and if he's satisfied that your need to see Massimov is important, he may let you talk to him."

McShane walked briskly back to his office, settled himself into his executive chair and dialed 5525.

"Powell," the gruff voice said at the other end.

"Mr. Powell, this is Brendon McShane. I believe Chase Barron mentioned my name and my request to you. I'd like to have about ten minutes with Massimov, if you'll allow it."

"Oh, yeah," Powell grunted. "I remember. What do you want to see Massimov about? What's your need?"

"I'm working on a special project for Barron. We're trying to come up with a new kind of profile for an outside courier, a profile that would be more obscure to KGB suspicions than those we've been using. As you're probably aware, we haven't had much luck with our couriers of late and Barron assigned me the project of developing a profile that would arouse the least amount of interest or suspicion on the part of the KGB. If I could talk to your defector, I thought he could give me some ideas of what the KGB particularly look for? I have a mental profile that I'm working on just now and want to test it against Massimov."

"Well, your call may be timely. We've just finished an interrogation and we're moving him to a safe house in a few hours where he'll be taken over by another division. Tell you what, jump in a cab and go over to the Bellevue hotel. I'll meet you in the lobby. Say in about 30 minutes? Ask at the front desk for John Bryant."

"Great, see you in 30 minutes." Ten minutes later, McShane left his office, hailed a cab and told the driver to take him to the Bellevue Hotel. He thought of the questions he would ask Massimov and prepared himself for the interview by writing notes in a pad in his wallet. He was surprised that it had been arranged so easily. He hadn't expected this kind of cooperation, but he was glad the other department was being so helpful.

The cab pulled up at the front door of the Bellevue. He gave the driver a $20 bill and told him to keep the change. He walked to the front desk and asked the clerk if he would page Mr. Bryant.

"Oh, that's Mr. Bryant over there," the clerk said. "He's been expecting you." He pointed to a balding, heavy-set man in his 50s, drawing on a lengthy cigar and reading a newspaper.

As he approached, he found Bryant relaxed in a comfortable leather chair. 'Mr. Bryant?"

The newspaper was slowly lowered, revealing two piercing, dark brown eyes underneath shaggy eyebrows. "Yes?"

"I'm McShane."

The man rose from his chair, held out his hand and said: "Hi, I'm Pierce Powell. Excuse the subterfuge. Let's go." The two men walked outside the hotel and a black Pontiac pulled up almost immediately. They sat in the rear and the car quickly took off.

"Are we going far?"

"Not far,' the fellow seated next to the driver responded without turning around and introducing himself. "We're going to have to ask you to put this over your eyes," he said as he handed a black mask to McShane.

"You've got to be kidding. Hey, I'm on your side."

"You wear the mask or we take you back to the Bellevue, which is it? We don't have a lot of time."

'Gimme the mask," McShane growled, feeling as if his loyalty was being questioned.

Nobody spoke after he had donned the mask, and another 10 minutes passed before he heard the car's tires pulling over crushed gravel indicating a private driveway.

"OK, Mr. McShane, keep the mask on. We'll guide you."

His arms were grasped as they helped him out of the car and then up some stairs. He heard a door open and close behind him and then felt himself being turned to the left.

"You can take the mask off now. Sorry, we have to play cops and robbers like that, but it's necessary."

The room was large and expensively furnished with an original painting of a Paris street scene above a fireplace and two comfortable dark blue easy chairs flanking a sofa. Mahogany paneling covered the walls, giving the room a somber aspect. Despite the hour, the shades were drawn and two floor lamps provided inadequate lighting.

"Sit over there," Powell said, pointing to one of the chairs. "Now here are the ground rules. We're going to sit in on the interview, and you've got five minutes. Just for the record, we don't usually do this sort of thing, but your boss, Chase Barron, pulled a couple of strings. Remember, you confine your questioning to the profile idea. Don't stray from that. Massimov doesn't know that this is a digression from his interrogation. Any questions about what I've told you?"

"No. I think I know the drill."

Powell nodded to one of the other men who left for a few minutes, returning with a burly, poorly-dressed man of medium height. He was balding with a fringe of brown hair turning gray. His ample nose was slightly crooked, suggesting that he might have been a boxer or a wrestler at one time. Worst of all, the man exuded a foul odor as though he hadn't bathed or changed his clothes for a few weeks.

"Ilya, please sit down," Powell said as he directed the defector to the chair opposite McShane. 'This is Joe Anderson who wants to ask you a few questions for a few minutes and when he's finished we'll be leaving by car. OK"

"This is good," the Russian said as he seated himself. "May I have a scotch and water, please?"

Powell nodded to one of the men in the room who immediately stepped to a built-in bar in a corner of the room and poured the Soviet a drink with lots of ice.

Powell noticed McShane watching the drink being poured and said: "Ilya has picked up our western ways. He likes ice."

The Soviet laughed as he accepted the drink, took a sip and sat back on the sofa. "Now I am ready."

"Mr. Massimov," McShane began, 'as you've heard, my name is Joe Anderson and my part of your interrogation is going to be brief. I only want to ask you a few questions that are very different from those you've been asked by my CIA brothers.

"We know that the KGB watches carefully all foreigners entering the Soviet Union. Can you tell me what sort of profile you have that draws your attention to one individual more than another? In other words, what do you look for when ferreting out the suspicious visitors?"

The Soviet laughed heartily, took another sip of his drink and placed it on a nearby table. 'We suspect everybody, even our brother officers."

"Yes, I know," McShane continued, "but you don't have the manpower to tail everyone. You must pick out a few who look suspicious to you and give them special attention. Can you tell me what you particularly look for? Are there obvious idiosyncrasies that draw your attention? Do you pay particular attention to clothing, hair, build, the luggage they carry? What hits your hot button?"

"Hot button? What is hot button?" the Soviet asked, obviously puzzled.

"Excuse me, Mr. Massimov, we Americans use a lot of slang and idioms and forget that people from other countries who speak perfectly good English are not always knowledgeable of our expressions. By hot button, I mean something immediately flashes a signal."

"Yes, of course, we have a profile as you call it, but I'm sure you know that we develop instincts that are more helpful to us than the actual profile. While I was not attached to airport security we did have some instruction in this area. I can tell you what we learned and then give you my personal thoughts. This will be satisfactory?"

"Yes, Mr. Massimov, that will be very satisfactory."

"Businessmen with leather briefcases and looking very successful and important are prime targets. Journalists, too, are watched carefully . . . all of them. The Soviets don't trust anyone connected with the press. We also screen tourists, but this is usually covered by the Intourist officials and guides who are with them all the time."

"You mean, then, that the KGB probably pays less attention to tourists than to other types of travelers?" "Yes and no. We certainly screen tourists, but because they are usually in groups and are taken around by our Intourist people, they do get less KGB attention than others. Remember, however, that Intourist people are also quasi members of the KGB, particularly those with titles. They don't hold high KGB positions, perhaps, but certainly they are required to watch carefully and report anything unusual to the Department. Additionally, tourists who visit the Soviet Union on their own, by that I mean who do not come with groups, are definitely targeted and carefully watched."

"Do you have a personal profile?"

"Yes, but here again, it's more intuition than anything else. For example, we are inclined to pay more attention to people with titles, such as president of vice president and who look successful, than we are to others. The Soviet Union is a country of proletariats, we are not inclined to be as suspicious of someone who does not dress well or who does not look so successful. But, again, that does not mean that we overlook anyone. We are a suspicious and xenophobic people, so we watch everyone."

McShane was impressed with the man's command of the English language. He spoke articulately without an 'umm' or the all-too-common 'you know'. Even his choice of words and phraseology was exemplary. Obviously, the man was the product of a sound education.

He felt he should ask more questions but he really had what he wanted and he didn't want to infringe any further on the time limit he had been given. Massimov had told him that tourists in groups were not as carefully or professionally watched by the KGB because they were, in effect, the responsibility of the Intourist people. Intourist, as he already knew, employed only party members because they were constantly being exposed to foreigners. But they were party members who did not have the training and the cunning of the KGB. Their job, as Massimov said, was to report anything unusual or suspicious to the KGB which would then take up the matter and assign it to the pros.

"One final question, Mr. Massimov. Does personality have any bearing on what you've told me. I mean by that, does the KGB react positively or negatively to personality? Would a pleasant individual be more likely to avoid their 'hot button' than a somber faced tourist?"

"I'm sure you know that the Soviets are not personality people, Mr. Anderson. We are characterized in the foreign press as dour with no humor at all." He laughed heartily then reached for his drink and took another swig.

"But to answer your question properly. I think that the Soviet people are more susceptible to a smiling face than to someone who tries to act imperiously and create a false front. Do I make myself clear?"

"Yes, Mr. Massimov, I think you do."

"Well, let me just add this. I would say that someone who has a pleasing personality would be less inclined to the full treatment, shall we say, as someone who is stand-offish, someone who indicates by his attitude that he is above others. Someone who is willing to listen to the Intourist people and politely converse with them would be more likely to escape attention than someone who appears to know it all. But the person must be careful not to ask political questions or be drawn into arguments with his hosts. You understand what I am trying to say?"

"Perfectly, Mr. Massimov."

McShane rose to leave and the defector got up from his comfortable sofa to take his hand and shake it vigorously.

"Goodbye, Mr. Anderson, or whatever your name is," he said with a wink and a wide smile. "I hope I have been helpful to you."

"Yes, Mr. Massimov, I think it was worth my time to speak with you. Thank you for sharing your viewpoints with me. Goodbye and good luck in our country."

Massimov was led from the room and as the door closed, Powell pulled the black mask from his pocket. 'Sorry, McShane, but you'll have to put this back on."

As they led him out of the house, McShane's mind was already occupied with what Massimov had told him. The Intourist officials and guides are responsible for tourists, not the KGB, at least not directly. He was positive now that he was on the right track.

"Well, was the visit worth your time, McShane?" Powell asked as he guided him through the front door, down the stairs and into the waiting car.

"Yes, it was, in fact it was much more so than I expected it to be. I'm grateful to you for the time. Hell, now I don't even mind having had to play Zorro for the chance to talk to him."

CHAPTER SEVEN

CIA HEADQUARTERS

Powell had two of his men drive McShane back to Langley. They removed the mask about a mile from the building and told him not to reveal anything about his meeting with Massimov.

"Where've you been?" Susan asked as he entered his office. 'There's a pile of telephone messages on your desk. And you turned your pager off."

"Which tells you that I didn't want to be found, doesn't it?"

Susan always got uptight when her boss took off without informing her where he could be reached. She knew, of course, that there were times when he did not want to be found, but this never stopped her from reminding him that she could relieve him of a lot of unnecessary calls if he would just take a few seconds to tell her when he would be back.

"Not now, Susan," be bellowed, "just get me the names of the guys in Records for both the CIA and the FBI. I need to make a couple of calls."

McShane looked through his telephone messages but could not see anything of immediate importance, certainly nothing that would transcend the importance of the calls he was about to make. The 'tourist courier' idea was now starting to consume him. He was finding it a real challenge, and one that he was enjoying.

His intercom sounded with Susan's voice on the line. 'I've got those names and numbers for you. Nigel Sherman is our man in Records and his extension is 4301. Orlin McKeon is the FBI contact and his number is 828-8700, extension 1102. Anything else, Grumpy?"

"No, thanks."

He dialed Sherman first and asked if there were any records on a Drew Cummins of 15 Harlequin Place in Minneapolis. Sherman told him he would need a few minutes and would call him back.

Next, McShane dialed the FBI and asked for extension 1102. Despite the stories that circulated about the two security services fighting to protect their territories, the agencies actually cooperated fully and got along very well together, at least in the middle management areas.

McShane had frequently been asked for assistance by his FBI counterpart and had gladly given it. And the FBI had always been helpful whenever he and others in his Department had needed information. McShane often wondered where these stories of inter-agency jealousy and rivalry originated. He had never seen any symptoms of problems in all the years he had been dealing with his fellow security officers.

"McKeon," the voice answered.

"Orlin, this is Brendon McShane over at CIA. I need some help in checking the records for a guy named Drew Cummins at 15 Harlequin Place in Minneapolis."

McKeon asked for McShane's rating to insure that he was entitled to ask and receive this information in case there was something confidential on Cummins' file.

"I'm H-2, and I can be reached on extension 2324."

"Right, I'll be back to you in a few minutes."

As soon as he replaced the receiver, Susan was on the intercom. "Sherman's on the line."

He punched the illuminated button. "Couldn't find anything on a Drew Cummins at the address given. Is there any other way I can be helpful?"

McShane thanked for his time and assured him that having no information on Cummins was already a big help.

Susan buzzed him a few minutes later to let him know that Orlin McKeon was on the line.

"Sorry, old buddy, but we drew a blank on Cummins. Nothing. If you have any more details, I'd be happy to check further."

"No, Nigel, I'm grateful that you don't have anything on him, so thanks for your efforts. They're appreciated."

"Any time. Always glad to help our higher-paid brothers."

McShane sat back in his chair, put his hands behind his head and his feet on the desk. He was feeling fairly good about his project and about the young man in Minneapolis whom he would soon be calling.

CHAPTER EIGHT

CIA HEADQUARTERS

McShane's next step was to relay the information he had collected to Chase Barron and the other committee members and to make his recommendation. He dialed Barron's extension and quickly got him on the line.

"Chase, I'd like to have a meeting with you and the 'Courier Committee.' I think I am ready to make a strong recommendation to you on the courier idea. When would be convenient?"

"How's three o'clock this afternoon?"

He assured him that three would be fine and Barron said he would alert the other members to be in his office at that time.

Brittany Kamden, Barron's secretary, was on the 'phone when McShane and the three other members of the 'Courier Committee' arrived. She motioned to them to be seated as she continued her telephone conversation.

"Yes, Mr. Millar, I'll certainly relay the message to Mr. Barron, and thank you for calling."

"Whew," she grimaced. "That's Mr. Barron's insurance man and he's like a shark when it smells blood. He never relaxes his hold."

George Hollis laughed and remembered an old line that he had heard one of the fellows in the cafeteria mention one day. The fellow said that when he is on an airplane and is tired and wants to relax and the fellow next to him is in a talkative mood, he uses a faultless plan to halt the conversation. 'It works this way," he said: "When, as invariably it will, the conversation turns to one's employment, all you have to say to your loquacious companion is that you are a life insurance salesman and you'll be surprised how quiet he becomes."

Everyone started to laugh when Barron's voice roared on the intercom. "Brittany is that a group of conventioneers out there? Send them in and let's get them back to work."

"Been eatin' pizza with meat toppings again, Chase?" McShane asked as he sat in one of the comfortable leather chairs.

"If I were, I wouldn't be as pleasant as I am," Barron growled. 'OK, let's get down to business. "What've you got, Brendon?"

McShane reported on his meeting with his friend in Customs and his comments on the young man from a midwest sales incentive company and how he traveled around the world. Next, he mentioned his conversation with Ilya Massimov, touching on the defector's comments about KGB's profiles and how Intourist was responsible for the tourists.

"Chase, I feel we have the type of man we're looking for, and I would like to proceed with recruiting this guy who lives in Minneapolis. There is no file on him; I checked with our Records Department and with the FBI's and he's clean. He sounds like a solid citizen. I would like to fly to Minneapolis to interview him and sound him out on helping us with our deliveries. If I find that his persona and career are exactly what we're looking for, we could subsequently set up a training school and hire him as the professor once he has performed a few errands for us."

Barron stroked his chin, a common occurrence when he was in a pensive mood, snapped his garish colored suspenders then sat upright in his chair. 'Why Minneapolis? Can't we find someone with an incentive company here in D.C.? There must be plenty of those companies around the east coast?"

"Chief, it's just a feeling I have. I don't want an easterner. I want someone from the midwest. It's a hunch I have. Easterners have a taint abroad. Mention you're from New York or Washington and foreigners immediately conjure up a vision of a smart-aleck, street-smart, loud-mouth type. Whether we agree or not, let's face it, that's what most foreigners think. The midwest has a different mentality, where people are not quite so . . . impersonal. New Yorkers are considered uncouth, rude. I hate to say that because I'm a New Yorker myself. But, nevertheless, that's how Europeans in particular view us. Not so the midwesterner."

"Besides, Chase, I checked and found surprisingly, that the three major sales incentive companies are in the midwest. The biggest is in St. Louis while numbers two and three are in Minneapolis. Another surprising statistic I found is that there are about twelve sales incentive companies in Minneapolis alone and that's more than any other city in the world."

"Why do we have to use a sales incentive company? What's wrong with a big travel agency or some other travel organization. Why an incentive company?"

Hollis felt it was time to jump in and give his cohort some support. He pointed out that sales incentive companies work with the giants of U.S. industry, as well as smaller businesses, and take their winning distributors and dealers, such as General Electric, the Big Three auto giants, insurance companies and almost every nationally-known business, around the world.

"That's right," McShane continued, "They don't concentrate on trips to the same destination, as most travel agencies do. The incentive companies' escorts, guides, trip directors, whatever they're called, travel to all the continents. They operate trips to the far corners of the earth . . . Australia, Europe, South America, China as well, of course, to closer in spots like the Caribbean, Mexico and so on.

"Incentive companies take their clients everywhere . . . north, east, south, west, and what's more, they are doing this several times each month. If this young man turns out to be as ideal a courier as I think he will be, we could use him wherever his travels take him. We could then consider recruiting other trip directors to give us the broad coverage we'd like to have."

Barron swung his chair around and stared out the window for a few seconds. "How do you plan to contact him? Do you intend to use the FBI in Minneapolis at first?"

"No, Chief, I want to make this contact myself and run the entire operation within our Department. I want this to be exclusively a CIA operation without any help from any of the other security agencies. Any objections?"

"No, none at all," Barron replied, still staring out over the Virginia countryside. Slowly, he turned his chair around so that he faced his committee. "It's kind of interesting Massimov's comment about tourists being left to the Intourist people. Never thought about that somehow. I guess they figure the guides can keep a close watch on their flock, but it's dangerous, too. If the tourists have a group visa, they must do everything together, so it wouldn't be too much of a problem watching them closely, but it would be difficult keeping tabs on them if they have individual visas and today I believe most tourists require individual visas, don't they? I mean, even if they are traveling with a group?"

'Yes, Chase, they do, but still many organized tours offer their participants, the group visa idea because if it's a Russia trip, it eliminates the need for the individual to go through the sometimes onerous rigmarole of trying to secure a visa from the Soviet Embassy."

"But we're talking here mostly about eastern Europe. Our couriers are going to be operating all over the world."

"Of course, Chase, but the KGB yields to Intourist in the handling of tourists visiting Communist countries or any other country in the world. Anything to do with tourism is the responsibility of Intourist. It's known that the KGB are more interested in watching the fat cats, not the little tourist who has saved up for years to make a trip to London or Rio or Paris. And, I've got to believe that it's the same procedure in China and other Communist countries.

The KGB is looked upon as the masters and their procedures are copied by other Communist countries. There are Intourist people in Russian embassies and consulates around the world, so any stalking or surveillance of suspected couriers or agents or anything to do with tourism is still an Intourist responsibility. Simply stated, the KGB doesn't want to waste its important time and top agents on the little tourist. And this also applies to other countries outside the Communist pale. There are Intourist agents attached to Russian embassies all around the world."

Barron looked at all the other members of the committee. "Do you guys all feel the same way. I mean do you think Brendon's approach is the right one? Do any of you have other suggestions?"

"I think Brendon's got something worth pursuing," one of the committee said, "and certainly I've heard nothing better. I just wonder if the trip director who travels in advance of his group is considered as a group member even though he is traveling alone much of the time."

"Interesting point, and quite frankly, I don't have an answer to that but I am relying again on my instincts that he will be considered in the same way. It's something we may have to find out by trial and error."

"We have to go with it," another committee member piped up. "It's the way to go. At least, it's worth the effort and it may just work better than anything else we've tried to date."

"Okay, go for it. Contact your Minneapolis man and report back to the committee and me on his reactions and whether he'll cooperate. I want you to give us a full report at our next meeting."

* * *

The normal procedure for contacting individuals on a secretive level is to bring in the local FBI and ask their cooperation in making the approach. But McShane wanted to do this on his own. He wanted to make the contact, interview the candidate and recruit him. This was to be a CIA operation, period.

"Susan, find me the names of sales incentive companies in Minneapolis. There are about twelve of them, I believe, but let's start with five or six. We can get more if needed."

Ten minutes later, Susan was on the intercom. 'The operator gave me Danbury Incentives and the Harrison Motivation Company. Their 'phone numbers are 763-930-8666 and 952-726-3313 respectively."

McShane lifted the 'phone and dialed the first number. "Danbury Incentives." The lilting voice of the operator sounded pleasant in his ear.

"Would you put me through to Drew Cummins, please?"

"I don't recognize the name, sir, what department is he in?"

McShane informed her that he did not know his department.

"Please hold and I'll check our directory."

She returned to the 'phone to tell him that there was no one of that name at Danbury incentives.

"Well, thank you. I may have the wrong company."

Checking his notes for the second number, he lifted the 'phone again and dialed 952-726-3313.

"Harrison Motivation Company, good afternoon."

"May I speak to Drew Cummins, please?"

"Yes, sir, I'll put you through."

"Hello, this is Drew Cummins."

"Drew, my name is Mel Sanders. I'm a vice president with the Cadillac Division of General Motors in Detroit. I'm flying to Minneapolis tomorrow on a business matter and would also like to have a meeting with you with a view to having your company bid on a special incentive program we are thinking of sponsoring. Would it be possible for you to meet with me tomorrow, Thursday, for lunch?"

The voice laughed gently. 'Mr. Sanders, it's not every day a potential client calls up and asks if he can have a meeting to discuss an incentive program. Usually, we have to spend months and sometimes years just to get in the door at the account and talk to the decision-makers. Of course, I will be very pleased to have lunch with you, but I should point out that I am in the travel department and you should really be speaking with someone in sales."

"I was given your name by my boss. He was on in an incentive program to Europe when he was with another company and Harrison Motivation operated it and he remembered you as being extremely efficient in the handling of the program and very popular with the participants. He said as I was going to be in Minneapolis to attend a sales meeting that I should give you a call and have a conversation with you. He had asked me to talk to you about possible destinations as he said he was impressed with your worldly knowledge and thought you would certainly have good ideas about where we should take this very special group. I thought it might be expedient to have lunch first and have you talk about some destinations. If it's not convenient, however . . . ."

"Oh, no, Mr. Sanders, the client is always right. As I said, normally this would be handled by an account executive in our Detroit office, but as you will be in Minneapolis, I would be happy to meet with you and later I can refer you to our Detroit office if that's agreeable with you."

"Yes, that perfectly satisfactory. I am staying at the Marriott Hotel downtown. One of our salespeople in Minneapolis suggested Murray's Restaurant and said it was almost next door to the Marriott. Would noon be OK?"

"Noon's fine, Mr. Sanders, and I am flattered that an automotive company would approach our company through me. I'm only a member of the travel staff and that's down the line a bit from sales."

"All I can tell you, Drew, is that you must have impressed my boss enough for him to ask me to contact you. Oh, one other thing. Perhaps it would be a good idea to keep our meeting to yourself for the moment. The program I want to discuss with you is very confidential. After our conversation, we can talk about approaching your account executive in Detroit. This way, no one in your Detroit office will get upset about the contact having been made through you rather than in Michigan. And as I said, the only reason for our meeting is that my boss thought it would be a good idea to have your ideas on destinations. OK?"

"I think that's sound thinking, Mr. Sanders. Do you want me to make a reservation?"

"No, I'll have my secretary do it."

"Then, thank you and I look forward to seeing you Thursday noon at Murray's restaurant. Goodbye, sir."

"Goodbye, Drew."

CHAPTER NINE

MINNEAPOLIS, MINNESOTA

McShane took an early morning flight to Minneapolis and hailed a cab to take him to Murray's restaurant. He did not have a reservation at the Marriott and did not intend to stay over. His plan was to meet with Cummins, discuss the important service he could render his country by being a courier and then return to Washington later that afternoon. He felt that he lent his story more credence by telling Cummins that he was attending meetings in Minneapolis and would be in the city for a few days.

Susan, his secretary, had made a reservation at Murray's in the name of Sanders and he gave that name when he arrived at the restaurant shortly before noon. He told the maitre d' that a Mr. Cummins, whom he hadn't met before, would be joining him and asked if he would show him to his table.

McShane watched the entrance, visualizing how Cummins would look. He had a mental picture of his potential recruit as a slim, fairly tall young man with blond hair, no mustache or beard and athletic-looking. The image he drew proved to be amazingly accurate with only the hair color being wrong.

Just before noon, he saw a young man enter the restaurant and approach the maitre d's upright desk. He looked to be in his late twenties, stood six-foot one with a strong, athletic build. He had a full head of thick, dark hair and was impeccably dressed in a navy blue suit, a pale blue shirt with a striped navy blue and gold tie.

His tanned, handsome face caused more than one of the young women executives dining in the restaurant to let their gazes linger on him as he waited for the maitre d' to finish his 'phone call and greet the guest in line before him. The maitre d' returned and Drew identified himself and asked for Mr. Sanders' table. "Yes, sir, Mr. Sanders has arrived," he said, flourishing one hand while the other held tightly on to several menus.

"Please follow me" he motioned with his hand and escorted Drew to a corner table. "Mr. Cummins, Mr. Sanders."

McShane felt confident that there would not be too many female Intourist guides who would not be charmed and beguiled by his looks and made less strict with their government rules and regulations.

McShane thanked him and held out his hand to Cummins. "Hi, Drew, I'm Mel Sanders." They shook hands and sat down as a waiter immediately handed each a menu. McShane invited his guest to have a drink, but Cummins said he preferred a mineral water.

"Good for you, Drew," he said, "because that's exactly what I'm having. Never drink during business hours; it clouds the mind."

They took a few minutes to decide which item on the menu to order then gave their choices to the waiter.

"As I said on the 'phone, Mr. Sanders, I'm flattered that you would single me out to discuss an incentive program. I've been thinking about this since your call and I know that this will help my career, whether we get the account or not."

"Well, let's exchange pleasantries and engage in what is known as 'small talk' then we'll get down to business after we've eaten. Do you have any time problem?"

"No, not at all. This is more important than what I've been doing in the office for the last couple of days. I have all the time in the world."

They consumed their entrees, declined dessert and ordered coffee.

"Drew, I have to apologize to you for something," McShane said as he drew a wallet from inside his coat pocket. He opened the wallet and showed his agency badge.

Drew looked at the badge and suddenly his eyes widened. "CIA? I don't understand. Aren't you with General Motors?"

McShane returned the wallet to his pocket and looked straight at Cummins.

"Drew, my name is Brendon McShane and I am an agent with a special department of the CIA. I am sorry that I had to use a subterfuge to lure you to this lunch, but I did not want to state my real purpose on the telephone. I want to talk to you about performing a very special service for the CIA and helping your country. You can walk away from this meeting and I assure you nothing will ever be said. We're not asking you to do anything particularly dangerous, but you are in a position to do a real service for the U.S."

As they sipped their coffee, McShane explained why he had chosen Cummins and the reason why someone in his position, traveling around the world with groups made him an ideal candidate for a courier's job. He told him that the CIA was confident that while the KGB watched every visitor to the Soviet Union very carefully, tourists traveling in groups were their Achilles heel.

"Not just the Soviet union and other Communist countries. We need someone who will be in an out of many countries without arousing suspicion."

The time was approaching two o'clock when McShane finally asked: "Will you help us?"

Cummins was obviously bewildered. "I honestly don't know what to say. I've never thought of myself as a spy and . . ."

"Not a spy," McShane interrupted him, "a courier. There's a difference. We're not asking you to engage in anything mysterious or dangerous. You will simply be carrying items to be delivered to people in foreign lands. I can't lie and say there may not be any danger, but I can say that the possibility of it is remote."

"What are these items you want me to carry?"

"They could range from microfilm, which we would hide in objects we would give you, such as a razor or hair brush, to money that will be cleverly concealed again in objects we will provide you."

"Mr. Sanders, er, I mean Mr. McShane . . ."

"My name is Brendon."

"Brendon, something's bothering me. I know that we have diplomatic bags and such. Couldn't these objects, if they are so small, be transported in them? Aren't these bags sacred in terms of the respect that countries give each other?"

"Yes, to a degree. No one is ever really certain if diplomatic bags go from the sender to the recipient without being exposed to some sort of tampering. The secret services of every country can also look at the contents of a bag without ever opening it. They do this with special x-ray machines. And we have couriers who carry pouches strapped to their wrists to insure that they are not looked at by any unauthorized person. But what happens when we want to deliver some of these items to people within a foreign country? Our diplomats are watched and tailed.

"We want someone who can slip in and out of countries and can make these drops without suspicion. Your job takes you around the world and you have perfect credentials. Do you want to think about our conversation before giving me an answer."

"Yes, I think I would like to mull it over. May I have a couple of days?"

"Here's my card. If you join us, we'll ask you to come to Langley to acquaint you more with what we expect of you."

"Just one more thing, Drew. Whether you decide to come with us or not, you must not say anything to anybody, Not a word. The success of the project is dependent on no one knowing anything about this conversation. We insist on total secrecy. I'll await your call . . . and I hope your response is an affirmative one."

Drew heard McShane ask the maitre d' to order a cab to take him to the airport. 'Don't bother," he interrupted. "I'll take you to the airport; it's not too far from my office."

As they drove to the Twin Cities international airport, McShane could see that his potential recruit was almost in a state of shock.

"I know our conversation is causing you some anxiety, Drew. Or maybe it's disappointment that you won't be instrumental in landing a plum account for your company. I wouldn't be overly worried about that just now. It's just possible that this meeting may do more for your career than you ever dreamed. I won't say more than that, but just let me say that we're not asking for something without being willing to do something in return."

Drew dropped him at the airport. They shook hands. "I'll await hearing from you. Goodbye."

* * *

Drew made up his mind that same afternoon. He wrestled with the glamour of the job as well as with the aspects of danger. He recalled that McShane had said there would be little danger, but Drew was smart enough to know that there would be an element of risk in surreptitiously slipping items to people in foreign lands, particularly eastern bloc nations. He also remembered McShane saying the meeting might produce more benefits in his job than he had realized. 'There's no doubt that the CIA has tremendous power and influence,' he mused. 'They could easily help me in many different ways.'

The next morning he dialed the number on McShane's card.

"Mr. McShane's office."

"May I speak with Mr. McShane, please. My name is Drew Cummins."

"Yes, Mr. Cummins, please hold on." Susan was aware of the name and that he may call.

"Good morning, Drew, this is Brendon."

"Brendon, I've given our conversation a lot of thought and I want to be brought in."

"Great," McShane bellowed into the 'phone. "What's your schedule like over the next few days. Are you able to get away?"

"Yes, I can easily do that. I don't have a trip scheduled until the end of the month."

"By the way, Drew, where is your next trip?"

"I'm going to London and Paris with a group of electronics distributors."

They settled on a date and a time and McShane told him he would pick him up at National Airport.

"We'll reimburse you for all expenses. Buy a ticket and keep receipts for all incidentals. I look forward to seeing you and I'm really pleased that you are coming with us."

CHAPTER TEN

WASHINGTON, D.C.

As the pilot banked the aircraft for its final approach into National Airport, Drew had a perfect view of the nation's capital from his window seat. He thought how spectacular it looked in the bright sunlight, and was able to pick out some of the famous landmarks. He had been to Washington on several occasions before, and each time he saw it, thought it looked even more beautiful than the time before. 'Maybe it improves with age,' he mused.

This was going to be a day trip, so he hadn't checked any luggage. He was able to go immediately outside the terminal and look for McShane. He had asked what model and color of car McShane had to make identification easier. He was not given any details but was assured he would be found without any difficulty. He had just arrived outside the Northwest Airlines entrance when a black car drove up. The window on the passenger side was lowered and he heard a voice call his name.

Drew waved his hand in recognition, entered the car and shook hands with McShane.

"Good flight?" he asked.

"Wonderful," Drew replied. "You know, I've been to Washington many times and I still marvel at the beauty of the city each time I come in."

"Maybe that's why I work for its preservation and the system that supports it. Maybe that's why you agreed to help us."

They drove along a tree-lined avenue for a few minutes until McShane pulled the Oldsmobile into a partially-wooded area with a guard booth manned by a stern-looking officer. McShane powered his window down and handed over his identification card. The guard scanned it on a machine just inside his door, returned it and asked for some identification from Drew.

He proffered his driver's license and provided his Social Security number. Again, the guard returned to his booth to check the validity of both items then waved them through.

"As you can well imagine, they are very careful about whom they allow to pass through to our building, and I'm afraid there is going to be some more investigation before we are permitted to enter the sacred halls," McShane said with a smirk on his face.

McShane parked the car and they entered the main building where all Drew's credentials were again checked and verified, and after they had passed through the metal screening gate, McShane suggested a late lunch in the cafeteria before giving a tour of only those areas of the building where he was authorized to take Drew.

Lunch was a quick event and despite McShane's frequent criticisms of the culinary skills of the cafeteria's chefs, Drew enjoyed the meal and mentioned that he would be very pleased if their cafeteria was anywhere near as good.

Despite the frequent stops that they had already made to check credentials, McShane had to slide his card in a few receptacles, press his hand against a pad on two walls and answer questions posed by a disembodied voice to explain the presence and purpose of Drew's visit.

"You've only seen about a tenth of our humble home," McShane said as he passed down a long hallway and entered a conference room. He pressed a button on the wall to alert would-be intruders that a meeting was being held inside.

"Drew, I don't plan to take you up to my own area on this visit because at the moment, the fewer people who know about you, the better. I thought we would conduct our business down here. Maybe when we bring you in on a subsequent visit you will be introduced to some of my cohorts."

"Now you're making it sound mysterious and more dangerous than you led me to believe when we had our first meeting."

McShane attempted a laugh and assured him that the courier job was no more dangerous than he first represented it to be but that he was known around his unit as Mr. Super Cautious, and stated that caution was an admirable quality in this business.

"As I said on the 'phone earlier, the reason I brought you into Washington was because there are too many things to talk about and I didn't want to discuss them over the 'phone. Okay, now Drew, here's your first assignment. You mentioned London and Paris as the destinations for your next trip. There is something I would like you to deliver in Paris.

"By the way, do you speak French?"

"Yes, I do. I studied it at the University of Minnesota and I was an exchange student in Paris for three months, so I also know Paris quite well."

"Great. That always helps," McShane beamed.

He gave Drew a black leather wallet with a built-in calculator. "On Friday morning, the 17th, I want you to go to the restaurant "Au Coin des Boulevards" on the corner of the Boulevard de Clichy and Boulevard Rochechouart near the Sacre Coeur, and order a café-au-lait. I want you to take an outdoor table. If it is raining, the restaurant has a canopy that covers the customers.

"I want you to be seated there by 10:25 a.m. I suggest you arrive early so that you are seated and sipping your coffee at that time. I want you to be reading a copy of the International Herald Tribune and reading the back page so that the front page is exposed to passers-by."

"At precisely 10:45 a.m., I want you to pay your bill and leave the café, turning left down the Rue des Martyrs. Walk slowly and put the wallet inside the newspaper which you must carry in your left hand. Someone will come along and overtake you. As he does, he will take the paper from your hand. That's all. Your first mission will have been completed. Any questions?"

"Yes, I have one. Why all the cloak and dagger stuff for Paris? Moscow or Beijing or some other foreign city, yes, but Paris is inside our friendly area of operation, isn't it?"

A soft smile creased McShane's face. "Sometimes it's the seemingly easy drops that are the most difficult and that need the most surreptitious means for delivery."

"It shows that I have a lot to learn, doesn't it?"

"Yes, but I have a very strong feeling that you're going to be a quick learner."

"OK, then, just so I have all the details properly, may I write down the time, date and place in the wallet's diary section?"

"Of course, but nothing more than the time and date. Just remember the name of the café."

"And that's all there is?"

"That's all there is. I told you there wasn't really too much to it. The only reason we are using you is that you're new, you're an unknown face and most important, we don't want to use anyone from the embassy or any of our other offices because they're constantly watched, even in friendly cities. This is really a simple chore you're being given—and much like that you will be given in the future."

"One other thing, Drew. I'm going to give you a special number where you can reach me at any time. I don't want you to write it down; I want you to commit it to memory. It's 222-555-1000. The operator will ask for your code access. Don't mention my name; give only the code access and you will be put through to me immediately or you will be required to hold for a short time while the operator locates me."

'What is my access code?"

"I've been thinking about that. I'm going to call you Courier Thirteen."

"What happened to the other twelve? I hope they are all still alive and well."

McShane smiled. We never use sequential codes; it's too obvious. I chose thirteen because it is the day of the month on which you were born. Right?"

"Yes." Drew paused for a moment then added: "I almost asked how you knew that, but I have a feeling there aren't too many things you don't already know about me."

McShane spent the next 30 minutes discussing CIA policies, techniques, systems and drills. After a while, Drew slipped his hand inside his coat pocket and took out a pad. He was about to write some notes when McShane grabbed his hand and said "No notes, Drew. It's not always a good idea to write down things of importance; better to train your memory and rely on it.

"I want to emphasize, Drew, that this first delivery is a test. If it's successful, and if you handle it well and if, after maybe a few missions, you feel comfortable with it, I want you to give me the names of other men and women in your office and any others you know well with your competitors that you feel might fit into this type of work. We want to develop a special outfit within our Courier Department organization that will do a lot of good for our country. We'll discuss this further in a few months so that we'll both know if the idea will work. OK?"

"That's fine with me, Brendon."

"I'll drive you back to the airport. I took the liberty of making a reservation for you on the flight at 5:35 p.m. I canceled the later flight you were holding."

As they drove back to the airport, McShane asked his new recruit why he hadn't mentioned money. "You know, you will get paid for these jobs and, of course, we'll cover all expenses. I have an envelope here for you with $1,000 as a permanent expense advance. Sign the slip attached to it and give it to me.'

"I don't know why I didn't ask about money. Maybe I just didn't think about getting paid. I was probably more concerned about doing something for my country. Does that sound too patriotic?"

"Not at all, but you will get paid. We'll give you at least $5,000 for each delivery, depending on the country. It's a little more than we normally pay but as we're not paying for your transportation, you should get a little extra. How does that sound"

"Great. Where do I send my expenses?"

"That is the last point I planned to discuss with you. I want you to write all your expenses down on a piece of paper. You don't need a printed form and you don't need it typed, longhand is OK. Include all receipts, where possible, and mail them to this address."

He handed a slip of paper to Drew who scanned the note which read: CIA, Langley, VA 23665 and the cryptic words CD 4-13 in the lower left-hand corner. "Memorize it and destroy the paper. Never mail it from Minneapolis. Mail it from any place you like, but never Minneapolis. If a receipt is just not possible, we'll understand why none is attached.

"Okay, Drew, here's National. You're on your own and I do mean your own. If anything happens to you, there's nothing we can do to help you. We can't say we know you, and we can't provide you any protection. If you do get in trouble, ask to see someone from the U.S. embassy. Plead innocent, no matter how damaging the circumstances and never mention anything about the CIA. Always be conscious of the fact that if you are speaking to a member of the embassy staff in a foreign jail, the cell will definitely be bugged and conduct your conversation accordingly. Oh, one other thing that may make you feel better. In every country, the worst that will happen to you is that you'll be expelled. They don't shoot couriers."

"You keep throwing in these zingers, Brendon. One minute I figure this is safe and simple and I get paid $5000 for doing nothing more than taking a walk. Next minute, you're telling me how to act if I get caught and that you can't lift a finger to help me."

"You can still bow out, you know."

"No, I said I was in and that's what I intend to do".

"Listen, Drew, we have to discuss all aspects of the job and that's why I brought up worst scenarios. I don't think you'll find yourself in any strange predicaments. Just follow my directions and you'll be in a safety mode all the way.

"When you have completed this task, call me at the number I have given you. Call me also as soon as you have been given your other trip assignments so that I can tell you whether we can use you on that particular program. By the way, are you able to pick the trips you want from the list of upcoming trips?"

"In most cases, yes. I have enough seniority that allows me to do that. It's not a guarantee that I'll get the particular trip I request, but in most cases I can get what I want"

"Do you get a list of upcoming trips on a monthly basis?"

"Yes, I get the list about four weeks in advance."

"Would you make it a point to send me a copy of the list as soon as you receive it? Send it to the same address as you would expenses. Is everything understood then?"

"Perfectly, Brendon. I don't suppose I could ask what's in the wallet, could I?"

"No, and don't try to feel it or bend it or do anything else to guess at its contents. Just treat it as a wallet and nothing else."

"Goodbye, Drew, and good luck. I'll await hearing from you after your first mission."

They shook hands. Drew opened the car door and headed for the Northwest counter to pick up his boarding pass.

CHAPTER ELEVEN

LONDON, ENGLAND

The Garfield Company program had been going well in London and this was their last day in Britain's capital city before traveling to Paris for another four days of lavish entertainment, interesting sightseeing and fine dining.

For their last evening in London, a special treat had been arranged for them. The group would have a farewell cocktail party in the ballroom foyer of the Grosvenor Hotel on Park Lane where they were staying, then the guests would move to the hotel's Great Room for a superb banquet followed by a special performance of Her Majesty's Coldstream Guards. The Great Room was the venue of choice of the Royal Family for any large, important banquets, particularly those involving foreign dignitaries.

Drew had seen the Guards several times before, but he still got goose bumps whenever the Master of Ceremonies, a Beefeater clad in his colorful, traditional uniform, banged his mace on the floor and intoned in a pleasant accent to the group:

"Ladies and Gentlemen, it is my honor and privilege to announce the band of Her Majesty's Coldstream Guards."

Suddenly, the huge doors to the room would swing open and in perfect synchronization, the musicians would strike their instruments and march smartly into the room.

Their performance never failed to evoke superlative comments while cameras clicked and movie cameras whirred recording the splendor of the musicians in their scarlet tunics, black feathery Busby hats and sharply creased black trousers.

Drew smiled as he recalled the fist time he had seen the Guards. He was on a program years before and the group was staying at the Hilton, just down Park Lane from the Grosvenor House.

The soldiers had arrived in their every day uniforms and were ushered into a private room where sandwiches, beer and tea had been arranged for them.

Drew met with the band's director to go over the selection of military and show tunes the musicians would play. As they spoke, he noticed the soldiers removing their gray uniforms to change into the smart dress outfits in which they would parade around the room.

He noticed that as many of them took off their shirts and pants, their underwear was sadly in need of bleach and many of their undershirts and shorts were badly in need of the services of a seamstress.

Later, as they marched through the ballroom of the Hilton, resplendent in their impressive apparel, they were the epitome of smartness. Their sartorial splendor hinted at sophistication and superiority. But he couldn't stop laughing to himself as he thought of the dirty, holy underwear hidden by their gleaming tunics.

He regretted that he would have to miss this evening's performance by the Guards. As many times as he had seen them, he still got excited watching them march and play in perfect harmony. The sights they created were as memorable as the sounds they produced.

But, he had to fly to Paris in advance of the group to ensure that when they arrived in the French capital the following day to confirm all the details for their stay in The City of Lights and that everything would be in readiness. This meant checking with Andre Gaulin, his company's representative in Paris, to ensure that the motor coaches and guides would be at the airport at the right time and would have the Garfield Company's logo and name on signs displayed on the motor coaches' windows.

He was also required to meet with the hotel staff to address the specific requirements of the group and go over the menus and locations of cocktail parties and dinners. All these arrangements had been contracted for many months before, but they still had to be confirmed and double-checked.

There would also be other myriad duties such as confirming that the hotel had responded to the special accommodations requests of the group that included some couples requesting king-size beds, others asking to have rooms close to their friends, rooms on the lower floors or higher up or near elevators.

Drew's schedule was planned weeks in advance of the trip, so he knew he would be in Paris one day ahead of the group which was scheduled to arrive at Charles de Gaulle Airport at 3:40 p.m. the next day.

This gave him the time he would need to deliver the wallet the next morning. He had followed McShane's instructions to the letter and had not tried to feel the wallet to determine just what it was that was hidden inside.

He was now experiencing the pangs of nervousness—or was it excitement? He wanted to do a good job on his first mission, but was conscious of the fact that something could go wrong and that he might be exposed. 'Better Paris,' he thought 'than Moscow or Bucharest or some eastern European city.'

CHAPTER TWELVE

PARIS, FRANCE

He awoke early and looked out the window of his hotel room to see what the weather was like. 'Hmm,' he thought, 'looks like the café won't need its canopy this morning.' The sun was shining from a cloudless sky; it was a beautiful morning in 'The City of Light'.

He showered, dressed in olive slacks and a white short-sleeved sports shirt and took the elevator down to the main floor to have breakfast. But he found when he arrived at the restaurant that he wasn't hungry. 'What's the use of going into breakfast when I don't feel like eating,' he thought. He was sure it was the mission that was taking the edge off his appetite.

He strolled to the gift shop and attended to the first part of his assignment, buying a copy of the International Herald Tribune. He had scheduled an early meeting with the hotel's convention manager to go over a few more points such as where the hospitality desk would be set up, and a blackboard on which he would put the group's itinerary for that evening. It was always put on a blackboard daily, even though a booklet with all the details of the program had been mailed to them two weeks before the commencement of the trip.

The meeting with the hotel official took only a half-hour, and the hotel's efficiency was evidenced by the fact that he had no need to change anything. All was in readiness for the group's arrival later in the day.

The hotel was not too far from Clichy and Rochechouart Boulevards so he decided to walk to the Café. He was going to be early but this would give him the time to find an outdoor table where his contact would have no trouble spotting him drinking his café-au-lait and reading the Herald Tribune.

Surprisingly, the café was quite busy when he spotted it shortly after turning on to the Boulevard Rochechouart, but there were two or three tables without occupants. He seated himself at one where he would be conspicuous.

"Bon jour, monsieur," the waiter said as he approached. "Bon jour," Drew replied. "Un café-au-lait, s'il vous plait."

"Toute-de-suite, monsieur," the waiter replied and turned to pick up some cups and saucers left by previous customers at the next table.

A few minutes later, the waiter brought his coffee. 'I must relax,' he told himself. 'I must appear like a tourist enjoying one of the pleasures of Paris—a coffee at an outdoor café in the world's most beautiful city while watching the Parisians going about their business.'

He had given the 'paper no more than a cursory glance before putting it down, concentrating on his coffee to give an indifferent appearance.

He had one more coffee before noting that it was just three minutes to go. He lifted the Tribune and appeared to be reading the back page so that the front page could be clearly seen by passers-by. He glanced at his watch and saw that it was time to leave. He slipped the wallet inside the newspaper and left a few francs on the table. He walked on to the Boulevard for a short distance before turning on to the Rue des Martyrs. The newspaper was held loosely in his left hand.

A woman with a small child approached and smiled as she passed. He thought more Americans should have moments like that and perhaps they would be less critical of the French.

There were several people on the other side of the street walking in opposite directions, but fewer on his side. He was now half-way down the street and no one had yet taken the newspaper.

He heard loud footsteps behind him. They were getting closer. Now they were right behind him and he waited for the newspaper to be taken, but the pedestrian passed him in a hurry.

Suddenly, the man who had overtaken him stopped to peer into the window of a store just ahead. Drew continued his walk at the same pace and passed the curious pedestrian.

The Rue des Martyrs ends at the Notre Dame de Lorette church where Rue St. Lazare and Rue Lamartin join, just another 100 yards ahead. He felt a stream of perspiration run down his back. Had something gone wrong? Had he followed all McShane's instructions carefully? Had he failed to . . .

Suddenly, the newspaper was smoothly taken from his hand and he could see the curious pedestrian walking smartly away from him, holding it as he quickly turned the corner on to the Rue St. Lazare.

When Drew reached the end of the street, he turned and looked ahead of him, but his contact was nowhere to be seen.

Mission accomplished. Now, he must return to the hotel, take another shower, change into his company uniform and drive out to Charles de Gaulle Airport with Andrew Gaulin to meet the incoming group.

CHAPTER THIRTEEN

JFK AIRPORT, NEW YORK

After clearing customs, Drew gave his bags to a porter who checked to see that they were correctly tagged to Minneapolis. He looked around to see if Airport Annie was anywhere nearby. He wanted to say 'hello' and have a few words with her; it was a good idea to maintain contacts in this business. She was not around, so he headed for the exit and gave his customs declaration form to the officer.

The complimentary yellow and white transfer bus was just pulling up to the stop outside the main building. He boarded it and relaxed while he arranged his thoughts. A call to Brendon McShane was the first thing he would do as soon as he got settled in Northwest's World Club Room.

It took the bus only a few minutes to arrive at the Northwest Airlines terminal and another five before showing his membership card to the receptionist. 'Where's Laurie?" he asked the woman behind the desk whom he didn't recognize.

"She has the day off. I'm Linda Dixon," the receptionist told him. "She must have a crystal ball and know the right day to take off because this has been a hectic one. All the airlines have had delayed flights because of bad weather this morning and many were canceled. We've had people wanting to switch either on to or off from our flights. I haven't had to look for work to do, I can tell you."

He settled himself in one of the semi-private telephone booths. The others were empty. It may have been busier earlier on, but it was fairly quiet in the clubroom now.

He dialed 222-555-1000. No voice came on the line to ask that coins be deposited. It was just like making a local call only he didn't even have to deposit a quarter. An operator came on the line and asked for his code.

"Courier Thirteen."

Please hold." There was silence for about 15 seconds then McShane's voice came on the line.

"Hi, Drew, how was the trip?"

"Fine. Very uneventful, just as you said. Everything went well."

"Yes, I know. I've been given a full report from the other end. Well done."

"I didn't really do much, but thanks for the kind words."

"Do you have any expenses?"

"No, not really. Just eight or nine dollars for the coffee. It's not cheap in Paris, you know. The amount's not worth bothering about."

"Drew, do you know where your next trip is?"

"Yes, I have a trip to Rio. I'm not sure of the dates, but I think it's sometime around the middle of next month. I should receive my monthly schedule when I get back to the office and will, of course, send a copy to you."

'Good, because I may just have another assignment for you. I want you to give me a call when you have the dates of the trip as well as the date you're leaving the States. If I do have a job for you, I'll let you know at that time. Thanks for the call."

"Goodbye," Drew said and hung up.

McShane replaced the receiver, and smiled complacently. The Paris pick-up had no danger attached to it. It had been a test to assess Cummins' nerves and determine his reactions and composure. The Paris agent informed McShane that his protégé had performed very well, showed no signs of nervous tension or agitation.

'Welcome to the CIA, Drew," McShane muttered to himself.

CHAPTER FOURTEEN

RIO DE JANEIRO, BRAZIL

The sun was just creeping over the mountains and had already cast sufficient light for Drew to distinguish some of the renowned landmarks of Rio de Janeiro as the Pan Am 747 slowly banked towards Galeao International Airport.

Rio's world-famous beaches were quiet but would be busy in another hour or so when the sun ascended in the sky and its warmth drew the Cariocas for their morning exercises, soccer and volleyball games and just plain soaking up its rays. The beaches of Copacabana, Ipanema, Gavea and Leblon quickly vanished under the jet as the engines' roar was reduced from a crescendo to a lower pitch in readiness for landing.

Coming up under the left wing of the 'plane, atop a mountain peak 2329 feet above the city, was the spectacular 1200-ton, 130-foot high statue of Christ the Redeemer, its arms stretched out to welcome the people from around the world to Brazil. It was an easily recognizable monument and several passengers on the left side of the airplane excitedly drew attention to it.

The pilot landed the 400-ton aircraft so skillfully that the touchdown didn't jar Drew from the thoughts of his next mission that were rolling around in his head.

The Belton Insurance Company would be taking almost 250 of its top customers to Rio in two more days and he had been assigned to the program as the lead trip director. He also had another job to do, another delivery, although this time the item to be passed to a contact was not a slim wallet as he had been given for the Paris trip. He was carrying a Pan American World Airways flight bag. Whatever it was he would be delivering was inside the flight bag, probably in a false bottom. He had been told to deliver the flight bag, and that's what he intended to do.

His instructions had been simple. He was to walk along Copacabana beach on his second evening in Rio, carrying the flight bag. At precisely 10 o'clock, he was to station himself opposite the Meridien Hotel as though gazing at the busy traffic and bright lights on Avenida Atlantica, the beautiful avenue that skirted the beach.

A man with a Brazilian accent and walking a small dog would approach, smile at him then say: "Be careful of the traffic at this time of night. It can be dangerous."

Drew was to engage in light conversation, bend down to pat the dog and release his grip on the bag. The Brazilian would lift the bag and walk away. Simple. Just like Paris.

As the jet nosed towards the ramp to which it had been directed, he smiled to himself as he remembered McShane's instructions for passage of the bag.

"Isn't that a dangerous thing to do," Drew had said, "carrying a bag on Copacabana beach at night? A mugger might target me as a good prospect, I mean, a lone person carrying a bag. The muggers down there work in packs, four or five together, and I would be no match for a bunch of teenagers who wanted to deprive me of my possessions."

But McShane had a ready reply. He pointed out that if Drew stayed in the general area of his hotel where the tourist police patrolled constantly, he should have no trouble. "And besides," he added, "there is so much pedestrian traffic in that area, you will be safe."

Drew picked up his bags from the carousel and hailed a porter who didn't even ask him which channel he would be choosing: Red for passengers who had exceeded their duty allowance; Green for those with nothing to declare. The porter matter-of-factly loaded the bags on his cart and proceeded to pass through the Green channel.

The Customs agents signaled to a couple in front of Drew whose tanned and swarthy complexions suggested they were Brazilians returning home from a visit to the U.S. No Americans had been stopped and asked to show their bags; they were walking briskly to the exit doors, sure that Customs officers would not want to upset tourists bringing much needed hard currency into their country.

Roberto Solleiro, the manager of the Brazil agency that worked with Harrison Motivation Company, waved to Drew as he came through the sliding doors.

"Welcome back to Rio, Drew," Mauricio said as he vigorously shook his hand while directing the porter to put the bags in the trunk of a new Oldsmobile.

"Very nice," Drew said as he seated himself in the passenger's front seat. "You must be doing well off the Harrison motivation Company to afford a car like this, especially in Brazil."

"Oh, we manage," Roberto smiled, "but remember, we have other clients, too." They set off for the hotel where the group and Drew would be staying. It was a perfect day and although it was not yet eight o'clock in the morning, the temperature was in the low 70s. The sky was clear blue.

It had been almost two years since Drew had last visited Rio and he quickly noticed great improvements, particularly the landscaping at the airport. He noted, too, that the streets seemed cleaner with no litter on the sidewalks.

But the traffic was still the same. Cars, buses and trucks vying with each other on the congested highways and consequently, the drive to the hotel that would normally take about 30 minutes in quiet traffic, took almost an hour.

The front desk staff of the hotel recognized him as he approached the counter and waved their hands in a form of welcome. "Ah, Drew," said Umberto, the front office manager, "welcome back. We're looking forward to having your group with us."

"Hi, gang," he replied, waving back to the three clerks behind the reception desk. "Yes, Umberto, it's nice to be back in beautiful Rio."

"We have a nice room for you, Drew. I hope you enjoy your stay with us." He called over a bellboy who picked up the bags and led the way to the elevator.

When they entered the room, the bellboy placed the bags neatly against the wall as Drew walked over to the windows and stared down in admiration at the beauty of Copacabana Beach that stretched in a magnificent crescent for more than a mile.

The beach was busy now as the fun-loving Cariocas frolicked on the sand chasing the girls in brief tangas, occupying themselves in the various volleyball and soccer games or improving their physiques on chin-up bars.

He handed the bellboy a couple of U.S. dollars, explaining that he hadn't had time to change his money into cruzeiros, the local currency. "This is much better, sir, thank you," the bellboy gushed as he closed the door.

He smiled to himself as he thought how the bellboy would change the dollars for many times the official rate of exchange so that his two-dollar tip could be increased through negotiations to the equal of eight or ten dollars in cruzeiros.

He took a shower, closed the drapes after one more lingering glance at Copacabana then slid under the covers and was asleep within seconds.

* * *

That afternoon, Drew met with the hotel's key staff and completed his pre-program checks and then met with Umberto to go over all the details for the group's arrival two days hence. He planned an early dinner in the hotel, refusing Umberto's kind offer of an excellent dinner at one of Rio's famous restaurants, and retiring early.

The next morning, he attended one more meeting with the hotel, finishing all his duties by noon. He lazed around the pool, enjoying the only free time he would have before the group's arrival early the next morning. And once more, he rejected Umberto's kind offer of a delicious dinner and a samba show saying that as he had to be up very early the next morning, he wanted to get a good night's sleep.

He had another job to do that evening. He looked at his watch. It was now 9:45, time to head for the mosaic sidewalk that edges Copacabana beach and his meeting with the man with the dog.

Picking up the flight bag, he walked to the elevators, pressed the down button and waited only a few seconds before one arrived.

He was tense and he couldn't explain why he felt that way. He had been nervous in Paris on his first mission, but not the uneasy gnawing in his stomach that he was now experiencing. Maybe it was the thought of muggers being around, although he had been assured by Umberto that such incidents were mostly things of the past, thanks to the increased police patrols. But he still remembered, from his previous visits, the serious problem with teenagers and young men in their 20s coming down each night from the favelas in the hills to search for prey.

Favelas is the name given to the slum quarters that have been erected on the slopes of the hills that form an ugly backdrop and a direct contrast to the extraordinary beauty of Rio. The favelas are crime-infested dwellings, few of which have any sanitary facilities, and are constructed of any materials the people can find or steal.

The aura of wealth and prosperity exuded by Rio's spectacular hotels, luxurious office buildings and sprawling private residences creates a dramatic contrast to the make-shift huts on the otherwise majestic hills. It is this skyline of wealth that draws the muggers to the city as moths to a flame. They are poor and unemployed and have no money to buy food or clothing. The only way they can exist is to pick up odd jobs or steal from the tourists. They seldom touch the local people because they are too smart to carry money in large amounts or wear jewelry that can easily be snatched.

Tourists, however, are another matter. They are easy pickings. They always carry money to buy gifts or pay bills for big meals in fancy restaurants, or have expensive cameras slung over their shoulders. And they wear designer jewelry, watches and gold chains which can be taken in a matter of seconds when a knife is put to a throat.

At one time, muggers would select a female victim carrying a shoulder purse. They would follow the tourist, then dash forward, grab the strap and pull it off her shoulder. But the ladies got wise to this tactic. They put their arm through the strap and held their forearm firmly against their stomach, thus thwarting any quick attempts to pull it.

So, the muggers changed their methods, too. Now, they use a very sharp knife to slash the strap, quickly grab the bag and relieve the hapless victim of her valuables. But the muggers seldom use violence, knowing too well the consequences from the police if caught.

These unnerving thoughts were going through Drew's mind as the elevator door opened on the seventh floor. He walked over to the escalator, descended to the main entrance, then turned left to Avenida Atlantica. The light turned green and Drew walked across the busy highway to the beach. He looked once more at his watch. It was five minutes to ten. He strolled a short distance along the well-illuminated walkway, then turned back to the spot where he would meet his contact.

He was comforted by the bright lights and the busy pedestrian traffic as he continued to wonder why he was so tense. He was not afraid of a tough Carioca approaching him, but he was sensibly cautious of not being a hero when accosted by six or seven youths brandishing sharp knives.

He looked at his watch one more time. The hands showed that it was now two minutes after the hour. Then he spied his contact. A slimly-built man in shorts and a tee-shirt and wearing open-toed sandals was about 20 yards away. In his hand was a leash controlling a small poodle that pranced unconcernedly at his side.

As he drew near, he smiled at Drew, nodded his head and said: "Be careful of the traffic at this time of night. It can be dangerous."

"Thank you, I will," he replied, stooping to pet the dog and putting down the flight bag.

"That's a lovely dog you have; a poodle, isn't it?"

"Yes, it is. I've had him almost four years. Good night, sir," the man said as he lifted the flight bag and was gone.

'Ho hum, another difficult mission successfully accomplished.' Drew thought to himself as he moved to the crosswalk, his confidence and composure returning. It seemed as though he had been waiting five minutes for the light to turn green when he heard a cry for help.

"Help me, please help me! It was repeated in Portuguese, the language of Brazil. "Ajude-me, ajude-me."

Drew could only make out some forms on the beach in the direction his contact had gone; the area from which the cries came was not so well lighted. He shouted "Police, Police!" then threw caution to the wind and ran to the spot where the mugging was taking place.

As he neared the hoodlums, he could discern two of them holding down someone on the beach. The muggers turned to face him then ran swiftly away as they saw the police come running from some distance away.

The victim was the man who taken Drew's flight bag. He was bleeding from two stab wounds in the chest.

'The bag," he sputtered, coughing up blood, "they got the bag. You must get it back. They saw me take your bag and . . ." he coughed hard several times and his tee-shirt soaked with blood.

"Listen to me. One mugger had a white tee-shirt with 'Samba School 113' in red letters. Another wore a black tee-shirt with 'Pepe's Bar and Grill' on it with the words in gold and in Portuguese, and in the left corner were the numbers 82. You must . . ."

He coughed violently as the police arrived. "An ambulance is on its way, Senor," an officer, speaking perfect English, assured him. "It will be here soon. Can you tell me what happened?"

But the man was dead. His little poodle was at his side, its head resting on its paws, staring at its master.

It was nearly two o'clock in the morning by the time he returned to his room and readied himself for bed. He had been questioned by the police for almost two hours and was told that he may be called to the police department for more questioning. He thought the police were very polite but very thorough in their investigation. They were disappointed that they were unable to glean anything important from their questioning of Drew and other people who were nearby when the murder took place.

He was exhausted when he got back to his room. His mind was filled with the horror of the murder and it was difficult for him to settle down, but he had to get some sleep and be up early in the morning to go to the airport and meet the group.

But sleep was difficult. He had never seen a man killed before, and tired as he was, he couldn't rid his mind of the vision of his contact using his last gasps to provide him with information to help identify the muggers who had stolen the bag.

He tossed and turned but eventually sleep mercifully relieved him of the tortuous thoughts racing around in his head.

CHAPTER FIFTEEN

RIO DE JANEIRO, BRAZIL

The guests of the Belton Insurance Company were now sleeping in their rooms after their long overnight flights from New York and Miami, and Drew was able to relax at the hospitality desk and give some thought to how he was going to find the bag. It was still difficult not to think of the Brazilian contact lying in the sand, the blood flowing from two deep wounds in his chest, and yet trying to give him some information to help him find his assailants.

He remembered McShane's warning not to approach the U.S. embassy or seek their help if he got into trouble. Such a move could blow his cover and render him useless for future trips because "the other side" would soon know his identity. He had to solve his own problem. But how? How does one go about contacting murderers who don't have an address and live in a mesh of nondescript and disheveled huts on a hillside? He was confident that this was not a political incident, just an unfortunate local killing.

He sympathized with the horrible conditions of the poor people who lived in the favelas, but he couldn't condone their cruel ways of finding money.

Thankfully, the hospitality desk was quiet, giving him the time he needed to sort things out in his mind. Four other travel staff members had traveled with the group and Drew had told them to get some sleep so they would be sharp for the evening's function.

In the past whenever he had a problem associated with the trip, he consulted the hotel's group coordinator, or the bell captain. But this was a very different matter.

The bell captain's desk was situated across from the hospitality desk. He rose and ambled over to the bell desk without really knowing why he did it or what to talk about.

"Has all the luggage been delivered to the rooms?" he asked one of the bellmen. It was the only thing he could think of that made any sense.

"Oh, yes, Drew," the bellman answered. "We delivered the bags to the last floor about half-an-hour ago. We left them outside the rooms as you asked so that we wouldn't disturb the guests by knocking on their doors."

"Thank you, Carlos," he said, trying desperately to think of something intelligent that would help him take the first step in locating the flight bag.

"How many people are there in the favelas, Carlos? Do you know? It seemed to me, as I was coming in from the airport the day before yesterday, that there were more than the last time I was here."

"Nobody knows that, Drew. But you're right in thinking there are more this time than last year. The huts are slowly covering the hillsides. They're ugly, no? It's a great pity that our beautiful city has to be scarred by those foul-smelling shacks."

"Everybody knows that all your mugging troubles are caused by the kids who live in those favelas, but can't the police do something to correct the situation? Can't your city government help the people find jobs so that they don't have to steal to exist?"

'I don't know, Drew. I suppose I should think of the poor people's problems, but I've got enough of my own trying to make a living. I'm lucky to have the job I have. But, you know, there are many good people up there, too. Not everybody who lives in the favelas is a bad person, only a small percentage. It's the young kids who don't want to work and have learned that it's easy to mug a tourist and make a few dollars who are creating this bad image. They know that the tourists are so scared that they won't resist, certainly not for $20 or $30."

Drew saw an opening. "Do the people who live in the favelas have jobs in town? You said that only a small percentage are bad, so do some of them work?"

"Oh, yes. Some of the huts are really not bad, and some even have toilets and running water. Those are owned by people who have steady jobs. It may surprise you to know that many of the maids who work in many of the hotels and in the shops live in the favelas. They are very nice girls, and very clean."

Drew was impressed with Carlos's command of the English language and asked him where he learned it.

"In school, but mostly talking with the tourists in the hotel. I picked up English very quickly and found it very easy to learn."

"Well, Carlos, I guess I had better get back to work. Nice talking with you."

A plan was forming in his mind. Slowly, but resolutely, he tossed ideas back and forth until he decided on an approach to take.

He looked at his watch. It was ten to one, just about the time the maids would be making up the vacated rooms.

He took the elevator up to his floor and glanced up and down the hallways looking for the carts the maids used in their cleaning duties. He noticed one next door to his room. A quick glance told him that his room had not yet been cleaned.

He knew the maid would be knocking on his door within minutes. He sat at the desk in his room, opened his briefcase and withdrew some papers to make it appear as though he was doing some work.

Ten minutes passed, then there was a knock on the door. He opened it and was immediately taken aback by the beautiful face that confronted him. The maid apologized and asked if he would prefer that she return later to make up his room.

"No, please come. I'm just doing some work at the desk and you won't be in my way."

He was taken aback by the beautiful face framed by shoulder-length black hair. Her slim body fit her uniform nicely and her breasts fully stretched the buttons near her shoulders. She had long, shapely legs that had been tanned by years in the sun.

He guessed her age at about 20. She smiled easily and moved about the room with the grace of a panther.

"I hope I will not disturb you, sir," she said as she proceeded to remove some objects from her cart.

"You won't bother me at all," he assured her. 'Well, not in the way you think,' he thought to himself.

He pretended to work for a few minutes then rose from the desk, stretched himself and moved over to the window.

"I've been working on and off all morning, so maybe I should quit." He was looking down on Avenida Atlantica, watching the Cariocas enjoying the sunshine on Copacabana beach. Without turning his head, he asked her name.

"My name is Maria." She stopped her work as though willing to engage in some light conversation with the handsome American.

"What is your name?"

"Drew, Drew Cummins. You have a very lovely city. It's a magnificent view from this window and I frequently just stand here and marvel at the gorgeous beach and the beauty of Rio."

"Do you live in Rio?"

"Yes, and I was born here."

"Whereabouts do you live?"

"Oh, not very far from here."

"Let me guess, probably in one of those posh apartment buildings on the Avenida Atlantica."

She giggled and nodded her head.

"What does posh mean?"

"Wealthy, luxurious, well-off."

"Oh, no," she said smiling, "not at all. In fact, I live in another world."

"Well, where do you live? Is it a secret? If it is, I can understand why. You're such a pretty girl, no, a beautiful woman, I'm sure you don't want all the young men who are chasing you to know your address."

Her head sank slowly onto her chest.

"Have I offended you, Maria? You look sad. I certainly didn't mean to embarrass you."

"I live on the hill. In one of those huts that the people call favelas. But I'm proud that my papa built one that has a bathroom and running water. My address is not so good, but I live in a decent place."

"I have a feeling just looking at you that you have a very nice home."

It was time to change the subject.

"Maria, would you mind if I asked you to have dinner with me tonight? I have been to Rio before but I have never been able to see much of it. I think it would be fun to have dinner with a Carioca. If you agree, after we eat, perhaps you could show me some of the interesting places in town. I know you have great samba restaurants where you can eat and listen to great music. Would you?"

She looked away from him for a few seconds then returned his gaze. "I would very much like to do that but I'm sure you could find much more beautiful girls in Rio than me."

"I doubt if I could find anyone more beautiful than you. Besides, you speak such good English it would make the evening more enjoyable having a companion that I could have an interesting conversation with. OK?"

Her face beamed. "OK. I think it will be better if I met you at the restaurant. It's called Antonino's. It is very nice and one that will not cost you a lot of money." She wrote down the name and gave him the slip of paper.

"Shall we say eight o'clock?"

"Yes, that would be fine with me."

"Eight o'clock it is then. Well, I had better get downstairs and let you finish your work. I look forward to seeing you tonight."

CHAPTER SIXTEEN

RIO DE JANEIRO, BRAZIL

A cocktail party and banquet in the hotel had been arranged for the group that night and while he would normally have supervised the events, he had a strong staff, all of whom had served as lead trip directors.

He asked Charlie Simmons, his second-in-command, if he would take over for the evening as he had to check out several restaurants and write a report on them for the office.

"Yeah, sure, Drew," Simmons laughed. 'I've never heard them called restaurants before."

He dashed up to his room, had a shower and changed from his uniform into olive slacks and a pale yellow golf shirt. He checked his appearance in the mirror on the back of the bathroom door and as he did so, a smile creased his face.

'Why am I so concerned about my appearance?' he thought. 'Could it be that I'm attracted to Maria?' He admitted to himself that she was a very pretty girl and there was something shy and becoming about her that appealed to him.

He dismissed the thought. 'This is business,' he reminded himself. 'I have a very serious matter to attend to.'

He was a few minutes early and Maria was two minutes late. He couldn't believe it was the same girl. As lovely as she was in their earlier encounter, she was now transformed into a stunningly beautiful young woman.

She wore a lemon-colored dress, tightened at the waist with a light brown cord belt and flat white shoes. She was gorgeous and he stared at her before she smiled and asked him if he was hungry.

"Yes, I am, but before we go, Maria, I must tell you that I don't think I have ever seen a more beautiful woman. You look . . ." He couldn't find the words as he struggled to think of an adjective that best described her.

"Oh, you mustn't embarrass me," she interrupted his thoughts. "Let's go because I am hungry, too."

'Ah, now, this is the Rio I want to see," he said as they entered the restaurant and walked past a huge kitchen where the chefs were busy fulfilling orders from the waitresses.

"I was hungry when I came in, but that delicious aroma has made me ravenous," he said to Maria as they were shown to a table.

They ordered drinks and Drew asked the waiter for recommendations. "Would you leave it to me, sir?" asked the waiter. "I assure you I can suggest something absolutely delicious for you and the young lady."

"Do it," said Drew, and the waiter took off ready to surprise and delight the young couple with a superb Italian meal with many of the restaurant's specialties.

The meal was so delicious that he ate much more than he normally would, and was surprised at his appetite. Maria, not surprisingly, ate sparingly, but still enough to show that she, too, enjoyed the several courses presented by the waiter.

Afterward, they hailed a cab and headed for the Plataforma II nightclub to see a fast-paced samba show that kept everyone tapping their toes to the hot rhythms. Afterwards, they danced to the vibrant Latin music before the band showed its versatility and played an American tune with a slow rhythm.

Maria pushed her voluptuous body close to him and he felt her firm breasts against his chest. He liked to put women on a pedestal and admire them and treat them like very special people. They were not objects of lust although sex was never far from his mind. But he felt that romance was important and that his female companions should be made to feel very special and desired before he made love to them.

When they returned to the table, he decided he had to bring up the reason for asking Maria to have dinner with him.

"What do you want to do with your life, Maria? You know, you really are a very beautiful woman. Have you thought of modeling?"

She laughed softly. "Are you teasing me?"

"No, I am not teasing or trying to flatter you. I have never been so serious in my life. I have seen women with much less to offer than you in television commercials and in newspaper ads."

"I'll tell you what I want to do with my life," she said, turning serious. "I want to get out of the favelas. I am going to night school to learn accounting and I hope that some day I can find a good job, one that will pay me well so that I can afford a nice place with a different address. Maybe not those posh apartments you joked about today, but a place of my own."

"Is it so bad living where you are?"

"Drew, do you know what the favelas are? They are the ugliest shacks in the worst part of Rio. Maybe I am more fortunate than most, but still it is my address. But not for long because I will be leaving there. I will graduate from my accounting classes in two more months and if I find a good job, I will be gone."

She spoke with such fervor that he could sense the misery she felt speaking about the favelas.

"Don't you feel safe there; is that the problem?"

"You're never really safe there, but that's not what bothers me. When you say to people that you live on the hill, they know exactly what you mean and they look down on you."

"I've heard they have a lot of muggings in Rio, particularly of tourists, but I guess you know how to look after yourself, right?"

"My father is a very strong man and is well known in our area. If anyone tried to hurt me, he would find them and they wouldn't hurt anyone any more."

"Well, there are toughs all around the world. We sure have our share in the States, so we can't condemn another country. I saw a couple of weird guys this morning who looked like real toughs to me. One was wearing a tee-shirt that had 'Samba School 113' on it. The other something in Portuguese on his tee-shirt. I remember thinking that I wouldn't like to tangle with either one of them."

Maria laughed. "That's funny and I'll tell you why. You know that we have samba schools in Rio, don't you?" she asked.

"Well, I've heard that the samba is the national dance of Brazil, so I suppose they have many schools where they teach the dance to the students."

"Not exactly. There are schools where they teach you to be a musician and play in the samba bands. The bands compete in our Mardi Gras celebrations and win very valuable prizes. The winning band ends up with contracts for radio and television and makes records that sell in the millions. All the band members become very famous and very rich."

Maria started to giggle again. She had a very pleasant way of laughing that appealed to him.

"I'm laughing because 'Samba School 113' is not a place to learn to become a musician. It's the name of a gang and a very bad one. If you saw someone with a tee-shirt with those words, you were right in thinking he was a tough. He was, and one you wouldn't want to tangle with."

"Do they exist in the favelas?"

"Yes, but not anywhere in my area, or even near it. They hang out at a restaurant called Pepe's. I don't know why they call it a restaurant. Nobody eats there, it's nothing but a gang hang-out."

It was the information that he needed. He felt closer to his quarry and although he didn't yet know them, he knew where they could be found and that was good for a start.

They finished their dinner and he paid the bill.

"Maria, I've had a wonderful evening and I've enjoyed your company so much. I would like to do it again before I leave next week. Would you like to have dinner with me again, say next Thursday?"

"You're so different, Drew. I don't think I've met anyone quite like you, not that I've had many dates. Oh, I've been asked out often, but I've seldom accepted. But you're different."

She looked into his eyes for a few seconds then nodded her head. "Yes, I would really like to have dinner with you again."

He called a taxi and gave the driver a handful of cruzeiros. "Take the lady to the address she'll give you. That should more than cover the fare and the tip," he said.

He shook Maria's hand. "I look forward to Thursday . . . if I don't see you in the hallway before then."

She smiled and bade him good night.

CHAPTER SEVENTEEN

RIO DE JANEIRO, BRAZIL

The group was scheduled to leave at 9 o'clock for a city tour followed by a visit to the tropical Tijuca forest and afterwards, stop at the awe-inspiring statue of Christ the Redeemer atop Corcovado mountain.

As they finished breakfast, they began to gather in the front lobby where Drew was talking to Umberto, his agent, awaiting the arrival of the buses.

The first motorcoach pulled up at the front door and Jeanie Egan, one of the travel staff, signaled the driver to open the door. She affixed a sign with 'Belton Insurance Co.' and the company logo printed on it, to the windshield.

The bus was now ready for boarding and Drew motioned to the group to be seated on the bus. Two more buses pulled up behind the first and Jeanie repeated the task of taping the company signs to the windshields.

When the last of the guests had been seated in the fourth and fifth buses, the coaches moved slowly away and the guides began their commentary on the magnificent city of Rio de Janeiro.

Drew watched the last bus leave before asking Umberto if he would like to join him for breakfast. They found a table in the coffee shop and studied the lengthy menu before giving their orders to the waitress. When she departed, Drew came right to the point.

"Umberto, you know how to get things done in this town, so I'm going to say something very strange. I want you to find me a tough kid, a really tough kid, who would like to make a few extra dollars. He's got to be tough enough to help me recover something that was stolen from me the other night.

"It was a gift I had bought for my girl friend and I had it inside a Pan Am flight bag I was carrying. Four young hoodlums mugged me and stole the flight bag and the gift inside. I've made a few inquiries and I know where the hoodlums can be contacted, but it's a place where I couldn't go without being mugged again, if not killed. Can you help me?"

Umberto seemed stunned at the news then puzzled at the request.

"Yes, Drew, I think I know the right man for the job, but why don't you just go to the police?"

While I know how to identify two of the hoodlums, the police would never be able to get my bag and gift back. Maybe it's more than just the gift. My pride is hurt and I am furious that hoodlums got away with something of mine. No, I need to do it my way."

He felt he had to say that an important gift had been inside the bag. If he had revealed that he only wanted to have a flight bag returned, Umberto would have wondered about his intelligence.

"I'd sure like to know what sort of gift it was, but it's none of my business," Umberto said, with a sly smile on his face.

"I know just the man for the job. Give him fifty bucks and he'll be really happy. His name is Juju. Don't ask me how he got that name, but he does odd jobs for me now and then. And believe me, he's reliable. A couple of years ago, my wife and I were leaving a restaurant when four thugs jumped me.

"They cleverly attacked when I was entering my car, catching me in a vulnerable position, half in and half out of the vehicle. They hit me on my back with some kind of pipe that almost broke my spine, pulled me out of the car and pounded me with their fists in the stomach. I don't think I ever hurt so much in my life. They emptied my pockets and saw I had only about thirty dollars in cruzeiros. They obviously expected much more because I was driving a big Oldsmobile, so they began to punch my wife mercilessly. She lost five of her teeth and had to have stitches on her cheek.

"A police whistle sounded and they ran away. I grabbed at one of them and tore the pocket of his trousers. Before the police arrived, I managed to pick up something that had fallen from the tough's pocket when I ripped it. It was a piece of paper and I put it under the front seat of my car to look at it more carefully when the police had gone. I didn't want the police to get the muggers; I wanted to get them myself. I was behaving just like you, so I understand your feelings.

"The paper had two names and an address on it. I located Juju through some friends and I gave him the names and addresses, describing the toughs as well as I could remember them."

"Let's just say that Juju found them—all four of them, one after another. I read in the 'paper two days later that four toughs from the favelas were found dead in an abandoned car. All had been beaten to death. I recognized two names as those on the paper I had given to Juju. Yes, Drew, I think he's tough enough to do the job. And he's been doing a lot of odd jobs for me ever since."

He asked Umberto to have Juju meet him across the street from the hotel on the mosaic sidewalk next to the beach. 'Tell him to look for a man in red shirt and tan slacks at exactly three o'clock this afternoon. Is that too early for you to make contact with him?"

"No, that should be fine, but if I have trouble locating him, I'll give you a call within the hour."

He had to advance the restaurant where the group was having lunch, check that everything was in readiness including the correct number of tables, the menu items, the wine selection and the location of the restrooms. It was always one of the first questions asked when the participants disembarked: "Where are the restrooms?"

After lunch and as they set off on the afternoon part of the city tour, Drew took a taxi back to the hotel. It was five to three, so he walked across the street to await the arrival of the man he hoped would help him retrieve his flight bag.

It was almost ten after three o'clock when a tall, powerfully-built man of about 25 approached and asked: "Excuse me, are you Drew?"

He was shocked. He had expected a dirty and tough-looking kid who would look as though he needed a shave and a haircut. This young man was neatly, if not smartly, attired. Huge biceps bulged from underneath his sport shirt and he definitely looked the type that you would shy away from and avoid irritating. His nose was slightly off to the side as though it had been broken more than once.

He was also surprised at the man's knowledge of English. His accent was difficult to understand, but he spoke the language reasonably well.

"Yes, I'm Drew. And you're Juju?"

"That's me, Juju, and I hear you need some help?"

Drew told him much the same story he had given Mauricio, but changing it a little. He said he had been carrying a Pan American flight bag with a gift inside it when two toughs put a knife to his throat, grabbed the flight bag and took some money.

He also described the tee-shirts that the toughs were wearing and had learned through some inquiries that they belong to the 'Samba School 113' gang and they hung out at Pepe's restaurant. "I don't know their names but maybe you can coerce them into boasting about robbing someone on Copacabana beach last Thursday night. That way you'll know you've got the right people."

He told Juju that one wore a 'Samba 13' tee shirt, the other a 'Pepe's Bar & Grill' with the numbers 82 on it. He also provided some physical descriptions of the thugs.

"Juju, I want the flight bag back. I'm sure they've sold the gift to some fence, but I'm not concerned about that. I want the flight bag back. That's important. I'm willing to pay them $100. That's more than they would get in a night's work. If you can pull this off, I'll give you $200. Is that satisfactory?"

Juju smiled and rubbed his chin. "For that amount of money, all I need to know is where you want the bodies delivered?"

"All I need is that flight bag delivered. I'm not asking you to do anything more, but if you were to beat the shit out of them, maybe I would pay a bonus."

"That seems an awful lot to pay just to get a flight bag back, but it's your money. If I get the flight bag without having to pay them $100, do I get to keep the whole $300?"

"And a bonus if you work them over real good."

He asked Juju to call him at the hotel when he had some news. "If I'm not in my room, ask the operator to put you through to the Belton hospitality desk and ask for me. If I'm not there, they'll know where I can be reached. Do you want to write the name of the hospitality desk?"

"No, man, I'll remember it. I have a great memory." He smiled and they shook hands. He had such a powerful grip that any remaining doubts Drew might have had that Juju could handle himself were quickly dissipated.

* * *

Drew wouldn't have recognized the Juju who entered Pepe's Bar and Grill. He was dressed in worn blue jeans with some holes and a scuffed tee-shirt. The tee-shirt had 'Samba School 113' printed on it.

"Hey, man," a curly-haired teenager with an ugly scar across his right cheek shouted to Juju. "Haven't seen you in a while. Where've you been? You missed a lot of meetin's and Tito is mad as hell at you."

"Oh, I was doin' a job in Recife. I needed the money an' I got a chance for some easy c's." In Brazil, c's is the slang term for cruzeiros, the local currency.

The air was filled with smoke and the dozen or so tables were occupied by a weird assortment of unkempt men and skimpily-clad women drinking beer and laughing loudly.

Juju spotted the two men he had been looking for. They were seated at a table with two empty chairs. When Drew had described the two men he wanted found, Juju knew exactly who they were. The men were as close as brothers and the descriptions of the tee-shirts told him all he wanted to know.

There were several 'Samba' tee-shirts worn by the gang, but only one black tee-shirt with 'Pepe's Bar and Grill' and the numbers 82 on it.

Chi Diago had the tee-shirt made just for him and the numbers 82 represented the year Diago had joined the gang. It was an exclusive, his and his alone and he considered it his lucky tee-shirt. He wore it only when he was going on a job—to mug or kill someone.

"Hey, brother, what's happenin',"

"Oh, I've been up in Recife on a job," Juju explained. "Well, I see you're goin' out on a job tonight, Chi. You're wearing your lucky black '82 tee-shirt."

"Yeah, me and the Toze need some bread so we're gonna find us a couple of nice tourists. Ah, but there's no hurry. Let's have another drink. Since you've just finished a big job up in Recife, Juju, you're loaded, so why don't you be nice and pick up the tab?"

Toze was Toze Volaco, the other hoodlum who had participated in the slaying of Drew's contact on Copacabana beach.

"Sure, why not," Juju laughed. "Hey, Simoes, how about service for some club members in good standing?" he shouted to a scruffy-looking man with string hair that fell half-way down his back.

Two minutes later, Simoes dropped three beers on the table and Juju pulled out a fistful of cruzeiros, peeled off a few and handed them to him. "Keep the change, Simoes," he said, "Juju's in a generous mood tonight."

"What've you been up to Volaco? Been makin' lots of money?"

"Not as much as you, by the looks of it," Volaco said, still thinking of the pile of notes he had just seen Juju take from his pocket to pay for the beers.

"Oh, I did OK up there in Recife. If you're interested in makin' real money, why don't you and Diago let me know?"

Volaco stared at him for a minute then his face broke into a sly smile.

"Hey, Diago, whaddya say? Wanna go to Recife and mug tourists up there?"

Juju laughed. "No, Volaco, it's not tourists. It's wastin' some shitheads for a dealer and that's all I'm gonna say about it. If you're interested, I can set it up."

"We're interested, Juju, but why are you bein' so nice to us? You've never done anythin' for us before?"

"Cuz you never asked, that's why. If you'd asked for help before, I'd've given it to you, but you never asked."

"Okay, let's talk."

"The job is taking out bums for Rui Parangua. D'you know him?"

"Never heard of him," Volaco answered. "Who is he and what does he do?"

"He's head of a bunch of top dealers in northern Brazil and neighborin' countries. They meet once a month in Recife. If they need anybody taken out, they give you the job. They pay very, very well for each dead body, like 50,000 cruzeiros, and there are plenty of them to waste."

"They supply the guns and all expenses 'cuz you might have to fly to Colombia, Venezuela, Ecuador or some other place. How's that? You see the world, hit a couple of bums and get paid real money for the job? Still interested?"

"You gotta be kiddin'" Diago shot back. "How do we get started?"

"Glad to hear you might want to join 'cuz that's what I'm doin' here. Parangua asked me to recruit a coupla more guys. Here's what you do. Pack a bag each with whatever you need and meet me at the corner of Santa Clara and Rua Bareta Ribeiro tomorrow night at 6 o'clock.

I'll be parked in a pale blue Oldsmobile. You'll be catchin' a 'plane for Recife, so if you have to tell anyone where you're goin', just say you'll be gone for a couple of months. That's the amount of time you have to stay before you can come back. OK?"

"Hey, that's great, Juju. We'll be there. A pale blue Oldsmobile? Shit, you really must've hit the big time."

"You'll be able to afford one just like me. Shouldn't take more than one stay in Recife. You'll see. Okay, now two more things; don't tell anyone where you're goin'. Parangua don't want any connections or loose ends. You don't tell anyone, get that? The next thing is I don't want you to do a job tonight just in case somethin' goes wrong. I don't want to explain everythin' to other recruits. Agreed?"

"Agreed, Juju. Say, you're a pal."

* * *

Juju stepped into the 'phone booth and dialed Umberto Solleiro's office.

"Mr. Solleiro, can I borrow your Oldsmobile for a couple of hours tonight, say from 5:30 to 7:30? It's in connection with the job I'm doin' for your friend Drew."

"Sure, Juju, come up to my office after lunch and I'll give you the keys. You can keep it overnight and return it to me tomorrow morning. I'll take a cab home."

* * *

Juju sat behind the wheel of the Oldsmobile which was parked on Rua Bareta Ribeiro, just off of Santa Clara. It was 5:55 p.m. on the car's clock. He had his plan all set. He would pretend to take them out to Galeao Airport, but before reaching it, he would say he had to make a stop to say goodbye to a woman he had been seeing.

When he approached a deserted area he had already selected, he would stop the car. He would order them out at gunpoint, shoot Diago in the leg to immobilize him, then turn the gun on Volaco.

He would remind them of the mugging they had done on Copacabana beach and the murder of the man with the dog. Then he would ask them for the Pan Am flight bag. If they refused to give him the information he would shoot Diago in the head and kill him.

He knew that Volaco would open up at that point. He would kill him, too, but not until he had the bag. A nice easy job, he thought, unless they had thrown the bag away, then it would be off on another merry-go-round.

Juju was confident that one of them would be carrying the Pan Am flight bag holding their personal belongings. Neither of them would have any decent kind of bag to take with them, so the new Pan Am bag would be a natural.

It was almost ten after six and they still hadn't arrived. 'Bums,' he thought, 'they're probably wearing watches they stole from tourists but don't know how to read them.'

He had just finished the thought when he saw them turn the corner in his rearview mirror. He couldn't believe his eyes or his good luck. Just as he thought, each carried a small bag, but the bag Diago was carrying was the Pan Am flight bag.

When they got in the car, Juju complimented Diago on his new flight bag. "Very nice. Where'd you steal it?"

Diago laughed and repeated the details of the mugging and the knifing on Copacabana beach. 'We saw this guy talking to an American who's holdin' this bag. The American puts the bag down to pet the guy's dog and the guy lifts the bag and walks away, just like that.

"We figured it must have something good inside and we jumped the old guy. He resisted pretty good for somebody his age and we had to knife him. The cops came and we ran like hell. When we were far enough away, we looked in the bag and, no kiddin', there wasn't a damn thing inside it. Just an empty bag.'

Juju smiled to himself. 'Well, whaddya say we go to Recife?"

"Yeah," the two chimed in, "let's try some good livin' and make some easy money."

* * *

Drew was early again by a few minutes, and Maria was late again by two minutes. She looked as beautiful as she had done on the first date and wore a pale blue dress, cinched at the waist by a dark blue belt.

"Well, this time I'm going to take you to a restaurant that's been highly recommended to me."

"Where?" she said with a hint of anticipation.

"To the Sol E Mar restaurant. Do you know it?"

"I've heard of it, of course, but I've never been there. I know that it's very expensive."

When they had been seated at an outdoor table near the water's edge, Drew gazed out over the bay and watched the lights twinkle on Sugar Loaf. It was an idyllic setting and enhancing the scene was a full moon, beaming from a cloudless sky and casting a wide shaft of silver on the water.

"This really is a romantic and magical city," he said, soaking in the beauty of the environment. They ordered drinks and Drew reached across the table and held Maria's hand as they stared longingly at each other.

They didn't talk much during the meal, but their silence eloquently described their feelings, their longing for each other and the closeness that was building inside them.

They finished their meal and he paid the bill. They stepped out to the entrance of the restaurant and the doorman asked if they wished a taxi.

Drew nodded and turned to look at Maria. "Well, where to now? The evening is still young."

Maria stared at him for several seconds before lowering her head. "Shall we go back to the hotel?"

He couldn't believe his ears. What he had been hoping for and what he had been thinking of throughout the meal had suddenly become a reality.

He looked at her tenderly and asked; "Is that what you want?"

She looked up at him and slowly nodded her head.

* * *

Drew had taken many women to bed and was not shy or lacking in the ways of love-making, but this was somehow different with Maria. Despite her background, her home and the environment in which she was raised, he was sure she was a virgin.

On entering his room, he put two chairs together next to the panoramic window, took two small bottles of wine from the mini-bar and extinguished the light.

They sat, held hands, stared down at the bright lights of Copacabana and the busy traffic, and talked softly. Soon, the wine glasses were empty. He took Maria's glass and put it with his own on a nearby table.

He touched her cheek and with his hand then gently turned her face to his and softly kissed her once, then twice, and slowly their passions rose. He touched her firm breasts, squeezing them and kissing them through her dress, feeling the hard nipples underneath. He undid the buttons and she stood up to let her dress fall to her ankles while she pulled his shirt over his head. They removed all of each other's clothes before moving to the bed.

He kissed her and rolled his tongue round her nipples and she began to moan. He curled his body over hers and her legs parted as she held his pulsating penis in her hand and guided it into her vagina.

As the head of his penis entered her, she moaned softly and began moving against him. The penetration was slow and difficult. 'She is a virgin,' he thought to himself as his full shaft was eventually buried in her. They thrust together again and again. He felt the oncoming of his sperm when Maria moaned loudly and quickened the pace of their love-making.

He ejaculated at the same time he felt Maria go limp under him. He kissed her tenderly on the lips and on her breasts before they disengaged and lay side by side in sheer exhaustion and ecstasy.

Neither spoke for several minutes and then Maria turned on her side and kissed him on the cheek and cuddled into him. They lay motionless, glorying in their love-making and in holding each other until Maria whispered in his ear: "I have to go, Drew, it's late."

She took a shower then dressed while Drew pulled on his clothes. "Do you want me to ride home with you in the taxi?"

"No, that's won't be necessary. I'll be perfectly safe. The driver will drop me right at my door and my father will be waiting up for me."

He hailed a taxi at the hotel entrance, paid the driver a generous amount, kissed Maria gently on the cheek and watched the cab disappear round the corner.

Returning to his room, he removed his clothes and prepared to take a shower. He turned on the television to watch the news although he knew he wouldn't understand any of it. The announcer spoke in Portuguese, but Drew looked idly at the pictures on the screen.

In one scene, two police cars with their lights flashing in the darkness gave a hint that an accident or a crime had been committed.

The camera then switched to an officer speaking to the television reporter and pointing to two bodies that lay on the ground behind them.

Drew froze. One of the bodies had a tee-shirt with 'Samba School 113' on it while the other had gold lettering on a black tee-shirt. Ken could see the number 82 in the corner of the tee-shirt and some Portuguese writing of which he could make out only one word: 'Pepe'.

* * *

The hospitality desk was busy. Guests of the Belton Insurance Company were looking over the menus of several restaurants which were being used that evening on a Dine-Around program. The guests had to choose which of the restaurants they wanted to dine in, as well as the time of their reservation. The travel staff was busy taking the names so they could make the reservations for them;

The telephone on the hospitality desk rang and Ed Reading, one of the travel staff, answered it.

"Belton hospitality desk, Ed Reading speaking."

"I would like to speak to Drew Cummins," the deep, accented voice growled.

"Just a minute; I'll pass you over to him."

He handed the 'phone to Drew. "It's for you. Sounds like the bodyguard you ordered."

Everybody laughed as Drew rose from his chair and walked over to the 'phone. He knew exactly who it was.

"This is Drew, can I help you?"

"Drew, this is Juju, I have your flight bag. When can we meet?"

"Great. That's wonderful news. How about this afternoon, say 3 o'clock? And why don't we meet in the hotel's coffee shop. Is that OK?"

"Sounds good to me. I'll see you at three in the coffee shop."

He replaced the receiver and held his hand on it for a few seconds as he thought about his next move.

* * *

He would have to take the money out of his safety deposit box at the hotel to pay Juju for his troubles. He had promised him $200 for his efforts and another $100 if he retrieved the bag without having to pay the thugs. He also promised a bonus if he beat up the muggers. How much of a bonus does one pay for a killing, he mused.

He tried to feel sorry for the muggers being killed, but all he could think of was his contact, soaked in his own blood, with two deep knife wounds in his chest. That made the muggers' deaths a little more tolerable.

"Drew, we know you're the boss, but we're busy over here," Marget Thompson, another travel staff, cried out with a little laughter in her voice to take the edge off her peremptory tone.

"Oh, sorry, I was deep in thought" he said as he returned to his seat.

When the guests had cleared away from the desk and the pace of work had slackened, Drew said he had to take some money out of his safety deposit box and would return in ten minutes.

He figured that if he gave Juju $500, he would be happy, or at least, he hoped he would be. He withdrew five $100 bills and put them in a money clip. It was going to be an interesting coffee break.

At five minutes to three, Drew entered the hotel's coffee shop and spied a table over in a corner. 'Ideal,' he thought, 'for private conversation.' He could also watch the entrance and know when Juju arrived.

It was well after three o'clock when he saw the big Brazilian sidle into the restaurant. He caught sight of Drew waving to him and ambled over to the table.

"Well done, Juju," he said noticing that he was carrying the Pan Am flight bag, "well done."

A waitress came over and asked for their orders. "I'll have a guarana," Drew said.

"I'll have the same," said Juju, adding. "I see you've caught on to our local soft drink."

"I tried one the first time I came to Rio and enjoyed it so much that I've become an addict."

Juju handed him the flight bag. "Mission accomplished," he said.

"How much do I owe you?"

"We agreed on $200 for me if I recovered it, and you said you would pay the bums $100 which I could keep if I didn't have to pay them. That makes $300 and I believe you said I would get a bonus if I roughed them up a bit. Well, I roughed them up real good, so good in fact that I think another $200, $100 for each roughing is fair. How does that sound to you?"

"Sounds very good to me." He handed Juju the five $100 bills which he folded and put in his pocket.

The drinks arrived and they had taken a few sips when Juju took control of the conversation.

"It's none of my business, but when I talked to those two idiots, they gave me a different story of how they acquired the bag. They said they took it from a man who had lifted it from an American on Copacabana beach. And they said they knifed the guy."

"Their story was the true one, but I had a very good reason for giving you the line that I did. No matter how it was stolen, you got it back and I hope you agree that you've been well rewarded?"

"Oh, yes, I'm happy. And if you ever need any more help of this kind, just ask Mr. Solleiro to get in touch with me."

He rose and extended his hand. Drew braced for the steel vice and grabbed it.

"See you," he said as Drew nodded. And he was gone.

CHAPTER EIGHTEEN

JFK AIRPORT, NEW YORK

After he had cleared Customs at JFK Airport, he saw a familiar face. "Hi, Airport Annie, how's the prettiest airline rep in all of JFK?"

"If you're talking about me, I'm fine, Drew. "how're you doing?"

"I'm doing fine, too. A little tired, but can't complain."

"Where've you been?"

"Rio, and even all those olive-skinned lovelies in their tangas pale when compared to you."

She laughed, checked the inter-line stub on his luggage and told him his bags were properly tagged for Minneapolis.

"Have a good trip," she said and moved on to four passengers waiting to ask for her help.

There was one olive-skinned lovely you couldn't out-shine, he thought to himself as he headed for Pan Am's Clipper Club where he could pour himself a cup of coffee and call McShane.

He had trouble erasing Maria from his mind. He wasn't in love with her, but he certainly had found her very attractive. He sighed as he thought how well such a beautiful young woman would do in the States where she would have a real chance in life. She would have a real struggle on her hands trying to make a go of it in Rio unless she changed her address. 'I wonder if I could help her,' he mused.

The night after the group's departure, he and Maria had gone out to dinner, then made passionate love again. He realized he was growing very fond of her and put a brake on his emotions. He couldn't get involved, but he thought how lucky some young Brazilian man was going to be one day.

When he kissed her a final time in his room, he said he would like to see her again when he returned to Rio. And he didn't fail to see the tears trickle down her cheek as she sat in the back seat of the taxi and whispered goodbye.

And now the mission—and what a mission—was almost over. He dialed the special number he had been given. An operator asked for his code. "Courier Thirteen," he muttered into the 'phone.

There was silence for about forty-five seconds before McShane came on the line.

"I have been desperately waiting to hear from you. I know you had trouble."

"Yes, but with the help of a brute in Rio, I managed to get the bag back. I didn't know whom to give it to, so I brought it back."

"You did get it, though?"

"Yes, but it cost me $500 which I'll put on my expenses."

"Don't worry about that. I'm just glad you got it back. You did well, Drew. Keep the bag until I call you and give you instructions on how to return it to me. I may even have it picked up."

"Brendon, I'm sorry I didn't deliver it. And I'm sorry about you losing one of your people. He was a real hero. Despite his painful wounds, he used his last breath to give me information that helped me to find the thugs who did it. Incidentally the two were killed by the gorilla I hired to locate them. I'll do a report and send it to you. By the way, Brendon, I just hope that whatever was hidden in the bag is still there. It was not torn or mishandled in any way."

"Au contraire, Drew. Let's just say you have returned everything intact. You may not have delivered the bag, but just retrieving it was well worth all your efforts, believe me. An important message was hidden inside the bag, and as the bag was not torn in any way, it's still there." You are a very resourceful young man, Drew. I think we're lucky to have a courier like you. I'll be in touch."

And the line went dead.

CHAPTER NINETEEN

MINNEAPOLIS, MINNESOTA

The door of the bathroom opened and the voluptuous young woman stood there, wearing only a thin robe. She was silhouetted by the bathroom light and Drew could see her sensuous form through the transparent robe. She pulled gently on the cord and the robe slipped to the ground.

Drew rushed to her, wrapped his arms around her and began kissing her as she reached down and unzipped his fly. She reached in and withdrew his fully erect penis, moaning s she stroked it.

He was wild with excitement and anticipation as he . . . .

Rrrrring, rrrrring, rrrring . . . .

Drew awoke abruptly, a film of perspiration on his forehead. The phone had interrupted what had promised to be a truly great dream. He had fallen asleep in an easy chair while watching television. He quickly switched off the set and lifted the receiver.

"Hello."

"Hi, Drew, it's McShane. Did I catch you at a bad time?"

"Brendon, you'll never know."

"Oh, then maybe I should call back."

"No, I had fallen asleep in my chair and was having a great dream. Don't worry about it. I commit enough sins while I am awake; I don't need any more when I'm asleep."

They both laughed before McShane discussed the reason for his call.

"Do you have any trips going to Egypt soon?"

"Let me check my Operations Outlook. Hold on."

He came back on the 'phone a few minutes later to say there was a program toward the end of the month going to Cairo, then Luxor and a cruise up the Nile.

"Good, are you scheduled on it?"

"Yes, I am. How's that for coincidence?"

"Great. I want you to call me a few days before you leave Minneapolis. I need something carried to Cairo. We can discuss the details when you let me have your departure date and your gateway city."

"Fine, Brendon, I'll call you."

* * *

Drew had been to Egypt several times before, so the prospect of the trip didn't have that same appeal he felt when going to a new destination. In fact, it had been quite some time since he experienced that feeling of excitement because it had been more than three years since he had visited a new destination.

Yet, there was always some excitement. He loved Egypt with its timeless antiquities and incredible monuments, and he liked the Egyptians because they were always such a friendly people. They were also an importunate people, especially the merchants who constantly urged and even tugged tourists into their stores with promises of unbelievable bargains. Still, Drew enjoyed their good-natured smiles even if you didn't take them up on their unbeatable offers.

He wondered if it was the thought of going back to Cairo that caused his lethargic feeling or the thought of another mission without much of a break in between the trip before it. Maybe both.

The briefing for the trip was held in the Harrison Motivation Company's conference room 'A', and after it was over, someone suggested that they all go to the local Italian restaurant for lunch. When everyone was seated and had ordered, Drew excused himself saying he had to make a call.

"Tell her I'm available when you leave for "Egypt," one of the travel staff said. Drew laughed. "I would be happy to do that but this one is kinda particular."

He closed the door of the 'phone booth and dialed McShane's number. "Courier Thirteen," he said as the toneless voice demanded his code.

"Good afternoon, Drew. How's everything in Beautiful Minneapolis?"

Drew chuckled. McShane had obviously heard that description of Minneapolis, too.

"Just wonderful. I'm checking in as you asked with the date of my departure from Minneapolis for Egypt. I'm leaving Thursday, the 10th and I'll be flying out of JFK. I am arriving in New York on Northwest Flight 435 which is scheduled to land at JFK at 4:45 p.m. I will be connecting to Pan Am flight 061 which leaves at 8:30 p.m."

"OK, Drew, listen. I want you to go to Pan Am's Concourse Clipper Club and at 6:00 p.m. you will hear your name paged to take a telephone call. The caller will give you your instructions. There are two Clipper Clubs at JFK, as you probably know, so be sure to go to the Concourse Club. Is that clear?"

"Yes, Brendon, very clear. Anything else?"

"No, that's all, Drew. Good luck, and remember to contact me as soon as you have returned to the States, just as you did on your return from Paris and Rio."

"I'll do that, but it seems rather redundant. When I've called you, you already knew everything that had happened."

'Yes, but that's not always going to be the case. Anyway, even if it's routine, please call me."

"Will do. 'Bye."

CHAPTER TWENTY

JFK AIRPORT, NEW YORK

The Concourse Clipper Club was situated on the departure floor of the Pan Am
Terminal and was seldom less than full. This was no exception. It was almost standing room only and Drew had trouble finding a seat to while away the time until the call came through.

He was immersed in the current issue of Time magazine when he heard the page. "Mr. Drew Cummins, please come to the front desk for a call."

He walked to the desk and identified himself. "I'm Mr. Cummins. You paged me, I believe."

"Yes, Mr. Cummins. There's a call for you. I'll put it in one of the booths around the corner. You can take it in booth number two."

He approached the booths, heard a 'phone ringing and lifted it.

"This is Cummins," he said.

"Drew, at 6:30, that's in about a half-hour, enter the duty-free shop that's right outside the Club. You will find a customer inside, a man with a camelhair overcoat and a brown velour hat holding a camera. Approach him and say your watch is broken and ask if he would give you the correct time. Walk out of the store and find a spot that's inconspicuous where you and he can talk. You pick the spot; he'll follow you. Understood?"

"Understood."

Drew returned to find that his seat had been taken. No surprise. 'Oh, well,' he thought, looking at his watch. 'It's only another 25 minutes or so.'

He saw an empty stool at the bar, took it and ordered a Perrier. The seat next to him became vacant for a few seconds before a burly man with a luxuriant beard occupied it. Speaking with a strong accent, he ordered a beer. He had a small almost imperceptible tattoo in the form of a snake between the thumb and index finger of his right hand.

Drew wondered to himself why people, particularly a successful businessman found pleasure in having his body painted with such ugly scars. He figured that anyone in this club had to be at least moderately successful to be a member.

He finished his Perrier, looked at his watch and saw that it was 6:27. He rose and slowly walked out of the Club and into the Duty-Free shop. There was no man with a camelhair coat and velour hat.

Drew noted that it was now a minute shy of 6:30. He glanced perfunctorily at the items which were for sale only to those travelers who were leaving the country. Some of the prices seemed inflated and he felt sure they could be obtained for less in Minneapolis.

"Do you have any of these items that are not duty-free?" someone asked. "They might be cheaper that way." Others in the shop laughed, but the clerk maintained a stony face. Obviously, she had heard the remark many times before.

Drew turned around and there was the man in the camelhair coat and brown velour hat. He approached him and said that his watch had stopped and would he please give him the time.

'It's 6:32," the stranger said and Drew thanked him for his courtesy.

He left the store and walked slowly, searching for a spot where they could speak without being overheard. The terminal was busy, so he stood in the middle of the hall, next to a display case exhibiting the wonderful things that could be purchased at even more wonderful prices at one of the duty-free shops.

The stranger was right behind him. 'You are . . . . ?"

"Cummins. Drew Cummins."

"Mr. Cummins, you are to take this camera. On the afternoon of Monday, the 14th you are to go to the Pyramids at 10:30 a.m. As you approach the Pyramids, you will be surrounded by camel drivers asking you to ride their camels up to the monument.

"Please wear a red, short-sleeved shirt, tan pants and put this baseball cap on your head as though to protect you from the sun. One of the camel drivers will say to you: 'That is a handsome camera. May I take your picture with it? Please sit atop my camel and I will give you a picture to remember.'

"Ask him if he knows how to operate a camera as complicated as a Kodak. He will say that he has had three Kodaks. You will stop the camel and the driver will pretend to take your picture. You will thank him, give him some coins and then leave. He will disappear with the camera, and your job is done. Understood?"

"Yes," Drew replied, "I understand perfectly, but let's go over the details one more time."

The stranger repeated the instructions then handed him the camera, turned and strode off towards the front of the terminal.

'A red, short-sleeved shirt and tan pants,' Drew murmured to himself. 'Everybody seems to know our company uniform.'

He returned to the Clipper Club and, luckily, there was an empty sofa chair. He opened his briefcase, deposited the small camera and pulled out his Time magazine. As he did so, he wondered to himself if all this 'cloak and dagger' stuff, with mysterious meetings and secretive 'phone calls was really necessary. This is the U.S.A. Surely there's no need for the clandestine hand-offs and codes. Maybe so, he thought, but he still wondered.

CHAPTER TWENTY-ONE

CAIRO, EGYPT

The tour group was staying at the luxurious Mena House Oberoi Hotel, a few minutes' walk from the Pyramids. The people had left earlier in the morning for a full-day tour to Memphis and Sakkara to see monuments and landmarks that vividly recall the truly incredible history of Egypt in a way even more graphic than the Pyramids.

It was Monday, the 14th, and Drew had just finished going over some of the bills with the hotel's accountant. He looked at his watch and noted that it was nine forty-five. He had about another half hour before starting out for the Pyramids.

He strolled over to the Oasis Restaurant and chose an outdoor table on the grassy lawn near the edge of the pool. He sat in one of the chairs that allowed him to gaze in admiration at the Pyramids, the tops of which peeked just above the trees at the hotel entrance.

He had seen the Pyramids a few times before, but his familiarity with the monuments did not mitigate the excitement he felt each time he saw them . . . huge landmarks built of enormous blocks of stone weighing from two-and-a-half to five tons each. He recalled a guide telling a previous group that nobody is really sure how the Pyramids were built or where the stones came from although there are many theories on these points.

The guide had also mentioned that when the Pyramids were built more than 5,000 years ago, the workers did not have the equipment, technology or superior skills that are available today. Yet, if they were constructed now with all of today's advanced equipment, they could not be better or more perfectly built or with any more precision.

The guide had also revealed that there were enough boulders in the Pyramids to build a three-foot fence around the whole of France. 'Might not be a bad idea,' he thought.

"Amazing," he muttered to himself, finding it difficult to avert his gaze from the Cheops pyramid, the largest of the three prominent structures.

He ordered a Turkish coffee, and soon was sipping its strong, black liquid. He had hated the drink the first time he tried it but had been told it was an acquired taste. He had asked himself, 'How could anyone drink it often enough to acquire a taste for it?' but he persevered and soon began to enjoy its flavor and ended up ordering it frequently.

Two pretty Middle Eastern girls were seated at a table next to him, laughing as they conversed with a swarthy, bearded man. He was holding the hand of the girl on his right and Drew noticed the tattoo of a snake between his thumb and index finger. 'The man at the bar in the Clipper Club', he recalled. 'Whatever he looks like to me, he certainly has some appeal for the ladies. Maybe he's a sheik with so much money that the ladies just flock to him.

He looked at his watch and saw that it was 10:15. He signed the bill to his room and skirted the pool as he crossed over the grassy area to the entrance. There were hawkers outside selling wooden carvings, parchment paintings and "genuine" ancient coins found in tombs in Upper Egypt thousands of years ago.

The coins were undoubtedly minted a week or ten days ago, but the hawkers never had any trouble selling them to the gullible tourists who couldn't believe that the cleverly aged coins could possibly have been of recent vintage.

It was a beautiful morning, as usual, and he decided to walk the short distance to where the Arabs waited with their horses and camels for those who wanted to ride the 150 yards up the slight incline to the Pyramids. His camera was prominently displayed at the end of a strap slung around his shoulder.

Most tourists arrive by bus but in agreement with the local "businessmen", the guides give everyone the choice of walking the last quarter of a mile, riding a horse or camel to the Pyramids or having the bus carry them to the monuments. Most opt for a camel or horse, particularly as it means the chance for a photograph with the Pyramids in the background proving that they had really been to the Land of the Pharaohs.

As he neared the spot where he had seen them congregate many times before, a bus pulled up and disgorged about 30 people. Like bees around a hive, the Arabs swarmed all over them, each assuring the tourists that their camel had the gentlest nature and they would enjoy riding it.

Camels have mean tempers and only follow the commands of their owner because they know that not to would earn them a powerful poke with a sharp stick or a kick in the belly. But they still do not like having these tourists climb on their backs and moving around in an uncomfortable fashion.

Three or four drivers ran towards him. He waved them off.

"That is a handsome camera you have," one said. "May I take your picture with it? Please sit atop my camel and I will give you a picture to remember."

"This is a Kodak camera. Do you know how to operate one so complicated as this?"

"It is no problem to me. I have owned many cameras. Please, sit on my camel and let me take a memorable picture."

Drew resisted briefly. That was not quite the answer he was to be given. The driver was to say that he had owned three Kodaks. His answer was not as precise as it should have been. He asked himself if the responses had to be exactly as they were given to him. He was in a quandary.

"Please, sir, I will give you a photograph to remember," the driver pleaded.

He had to make a quick decision. The other drivers were still urging him to ride their camels or horses.

The driver's answer was close enough, he decided. I'm sure this is the right man. Who else could have known the first part of the exchange? No, he convinced himself, this is the right man.

"Okay," he said, "you look like you know how to take a good picture."

He gave the driver his camera and as he did, he noticed the man had a small tattoo of a snake on his right hand, between the thumb and index finger. It looked exactly like the tattoo on the right hand of the bearded man whom he had seen in the Clipper Club in New York and again at the pool of the Mena House Hotel.

Drew accepted the driver's help in mounting the beast which turned to look at him. He could smell its foul breath which made him feel more like regurgitating than mounting it.

The driver held the camera to his eye and asked Drew to smile. He pretended to focus the lens, select the right aperture and click the button.

He descended, thanked the driver and gave him a few coins. The driver bowed and muttered 'missouri' ('thank you') three times before taking his camel and the camera and disappearing the among the other drivers.

He headed back to the Mena House, content that he had completed mission number three. He thought how much easier this assignment had been and hoped that all in the future would be just as devoid of danger as Paris and this one had been.

As he entered the hotel, he saw the Director of Food and Beverage. He had an appointment with him to go over the details for the group's cocktail party and elegant dinner on the hotel lawn this evening.

* * *

A loud ringing noise split the air, startling Drew from a deep sleep. He lifted he 'phone and managed a tired 'hello'.

"Please go to another 'phone, one outside the hotel, and ring your access number. Please do this now," the voice on the other end told him. It was a heavily-accented voice and one he did not recognize. Before he could ask what this was all about, there was a click and the line went dead

He was still groggy as he entered the bathroom to throw some water on his face. He put on a sports shirt and slacks and pushed his feet into his sneakers.

He was thinking of what the voice had told him. Ring your access number, it had said. Why would a Middle Eastern voice be telling him to ring his access number? McShane must have another job for me to do here, he thought. But why roust me from a sleep in the middle of the night? Why couldn't he have had the Egyptian, if that is what he was, call me in the morning?

He took the elevator to the lobby and walked across the hall to the front door where he hailed a taxi. "Take me to the Jollyville Hotel, please," he told the driver. The Jollyville hotel was less than a mile away and the walk would have done him some good, but he didn't feel like walking; he still had cobwebs in his head.

He approached the front desk and said he would like to make a collect call to the United States.

"Yes, sir," the clerk replied. "May I have the number you wish to call?" Drew gave him the number and asked how long the call would take. "At this time of night, sir, it shouldn't take too long."

That was comforting. Drew was well aware that calls to the States often took as long as two hours during the day and sometimes you just couldn't get through at all.

"Is the lounge still open?" he asked the clerk.

"Yes, sir, there is a waiter on duty who will take your order."

"Would you please have someone notify me in the lounge when the call comes through?"

The clerk told him he would do it personally.

He walked into the deserted lounge. No waiter was in sight. He clapped his hands and a dark head appeared above one of the sofas. He had been sleeping soundly. 'I know the feeling,' he murmured to himself.

"I would like a Turkish coffee, please," he told the waiter who smiled and disappeared. He returned five minutes later with the steaming coffee. It was excellent.

All the possible reasons McShane had for contacting him at this ungodly hour began to flood his mind. Suddenly, he thought of the delivery at the Pyramids. Was there something wrong with the delivery. Should I not have given the camera to the driver because he did not give me the precise answer? He couldn't expunge these thoughts from his mind as he sipped the black liquid.

"Sir . . . sir." It was the clerk. He was waving to him from the door of the lounge. "Your call is ready. Please take it in booth number one next to the front desk."

Drew was surprised at his energy as he sprang up and ran towards the booths and entered the first one.

The 'phone rang and he lifted it. The operator repeated only the number he had dialed. "This is Courier Thirteen."

"Please hold," the voice said.

Within 10 seconds, McShane was on the line. "Drew, we've got trouble. Did you make your delivery?"

"Yes," he almost shouted into the receiver. Didn't you get a report that I had delivered it?"

He repeated everything that had happened and mentioned that the driver had not given him the exact response at the end of their conversation.

"I wondered whether I should give him the camera but he was correct in every other word he said and I thought that perhaps responses didn't have to be precise."

McShane told him that the camel driver who should have approached him was found murdered, strangled with a cord that is used as camel reins.

"Drew, we have to get that camera back. It contained some very important information on our spywork in the Middle East. I will have a CIA man from the Cairo station call you at your hotel. Be prepared to cooperate with him fully. He will identify himself and show his credentials. He will want you to go over every detail. Drew, we have got to get that camera back."

CHAPTER TWENTY-TWO

CAIRO, EGYPT

Drew was the trip director on the program, so he called Lois Friederich, one of the travel staff, to ask her to take control of the program for a few hours to enable him to do some accounting. This would give him the necessary hours to spend with the CIA man who would be calling soon. He mentioned to Friederich that he would be in his room going over the bills for about an hour before meeting with the hotel accountant and could be reached there in the event of an emergency.

"If anyone calls for me, put the call through to my room," he told her.

Almost immediately his 'phone rang. "Mr. Cummins, my name is Colman, Holden Colman. I believe a mutual friend in Washington mentioned that I would be getting in touch with you."

"Yes, Mr. Colman. I'm in room 159. Perhaps it would be better if you came up here."

Colman, who spoke with an American accent, acknowledged the wisdom of the suggestion and said he would be there in about 40 minutes. It didn't take him that long, and a half-hour had elapsed when there was a knock on the door and Drew admitted him.

Colman was a tall, solidly-built man in his middle thirties with a full mustache. He had an olive complexion which made him fit easily into the local scene. 'The CIA obviously coordinates its men with the culture of their assigned destinations,' he thought to himself.

"Drew, please go over every detail, even anything you think is insignificant. There may be something important that appears trivial or even ludicrous to you that could shed some light on our problem."

He carefully recapped his movements that morning including the Turkish coffee at poolside, the walk to the camel drivers' meeting spot, his conversation with the driver who pleaded to take his picture, as well as his slow walk back to the Mena House.

"What I can't understand is how this fellow knew the questions to ask. How did he know to contact me?"

"That's the easy part of the puzzle, Colman told him. "Our contact was murdered, as you already know. What hasn't been reported is that his body bore the unmistakable marks of torture. He was forced to give the information to his captors. Shrewdly, he did not give them all of what they wanted to know. The impostor did not know that he should have told you he once had three Kodaks. That was our contact's way of warning you. Of course, you should have been made aware that the answers must be precise. It's not your fault."

"Holden, there is one thing I should mention. When I was in the Clipper Club at JFK awaiting a call from my contact, I sat next to a burly, swarthy Middle Easterner at the bar. He had a small tattoo of a snake between the thumb and index finger of his right hand. I remember wondering why people disfigure their bodies with such ugly marks, even though it was not an obvious one and was difficult to see without close inspection.

"Anyway, when the phony camel driver took my camera from me, I noticed that he, too, had a similar tattoo and in the same place. Is that a common type of tattoo in Egypt, do you know? I've been here a number of times before but I don't remember ever seeing such a tattoo."

"No, I've never seen that in Cairo and I've been stationed here for almost two years."

"What might make this even more important is that I saw the same burly man, who I forgot to mention had a full beard, at poolside yesterday morning when I was having my coffee. He was obviously on the make with two very attractive young women, both of whom I'd guess to be Egyptian."

Colman was thinking seriously about the coincidence. He was quiet for a few seconds. He pulled a pager 'phone from inside his pocket and dialed a number. He asked the person at the other end of the line to check for information on any gang whose members had a tattoo in the shape of a snake and worn on the right hand between the thumb and index finger. "Do we know of anyone or any sect carrying such a tattoo? Is there some secret society that uses the tattoo as a symbol of their membership. Call me back in room 159 at the Mena House as quickly as possible. This should be given urgent status."

"We've nothing on it here, Holden. I'd better get in touch with Langley to put them on it."

He hung up and turned to Drew. "Your observance of the tattoo might mean something. I have a feeling there's a connection. You say you saw the man at poolside yesterday morning. There's a good possibility he's a guest in this hotel. Let's see, it's 8:15. Maybe he's having breakfast. I want you to go down and walk through the dining room, the other public rooms and poolside. If you spot him, come back here and let me know immediately."

Drew left the room and descended the stairs to the lobby. He entered the dining room and began searching for the bearded man.

"Hi, Drew, who're you looking for? Me?" It was Henry Castle, the vice president of marketing for the company sponsoring the trip.

"Oh, no, Mr. Castle," he replied. "I'm looking for the hotel accountant. I have to go over some of the bills with him. His assistant said he was having coffee and I thought he might be in the dining room. Perhaps he's at the pool, so I'll try there. Are you enjoying the trip?"

"Indeed I am. Fantastic place. I still can't believe I'm here in Egypt looking at 5,000 years of history."

"Good," Drew responded. 'Well, I'll see you later."

He walked over to the hotel's other dining room, but the bearded man was not there either. He walked out the front door and crossed over the pathway to poolside, but there was no sign of the man. Returning to the hotel, he decided to look in some of the other public rooms. Just as he was crossing the lobby, he saw his prey leaving the elevator. He stepped out of sight and heard him ask the bell captain to call a cab.

He raced up the stairs to his room, turned the key in the door and called out: "Let's go. He's leaving the hotel by taxi."

They didn't bother waiting for the elevator, but rushed down the stairs, taking them three at a time. "Stay out of sight while I get my car. Remember, he has seen you, however briefly, and may remember you. When I pull up in a gray Fiat, jump in. I'll wait 'til he's boarded his cab before I pick you up."

Drew watched as Colman passed their quarry whowas still waiting for his taxi. "Your cab is here now, sir," the bell captain said as he touched his cap in deference to the importance of the guest. The Middle Easterner gave him some coins and the bell captain thanked him profusely.

'Must've been a great tip,' Drew thought as he looked at the wide smile on the bellman's face.

The bearded man entered the cab and Drew moved closer to hear the directions he was giving the cab driver, but he couldn't get near enough without exposing his presence. The cab took off but Colman was right behind him and stopped briefly to let him jump in.

The cab sped down the Giza Road towards the city, ignoring red lights as well as any lanes that could only appear in one's imagination. If there were once lines painted on the highway, they were long gone.

The traffic was in its usual, disorganized, congested state, and the cab was moving slowly. Colman kept the Fiat at least three lengths behind, with the taxi always in sight. They moved past the home of the late Egyptian president, Anwar Sadat, and the nearby Cairo Sheraton Hotel and crossed over the El Galaa Bridge into the downtown area. The traffic was even worse at this point, but Colman kept his car close enough that the cab was always in view.

Suddenly, the taxi turned right on to another main street just as the lights changed. None of the other cars drove through as they usually did; instead, they stopped. Colman soon saw why. A cop was directing traffic, even though the lights were working. He was holding his hand flat out signaling for the oncoming traffic to stop.

"Damn," Colman cursed, "of all times for a cop to be directing traffic. Some times they'll hold a line of cars for as much as five minutes before allowing them to continue."

They waited nervously for what seemed an eternity before the cop waved them on. There were still cars ahead of them but the one in front didn't move. It was obviously having a problem, again a frequent occurrence in the choked streets of Cairo.

It took another two or three minutes for the stalled car's engine to ignite then cough and sputter as it moved slowly forward. Colman gunned the Fiat's engine as he turned on the same road the taxi had taken.

"Well, any ideas?" Colman said as they drove along the boulevard, looking on both sides and down the cross streets they were passing. The cab was nowhere in sight.

'Would it be worthwhile cutting down one of these streets and driving up and down them in the hope of spotting him?"

Colman agreed. "It's a long shot, but I can't think of anything better to try, so let's do it."

They turned left on to a wide street where store merchants were displaying their wares on the sidewalk. It made for good business, as the pavements were full of shoppers jostling with each other to see what was available on the stalls.

Colman turned right at the bottom of the street and turned right again at the next one, driving in the direction of the boulevard they had just left.

"There he is," Drew shouted at the top of his voice. "There he is, talking to someone outside that store. Look over there."

"Got him," Colman answered. "Get out here and keep him in view while I try to park this car somewhere. Don't lose him. If he moves and you have to leave, tail him at a discreet distance and when you think he's reached where he's gonna stay put, we'll meet back at this spot."

Drew jumped out of the car as Colman moved forward in search of a parking spot, almost an impossibility in downtown Cairo. Drew was easily hidden in the bustling crowd and managed to keep the Middle Easterner in his vision. He moved very slowly with the crowd towards a vantage point that placed him directly opposite the store where the two men were talking.

They shook hands and the bearded man entered the store while his companion walked away. He decided against moving closer lest he be spotted. He was well hidden where he stood, yet could clearly keep the store under surveillance.

Fifteen minutes passed before he saw Colman. He was coming towards him and just as he was about to pass, Drew grabbed his jacket. "Have you seen anything?" Colman asked.

"Yes, the two men for a few minutes," he replied, "before the Middle Easterner entered the store and the other man walked off as another man approached.

Suddenly, Drew stiffened. "Look," he pulled at Colman's shirtsleeve. "It's the camel driver. That's the guy who spoke to me at the Pyramids. I can see his face clearly now; it's definitely the camel driver."

"Are you positive?" Colman said, hardly betraying the excitement he felt.

"Absolutely," Drew replied. "That's the man with the tattoo. Now we know there's a connection."

Colman was sweating profusely in the 96-degree heat and wiped his forehead with a handkerchief. "I think we have to make a move and quickly. We don't have time to do some scouting and plan a cute maneuver. I have a feeling our burly friend has the camera now. That's why the camel jock is leaving. They have had a meeting, it's been turned over and the pseudo camel driver has undoubtedly been very well paid.

"I'm going to cross the street and sneak a glance inside the store. You wait here for my signal to come over."

Dodging the endless traffic, Colman reached the other side of the street that was still busy with pedestrians and shoppers. The store had several people milling about its door, some were looking in its windows while others were picking up and evaluating objects on the sidewalk stall.

Colman saw three clerks inside the store; all were haggling over prices with customers. The burly man was nowhere to be seen. Colman moved away from the store and waved Drew over.

"I'm about to suggest a simple action that is definitely not in the training books of the CIA. We're taught to study the quarry, plan a clever and foolproof maneuver and act on it. But we don't have the time for cuteness and besides I think the very simple plan I have in mind will be the most effective one. When the burly guy comes out, I feel confident he will have the camera and its contents on him. I think he's going to come soon, return to the hotel, pack his bags and head for the airport to fly to his home base.

"Let's go back to the hotel because that's where we're going to move on him."

They returned to the car which Colman had parked nearby, its exit partially blocked by a beat-up old Chevy that had obviously been through many wars. It was impossible to drive away without moving the museum piece, and there was no time to waste.

Colman hailed a couple of robust-looking men who were more than pleased to lend a little muscle to help move the vehicle, particularly when he showed them a few Egyptian pounds. He told them they could have all of the money in his fist if they would quickly push the Chevy to the side. With little more encouragement, the men lifted the rear and pulled the car out into the road it was a sitting target for the mad drivers of Cairo.

Colman dispensed the money and both climbed into the Fiat. They had moved no more than 50 feet when they heard a horrendous, metal-crunching sound. They turned to see the Chevy squashed into a quarter of its size. "That's one shock for an idiot driver," Colman said. "I wish I could see him to tell him that I would like to bet that he won't make the same parking mistake with his next car."

Colman mentioned that had to stop at his apartment to pick up a few things before they drove to the Mena House. "My apartment is actually on the way," he aid. "I shouldn't take more a couple of minutes."

"Do we have the time?" Drew asked.

"Believe me, for what I am going to pick up, we have lots of time," Colman assured him.

Shortly after they crossed back over El Galaa bridge, Colman turned right into a fashionable but narrow street and stopped in front of an elegant old building. He dashed up the stairs leading to the front door and was gone in an instant. He returned two minutes later, descending the stairs two at a time, and jumped back into the driver's seat.

'What did you pick up that was so important?" Drew asked. "I don't see anything."

Colman smiled and patted the breast pocket of his jacket. "Ah, but you will when we get to the hotel."

Thirty minutes later, they turned into the driveway of the Mena House and passed the front door of the hotel before parking the Fiat in the shade of some pine trees.

"First, we have to find out who our bearded friend is. We don't even know his name."

Colman approached the bellmen's desk and sought out the bell captain who was reading a newspaper. He thrust a twenty-pound note into his hand. 'Say, who was that bearded man who asked you to get him a taxi this morning. He wore a white suit with a red handkerchief and . . ."

"You don't need any more description, sir, that was Mr. El Fahoud."

"Are you sure? I thought he was a man I had done business with several years ago, but I don't recognize that name."

"Oh, I'm sure, sir. He stays at our hotel three or four times a year. He comes here to have a little fun away from home, if you know what I mean."

"If he's who I think he is, he's from Upper Egypt and he's a gold merchant."

"Oh, no, sir, Mr. El Fahoud is from Damascus, but I don't know what his business is. He has never said. But I do know that he has a lot of money," the bell captain said with a huge grin on his face that bespoke many big tips."

"No, it's not the man I'm thinking of. My man was from Upper Egypt and he's definitely not a big tipper. He would haggle with me over a few pounds. Thanks anyway." The bell captain touched his cap as a gesture of respect and returned to catching up with his duties.

Colman and Drew walked into the lounge and sat down. "I don't want the bell captain to see me going over to the front desk lest he get suspicious," Colman whispered. "You sit here and I'll slip over unobtrusively and try to locate Mr. El Fahoud's room number."

The front desk clerk was staring intently at a rooming list. Three keys were lying on the counter and had not yet been put in their boxes. Colman lifted one without attracting the clerk's attention, then coughed politely.

"I am sorry, sir, I didn't see you standing there. May I help you?" the clerk inquired.

"Yes," Colman began. "I had lunch with Mr. El Fahoud this afternoon and I think he took my room key by mistake because I'm sure I have his key. Would you check, please?"

The clerk turned and took the key out of the box for the Nile Suite and looked at it. "No, sir, Mr. El Fahoud's key is in the correct slot. Let me see the key you have."

He gave the key he had picked up to the clerk. It was for room 331. "What is the number of your room, sir?"

"It's . . . . oh, I am embarrassed. I have it in my coat pocket. I thought I had got it mixed up with Mr. El Fahoud's key. But whose key is 331, then?" My, my, this is a mystery. I must have picked up someone else's key. Here's something for your trouble." He slipped the bewildered clerk a twenty-pound note which brought a wide smile to his face.

"No trouble, sir, and thank you. You wouldn't believe the mix-ups we have with room keys."

He returned to the lounge and caught Drew's eye. He jerked his head to indicate that he should quickly follow him. They walked to the elevator, got in and punched the button for the top floor.

"He's in the Nile Suite, the best suite in the hotel. Why doesn't that surprise me? Now you'll see why I stopped at my apartment. This is what I picked up."

He took a small piece of metal like a nail file from his pocket. "I'll pick the lock and then we wait for that wonderfully generous Mr. El Fahoud to return."

It took Colman no more than 10 seconds to open the door. Once inside, he suggested that Drew hide in the bathroom.

"When he comes in, I plan to hit him over the head without giving him a chance to see me. Don't budge until I call you."

They waited patiently, without conversing with each other, for about 20 minutes when there was a click in the lock. The door opened and Colman, positioned behind the door so he couldn't be seen, slammed a black cosh on El Fahoud's head. As he sagged, Colman caught him and simultaneously closed the door with his leg.

He called softly for Drew who came out of the bathroom to see Colman sifting through El Fahoud's briefcase. It was locked, but the same thin metal instrument soon opened the catch. He carefully looked through the case and whispered 'bingo'. He pulled out his hand, opened it and displayed the roll of film.

"Are you sure there is no other film in the briefcase?"

"No, this is the only one and I'm positive this is what we want. I just wish we could have it developed on the spot to know for sure, but that's one gadget the CIA hasn't yet provided us."

Colman looked through the papers to see if there was anything interesting. Everything was in Arabic and while Colman was conversant with Arabic, he was not sufficiently strong in the language to be able to translate the contents. I'm taking everything because our boys might find much of interest in them."

He looked at El Fahoud's right hand and studied the small snake tattoo. "I wish I knew what society this is. It's obvious that it is an identification of some kind, much like the SS had their blood type tattooed on the inside of their right forearm. It let everybody know that they were proud members of a very exclusive group."

"I should be hearing from my office soon concerning what they've learned about the tattoo. They are probably waiting to hear from Langley."

They moved downstairs to Drew's room where they could talk in private without fear of interruption.

'There's going to be one helluva flap in a few hours so we have to finalize our plans fast. You have to take the film and the papers and get out of Cairo tonight. There's no flight to the States at this time, but will be later tonight, but I don't think you should hang around 'til then. There's a flight to Rome that you could take, then overnight at the airport and catch a flight to New York tomorrow. Can you leave your group just now?"

"I think I can do that, but why should I take the film back to New York. Shouldn't I leave it here? This is where I was supposed to take it in the first place."

"I was told that if we located the film that you should carry it back to the States. Perhaps Washington wants to find out if it has been tampered with in any way. Maybe they are concerned that the information on the film has been viewed thus exposing the details. Anyway, I was given instructions to have you take it back with you so that's what we're gonna do."

"You know best,' Drew said. "As for leaving the trip, I could say I received a call from the States that my father is seriously ill. I have a strong staff here and Lois Friederich could take over. Emergencies such as this have happened before and usually we send a replacement from our office, but we have enough staff here so I don't think that will be necessary. Quite frankly, I don't want to stay around here any longer than I have to."

"Great, then pack as fast as you can and let's go."

Drew picked up the 'phone and called the group's hospitality desk. Lois Friederich answered and he told her he had just received a call from home and that his father had a serious heart attack. 'My mother was in a panic on the 'phone. I have to get back to the States immediately. Can you take over?

"Sure, Drew, I don't think you need to call the office and request another staff. The trip is going well and there are no particularly tough areas that would require any more help than we've got. Just go and don't worry about a thing. I sure hope your dad recovers fully."

"Thanks, Lois," and good luck."

Colman told him he would get the car and pick him up at the front door in a couple of minutes.

Drew threw his clothes into his case. He didn't pack them as neatly as was his custom. He just jammed them in and closed it.

He felt the perspiration run down his chest and back. His heart's normal pulse rate of 57 a minute was racing, close to 100. It was only three floors to the lobby, but as he had three pieces of luggage, he decided to take the elevator. It seemed that the elevator was taking longer in its descent when the buzzer sounded and it stopped.

'Oh my God," he thought to himself. 'The elevator has stopped.' The passengers began to panic. "The elevator has broken down," one screamed. "Oh, help us, please help us," one moaned. "There are too many damn people on this thing,": another yelled. One woman looked at Drew and said: "Why did you get on with your cases when you could clearly see that the elevator was full. It's your fault that it's stopped."

As coolly as he could, Drew opened the small emergency door above the panel of buttons, pulled out the 'phone and dialed the operator.

"Can someone help us, please? We're stuck in the elevator between the first and second floors. Hurry, please, hurry."

'Right away, sir, right away," the operator answered. "Please stay calm."

He waited for five minutes, all the time wondering how long El Fahoud would be unconscious. He found himself hoping that Colman had given him a really good whack, one that would put him out for hours. 'How long does one remain unconscious from a blow on the head?' he found himself wondering. He looked at his watch and saw that it had been approximately 35 minutes since Colman had slammed his cosh down on El Fahoud's head.

'God, how much longer?' he thought. Suddenly, a woman fainted and everybody struggled to help her, not really knowing what to do.

"Fan her, somebody," Drew shouted. 'Wave something over her face to keep her cool."

Next, a man passed out and slid to the floor. Another guest loosened the man's tie and collar then began to fan him.

There was a sudden lurch, and the elevator began to descend.

"Oh, thank God," everyone shouted, "thank God." "Allah Akbar," Arab voices cried out. "Allah Akbar."

The doors opened and several hotel officials were waiting to help the guests, immediately rushing forward to offer assistance to the two guests who had fainted.

Drew rushed forward carrying his suitcase. He stepped smartly out the front door, descended the steps to the driveway. He tossed his suitcase in the back seat of the Fiat and jumped wildly into the front seat. The car sped forward before he even had time to close the door properly.

"What took you so long?" Colman asked. "I was getting nervous."

Drew quickly relayed what had happened as Colman muttered that he hoped the rest of the evening would be an improvement.

"There's a Rome flight leaving at 9:25, he said, looking at the clock on the dashboard. That's about a little over two hours from now. There will be probably be others, let's hope so. Thank God the traffic is only just awful tonight. Most times it doesn't move at all."

Fifty minutes later, they reached the airport. Colman let him out with his bags and told him to look for the first flight to anywhere in Europe and buy a ticket while he parked the car.

Drew checked the Flight Departures board and saw that there was an Air France flight leaving for Paris at 7:30 and an Alitalia flight departing at 9:25 for Rome. But next to the Rome departure time was a note explaining that the Alitalia flight would be delayed one hour.

Rushing to the Air France ticket counter, he asked if there was space on the Paris flight. "Do you have a ticket?" the agent inquired.

"Yes, I have a ticket, but it's TWA to New York and I have had to change my plans because of a medical emergency at home. Because of the time shortage, I'll just buy a ticket and I'll see to a refund when I get home."

"May I see your ticket?" the agent asked, a suspicious look clouding his face.

"Of course," Drew replied, searching his jacket pocket. "Here it is."

The agent looked at it, noted that it was an economy ticket, then returned it to him. "All right, sir, I can book you in coach. Shall I book you on the flight from Paris to Washington tomorrow?"

"Yes, please do that."

"How will you be paying for it, sir?"

He produced his American Express credit card. The agent took it and began to write a new ticket.

"Ah, there you are, Drew, I thought I had lost you." It was Colman, appearing very cool and collected. "When I dropped you off, I couldn't remember if you said you were hoping to fly on Air France or Egyptair."

Colman was making it appear to the agent that there was no great urgency about Drew's departure so as not to arouse any suspicion, particularly as he was making a reservation and purchasing a ticket at the airport. Most people handle such details long before taking an international flight.

"Here is your ticket, sir, and thank you. I would suggest you go through passport control immediately. Security can take a lot longer than it does at other major airports. Have a good flight."

As they advanced to passport control and out of hearing distance, Drew explained why he had chosen the Air France flight. "Good thinking," Colman replied. "The sooner you are out of Cairo, the better. I think it would be wise for me to say goodbye here. I want to keep watch on the entrance and if our friend shows up, I'll do everything I possibly can to delay him."

Drew gave him the flight number of tomorrow's flight to Washington and asked him to pass it along to McShane and reminded Colman about the film.

They shook hands and Drew felt the film being pressed into his hand. "Oh, here's a newspaper to read on the flight," he said shoving it into the pocket of Drew's light raincoat. The inside pages are particularly interesting, you'll find."

Lowering his voice, he aid: "I'll call our friend in D.C. and give him your flight number and arrival time into Washington. All the credit for pulling this off is yours, Drew. Congratulations and good luck."

Colman watched until Drew had passed through passport control and moved towards the terminal entrance. The time passed slowly but eventually he noticed that the flight board indicated that Air France flight 210 for Paris had departed on time at 7:30.

He heaved a sigh of relief. There had been no sign of El Fahoud and he wondered if he had applied too much pressure hitting him and had killed him. 'It would serve the bastard right,' he thought to himself.

CHAPTER TWENTY-THREE

CIA HEADQUARTERS
LANGLEY, VIRGINIA

The Air France flight touched down at Dulles International Airport 10 minutes ahead of schedule. When Drew cleared Customs, he quickly spotted McShane who was standing off to the side of the crowd that had gathered to welcome relatives and friends back from European vacations.

He signaled Drew to make sure he saw him, then moved forward to help carry one of his cases. "I've got a car outside," he said, motioning for him to follow. As they drove away from the airport, Drew opened the conversation by giving McShane a complete and detailed report of the happenings in Cairo.

"Well, you had another rough one, but Colman called me and he is full of praise for the way you picked up on the snake tattoo. He says you deserve all the credit for recovering the film. You do have it with you, don't you?"

"Yes, of course. What did you think I would do? Leave it in Paris in a hotel safety deposit box?"

McShane laughed at his fighting spirit. "I meant do you have it on your person or did you pack it in your case?"

"No, I have it in the inside pocket of my jacket, and I have the papers in my briefcase, tucked inside my appointments calendar."

He was experiencing that out-of-sorts feeling again. The fatigue made him fractious, and that was not his usual behavior.

"Sorry for snapping at you, Brendon. I'm just tired. With all the traveling I do, you would think I would be inured to time changes and lengthy airplane flights, wouldn't you?"

"No sweat, Drew. I once traveled as much as you, maybe more, and I never was able to slide into a regular schedule right away. Always took me a day or two and in some cases much longer."

McShane told him that he was going to suggest something that he figured was about two or three years ahead of plan. He was taking him to CIA headquarters at Langley.

"I know you're tired, Drew, but I think we have to go over, very carefully, what happened to you in Cairo. I'm baffled how they knew of your arrival. We know they must have beaten the contact phrases out of our man at the Pyramids, but how did they know of the date and time? He definitely wouldn't have given them that information. He could easily have claimed that it was not passed along to him. I can't figure our man giving them that information, too. I would have thought he would give them a false date and time. Poor bugger, they must have made him suffer terribly. Middle Easterners are not averse to using the most cruel and painful means to get what they want."

"Are you up to an hour's meeting?"

"You know, Brendon, when I come back from overseas, I feel tired and crotchety and am definitely not the social person I normally am. Not at least for a day or two anyway, but if you think it's important, I'll go along."

McShane stopped the car at the gate of the CIA headquarters and presented his identification card. The guard took the card, pressed it into a metal receptacle then withdrew it. There was no sound from the receptacle, so McShane's card was valid. The guard pressed a buzzer inside his kiosk, the gate swung away and McShane drove inside.

The road to the main building was through a forested area which lent a sense of tranquility to the scene. 'Strange,' Drew thought, 'that the world's most vaunted intelligence agency, the hub of action and constant on-the-go agents is situated in such serene surroundings. Or maybe it isn't so strange.'

There were several empty parking spots, each with a number painted on the ground. Drew noted that there were no names on the obviously reserved areas, just numbers.

McShane steered his car into the slot marked number 92, shutoff the ignition, released his seat belt and stepped out. He presented his ID card to the guard just inside the door who repeated the same process as his fellow officer at the gate. The card was returned to McShane who asked that a visitor's pass be issued to Cummins.

Drew was given a sheet to fill out with numerous questions which he completed. He was given a pass and asked to clip it to the breast pocket of his jacket. McShane gave the film to the guard. They both passed through a sensitive metal detector. Drew was surprised that he hadn't been asked to remove his jacket, shoes and belt and commented on that fact to McShane.

"This detection system is 'way beyond what is used in airports," McShane confided. "Nothing damaging, and I do mean nothing, could possibly get past it."

The guard returned the film to McShane.

They walked to an elevator and slipped inside the doors just as they were closing. The elevator stopped at the fourth floor where they exited.

McShane stopped at a door, pushed his identification card into another metal receptacle on the wall and the door automatically opened. "This way," McShane said as he entered a small conference room obviously designed for just a few people. "Wait here. Do you want some coffee?"

"Yes, I would . . . black, please."

McShane returned a few minutes later, holding two cups of coffee. Drew's mug brought a smile to his face. It had a picture of what the public humorously imagines a man of intrigue to resemble. It showed a caricature wearing an ear receiver and a bulge in his jacket revealing the tip of a revolver. The figure was speaking into a tiny microphone attached to the lapel of his jacket and wearing a Sherlock Holmes cap while holding a magnifying glass. A pipe drooped from his mouth and he held the leash of a bloodhound. The words: "The Compleat Spy" appeared at the bottom of the mug.

"We're going to be joined by two other people, Drew. They are Chase Barron, who is my boss, and George Hollis, who has the same rank and works in the same department as I."

"Am I going to get the third degree?" Drew asked with a smile.

Before McShane could offer a humorous rejoinder, Barron and Hollis entered the room. They were introduced to Drew then sat down at a round table designed for no more than six people.

"Drew," McShane opened up the meeting, "we're going to record your statement. This is normal procedure. We know you're tired and we won't prolong this more than necessary, but we need to hear everything that happened in Cairo. Would you go over all the details again from the beginning until your departure from Egypt? Don't leave out even the smallest details because some times insignificant little occurrences turn out to be very important."

Drew slowly and meticulously relayed the whole story, taking almost a half-hour to cover every detail.

"I would say that's very thorough coverage," Barron smiled as Drew finished. "What puzzles us, Drew, is the snake tattoo. We have absolutely no information on this sect. Our Cairo office cabled us requesting information on it, but our voluminous files came up zero. It must be a new group. Perhaps it is a recently-established Middle Eastern terroristic movement, probably allied to Iran or Syria. Maybe even the Palestinians. One thing for sure, you did a mighty fine job of recovering the film. May I have it now?"

Drew reached inside his pocket and withdrew it. He also opened his briefcase and took the papers from inside his appointments calendar. He turned them over to Barron.

"This is one for the book," Barron continued. "I don't think I have ever heard of us losing such valuable information and recovering it in 24 hours with perhaps a bonus thrown in," he said, riffling the papers. "You did one helluva job, young man, yes, sir, one helluva job."

"Mr. Barron, there is one other thing I would like to mention and that concerns Holden Colman. He is giving me all the credit. He and I worked so effectively together, and he deserves as much of the credit as I do. Without his great cooperation, I don't think we could have done as well as we did, so I hope that something creditable will be put in his record."

"Well, you just put it on the record with that statement because it has just been recorded."

Drew fidgeted in his seat and ran his fingers through his thick hair, waiting for the all-important question he knew would be asked.

"How do you feel about continuing to help us?" It was McShane asking the question and looking him straight in the eyes.

"I was wondering when that would come up because I've been mulling it over in my mind. I won't tell you I wasn't scared because I was. Not at what I might encounter as we chased El Fahoud all over Cairo, but at the fact that I had failed in my mission and had let you down. That bothered me more than anything else.

'And another thing that disturbed me is that in my last two missions, I've had to bring back the damn things I was carrying. I didn't complete my tasks and that doesn't sit too well with me. Tell me, is my cover blown . . . or is that the right phrase?"

Hollis smiled and a chuckle could be heard in his throat.

"No and yes," Barron replied. "Your cover is not blown and it is still a phrase we use here at Langley. I believe that encountering the bearded man in the Clipper Club was an accident. He would not have shown himself to you if he had known who you were. It was pure coincidence, and I might add, lucky for you. From what you have said, I doubt that he had a good look at you. Certainly not in the bar, and I would imagine he had other things to look at when you were at poolside."

"Incidentally, we checked his entry papers into the U.S. and he used the same name, El Fahoud, so we are assuming that it is indeed his real name. He listed his occupation as an importer-exporter. We can't find anything else on him in our files that could be helpful. As far as we're concerned, the only one who can recognize you is the phony camel driver and we've sent a top priority message to Colman to try to find him and minimize his effectiveness. I'm inclined to believe that you're a natural for this business, so we're hoping you'll continue to work for us."

"Oh, one other thing. You're far from being a failure. We've had couriers frequently bring back the information they were asked to deliver abroad, and for many different reasons.

"We don't look on your so-called unsuccessful efforts as failures; I think of your last mission as assisting us in recouping valuable documents that would have been of great help to the other side if they had gotten their hands on them."

"In that case, I would like to continue because I really feel that I am doing something worthwhile for my country, and that means a lot to me. However, I mean it when I say that I hope my future missions are all completed satisfactorily."

"I'm very pleased to hear you say that, Drew, and I mean it when I say that if you ever tire of traveling all around the world with your groups, I hope you will consider maybe joining the CIA and our division in particular. You're exactly the type of individual we need in this business, so give me a call.

"I was impressed with your comment that you were more scared of failure, of letting us down than of bodily injury. That, my friend, is the mark of a pro. I'm going to leave you in the capable hands of Brendon and George who want to question you further."

Barron shook hands with Drew and left the room.

"Wow, said McShane, "I've never heard the old man gush like that before. He obviously thinks very highly of you, Drew. Now, I want to suggest that you maintain a low profile until I contact you. I'll feel much better sending you on another mission when we know that the camel jockey has been removed from the scene. So, why don't you return to Minneapolis and when I have something to report, I'll contact you. OK?"

"Fine," Drew replied, happy that he might be nearing an opportunity to collapse in a bed and get some sleep.

"George will drive you over to the Marriott. I've made a reservation there for you. Just sign the bill in the morning when you leave and it will be sent to me for payment. Enjoy a good dinner and breakfast, watch an in-room movie, order a few drinks and charge everything. You've earned it."

"Another thing, Brendon. This may sound funny, but Holden and I can't offer irrefutable proof that the film you have there is one I carried over to Egypt. I'd like to know for sure that it's genuine."

McShane and Hollis looked at each other dumbfoundedly.

"Hell, that never dawned on me," McShane gasped. "Of course, how could you know for sure? I'll call you at the Marriott. I'll have it developed immediately and call you before you're settled in."

* * *

The bellman pointed out the climate controls, explained the operation of the television and handed Drew the room key, adding that if there was anything else he wanted, just to dial #4 on his telephone. Drew slipped him two dollars as he left the room.

The 'phone rang. It was McShane. "Sleep well, Drew, the film was the genuine article."

He heaved a sign of relief. "I will now. Thanks for the call."

Drew looked at his watch and noted that it was almost seven o'clock, six o'clock in Minneapolis. He dialed Cole Tennant's direct number, thinking it would be a good idea to let his boss know he had come back early from the trip. Unless, that is, Lois Friederich had made contact with him in the meantime.

"Tennant," the gruff voice answered. 'Good,' thought Drew, 'he's still in the office.'

"Cole, this is Cummins."

"Why are you calling from Cairo? It must be the middle of the night there. Is anything wrong?"

"No, Cole, the trip is going fine, but I had to leave. I had a call from my sister to tell me that my father had had a very serious heart attack and urging me to come home. She said my mother was in a state of panic, as I could well have imagined. I had a conversation with Lois Friederich who felt she could handle the trip without any replacement being flown over from Minneapolis. Everything is going very smoothly."

"Gee, Drew, I'm sorry about your father. Has there been improvement?"

"A little. The doctor feels he will recover but there may be some damage. He's ordered complete bed rest for him."

He hated to lie, but felt he had no choice. They spoke for another five minutes then Drew said he would be in the office in a couple of days.

"Don't hurry, buddy, just take your time and stay with your dad. I don't have you scheduled for another trip until the beginning of next month. Thanks for calling to keep me informed."

It was now 7:25 p.m. He wanted to go to sleep right away but knew that if he did, he'd wake up in the middle of the night. He decided to have a meal on the government then return to his room for a hot bath and then it would be close to 10 o'clock before he got to bed. That would probably insure that he would not wake up until a decent hour in the morning.

CHAPTER TWENTY-FOUR

CAIRO, EGYPT

Colman stared at the decoded message brought to him by Judy, his American secretary. *Top Priority*, it read. Do everything possible to locate and render ineffective the pseudo camel driver who took the camera from your recent companion.

He sat back in his chair in his office at the embassy. His feet on his desk, gazing at the ceiling and thinking of the best way to fulfill his assignment.

After fifteen minutes of immobility, he had formulated a plan. He drove to his apartment and changed into blue jeans and a short-sleeve shirt. Pulling on a baseball cap with Monte Carlo on the visor, he grabbed his camera and slung the strap over his shoulder.

Colman sat in the gray Fiat, pressed the starter and the motor coughed obediently. He put it in first gear and steered it towards the Giza Road and the Pyramids.

Entering the grounds of the Mena House, he easily found a parking spot. 'This must be one of the very few places in Cairo where you don't have too much trouble finding a parking spot,' he mused.

He locked the car and set off on foot for the Pyramids. He slowed his pace, waiting for a tourist bus to arrive so that he could blend in with the other tourists.

Soon, the roar of a straining engine announced the approach of a vehicle and Colman turned to see a bus slowly ascending the slight incline leading to the Pyramids. It belched thick, black smoke as it slowly passed him. He quickened his step, arriving just as the door opened to disgorge the tourists eager to suffer the pain of a camel ride up to the Pyramids.

With the camera covering his eyes, he pretended to be focusing the lens and snapping the color of the camel drivers and their snorting beasts.

"Please, sir, you try my camel. It's the gentlest beast in all of Egypt. Look," he said, pulling the creature's face around with a sharp tug on the rein, "see what a beautiful and contented face he has. He would love to have you ride him up to Cheops." Cheops was the Pharaoah who built the largest of the four Pyramids that dot the landscape and frequently the locals used the words Pyramids and Cheops interchangeably.

"Tell you what," Colman said to the driver. "I'll take your beautiful and contented camel, but I want to ask you something. I was here about two years ago and I made friends with one of the camel drivers. He loved American cigarettes and asked if I would bring him some Camels, no pun intended, when I returned to Egypt. I did have his name written down but left it in my hotel room. He had a small snake tattooed on his right hand, right here," Colman said, pointing to the area between his thumb and index finger. 'Would you know him by chance?"

"No, my friend, I don't know of anyone with a tattoo on his hand. Here, let me help you get up on my camel. His name is Sakka." He grabbed Colman's arm to assist him on to the saddle, but Colman resisted.

"Say, ask one of your friends if they know the man I speak of. If you get his name, I'll make it worth your while." He showed the driver a 20-pound note. The Arab's eyes swelled. "Just a moment," he said, and moved a few feet away and spoke in a loud voice to the other drivers. They shouted back and forth in Arabic and then he returned.

"One of the drivers knows your man, but he says he is not a regular camel driver. In fact, the other driver said he only saw him here once and that was just a few days ago. His name is Samir and he mentioned that he lived in the area of El Khalili bazaar. Strange, we all live here in Giza. I never heard of a driver living in the city. Anyway, sir, you promised me the 20-pounds for the information, right?"

"Right, and here's another 10-pound note for your time. I've decided not to ride your beautiful and contented beast. Go grab another tourist."

The camel driver was not dismayed by the fact that his camel would not carry this tourist up to Cheops after all. He was delighted with the 30 pounds he had just earned. That was more than he made in a whole day of hard work.

It was not a lot of information, Colman thought as he drove back to his office, but it just might be enough. He parked in his space in the U.S. embassy compound, showed his ID to the marine guard and ran up the stairs two at a time. He eschewed the elevator most of the time, preferring the exercise the stairs afforded him.

"Holden, there's another message from Langley here for you," Judy said, handing him the decoded cable. The message informed him that the papers he had taken from El Fahoud's briefcase were of some importance, and one sheet did reveal that the camel driver was probably a man named Samir Fayez. There were notes promising that 1000 pounds would be paid to Fayez for removing the CIA "stooge" while impersonating his contact. Another 1000 pounds would be paid for safe delivery of the camera to El Fahoud at an address that was obviously the store where he and Cummins had spotted them. The papers also indicated that Samir was a member of the Reptile Society and could be trusted to perform his tasks satisfactorily.

The only other important piece of information was that Samir's telephone number was 330-14.

The pieces were falling into place. Colman asked Judy to have one of the Egyptian secretaries come up to his office. "Don't ask me why," he said, "but pick one of the better-looking ones."

Three minutes later, an attractive young woman knocked on his office door. "Come in and have a seat."

He told her that he wanted to find an address and asked her if she would use all her wiles to get it. 'I want you to call 330-14 and ask to speak to Yassouf. 'There is no such person, but I want you to force the speaker on the other end of the line to reveal his address. Can you do it?

"I can certainly try, Mr. Colman."

She asked for a few minutes to mentally prepare herself and think of a few questions, then lifted the receiver and dialed the number. Colman listened in on another line. It rang four times before a man answered.

"Allo," the male voice answered.

Speaking in Arabic, she asked to speak to Yassouf. "There's no one by that name at this number," the voice informed her.

'Oh, please, this is Janna. I know he's there. Just tell him I want to speak to him and you'll see that he'll come to the 'phone."

"Listen, my pretty sounding one, if I were Yassouf, I, too, would come to the 'phone, but I swear by Allah that there is no Yassouf here. Why not speak to me? I don't even know Yassouf but I can tell you I am much more handsome and far more intelligent than he."

Janna started to laugh. "All right, then, what is your name. I've told you mind is Janna."

'I am Samir. What did you want to speak to Yassouf about?"

"Ah, so Yassouf is there, then."

He laughed. "No, again I say that there is no Yassouf here. I only wanted to know why you were so impatient to speak to him."

"He asked me to have dinner with him tonight, but I have to postpone it, that's all."

"At what time and where were you to have dinner with him?"

"At the Caravanserai Restaurant at nine o'clock. I wanted to suggest that we make it tomorrow night. So, now may I speak to him?"

"By the name of Allah, I swear yet again that there is no Yassouf here. You must have dialed the wrong number."

"Maybe I do have the wrong number. Is this 14 El Kamaan Street I am calling? The number I wanted is 338-13."

"No, my sweet one. This is 330-13 and I don't even know where El Kamaan street is. You've misdialed but maybe this is a blessing from Allah. If you look as good as you sound, I would very much like to meet you. Would you mind having a coffee with me this afternoon at the Merata Café, say four o'clock? You will find me very charming and a man of the highest character."

Janna chuckled softly on the 'phone. "I must admit that you do indeed sound charming. But what would you think of a woman you pick up on the telephone?"

"I don't think of it as picking you up. I am merely suggesting a coffee in a public place with many people around."

She laughed softly again. "Very well, then, a coffee just to satisfy my curiosity. How will I know you?"

"When you arrive at the café, just ask for me, Samir Fayez. The proprietor is a good friend of mine. He will show you to my table. Until then, Janna, goodbye."

"Goodbye," she whispered into the telephone and turned to face Colman. She asked if she had done the right thing. "I couldn't get him to reveal his address, but maybe I can draw this from him over coffee."

"Janna, you are indeed a sweet thing," Colman said. "I would like you to meet him and have a coffee, but don't worry about getting his address. I plan to follow him after your rendezvous. He'll probably suggest dinner, but tell him that you can't tonight and remind him that was why you were trying to call Yassouf. Suggest tomorrow night and let him come up with the arrangements. And don't worry. You won't have to meet him, I promise you."

She rose to return to her own department.

"Thank you, Janna, you have been very helpful. Just one more thing. I want you to look, discreetly, of course, at his right hand and note if there is a tattoo of a small snake on it. Will you do that?"

"Of course, Mr. Colman. I'll report back to you tomorrow morning."

After Janna left the room, Judy asked if she would be safe. "There's no danger to her, is there?"

"None, whatsoever, Judy, none whatsoever. What's more, I don't think that Mr. Samir Fayez will make any more dinner appointments with ladies he speaks to on the 'phone. He'll be too embarrassed after we're through with him."

Colman had no intention of embarrassing Samir Fayez. He planned to eliminate him, but he couldn't reveal such a plan of action to Judy. The less she knew, the better.

CHAPTER TWENTY-FIVE

CAIRO, EGYPT

It was just a few minutes after four when Janna, wearing a pale yellow cotton dress, asked at the cashier's counter if Mr. Samir Fayez had arrived. "Oh, yes," one of the waiters behind the counter said. He told me to show you to his table. Please follow me."

The waiter walked into the gardens, where the tables were all occupied, to one where a man was idly watching the people pass by. "Samir," the waiter said, "I believe this is the young lady you've been waiting for."

He quickly rose from his chair. "Indeed, I hope that you are right," he said, appraising the lovely young woman before him. 'Janna, I am Samir Fayez. How nice to meet you. Will you please sit down. Makee, two Turkish coffees, please."

"Well, I must tell you that you are even an improvement over Yassouf," Janna said, showing her white, even teeth in a pleasant smile. "I confess that I was a little nervous meeting you, a stranger, like this, but there was something in your voice and in your manner that aroused my curiosity, and now I find myself glad that I decided to come."

"I think the pleasure is all mine, but I must admit that I fully expected you to be just as lovely as you are."

As they talked, the waiter brought their coffees, and they sipped them slowly, all the while engaged in animated conversation. Seated alone at a table nearby was Colman, pretending to read a newspaper and straining to hear what they were discussing.

"Then, we must have dinner together. I remember that you said you could not have dinner with that unfortunate man, Yassouf, because something else had come up. So, may I ask if you will dine with me tomorrow night?"

Janna pretended to be considering his invitation for a few seconds. "I think that I shall accept. After all, you're not a stranger now, are you? Where shall I meet you and at what time?"

"Nonsense, Janna. A gentleman does not invite a lady to dine with him and meet her at the restaurant. He calls for her, and that is exactly what I will do. What is your address?"

Janna had been anticipating the question and was ready with a phony address. "My apartment is at 434 Dr. Shabeen Street, not too far from the Agricultural Museum in the El Agouza district."

"Wonderful. I shall call for you at 8:30 p.m. and make the dinner reservation for nine o'clock."

They talked for almost half-an-hour until Janna said she must leave.

As she rose from the table, he asked her if she had a car and she told him that she did not. "Well, may I drop you at your office?".

"No, thank you, Samir, I want to stop in at the shop next door to buy a few things. I shall see you tomorrow night at 8:30."

Colman left a few coins on his table and walked out to the sidewalk where he had parked his car. He had heard Samir ask Janna if he could drop her somewhere, so he must have his own automobile. He drove around to the front door and noticed Samir shaking hands with Janna. The erstwhile camel driver walked over to a new Mercedes, unlocked the front door and drove off.

He appeared not to have a care in the world as he drove down El Tahrir Street towards the Hilton Hotel. He parked on a side street next to the Egyptian Museum and locked his car.

Colman was not so lucky. He couldn't find a parking spot and decided to invoke his diplomatic immunity and left his car at a 'No Parking' sign. He positioned his "diplomat" sign in a prominent spot on the windshield.

He was just a few steps behind Fayez. The streets were crowded with people moving in every direction, pushing and bumping into each other. Fayez turned into a narrow street and walked about 50 yards before turning on to another narrow alley. He took out a key and let himself into an apartment building. Colman noted the address and walked quickly over to the Hilton Hotel to use a telephone.

He called the embassy and asked for Janna. "This is Janna. May I help you?"

"Janna, this is Holden Colman. I had you under observation all the time you were having coffee, but I was not close enough to observe if our friend Samir had a tattoo. What can you tell me?"

"Yes, Mr. Colman, he did have a tattoo. It was of a very small snake, not too visible, but very definitely a snake. He asked me to join him for dinner tomorrow night and I accepted, as you suggested. I assure you, I have no intention of keeping the appointment. I hope you realize that."

"Don't worry, Janna. You won't have to keep the appointment. I think Mr. Fayez will be leaving Cairo when he learns what we know about him. I just had to be sure I was targeting the right Mr. Fayez, and I was. Your help was of great importance. You did very well. Thanks."

He hung up and began to formulate a plan to dispatch Mr. Fayez.

His instructions from Washington had been to act quickly. He returned to the Hilton and entered a 'phone booth. He dialed 330-13. "Yes?" a voice answered. Colman affected an accent and spoke in broken English.

"Do you speak English, please?"

"Yes, I do. Who is this?"

"Is this Samir Fayez?"

"Yes, it is. Who's speaking?"

"I am calling for Mr. El Fahoud. He has asked me to deliver a package to you. I bring it to your home?"

"Yes, of course. Do you know my address?"

"Mr. El Fahoud gave it to me. I can be there in 10 minutes. Is this OK?"

"I will be here."

Colman hung up and walked over to a nearby fruit stall where he bought two oranges. He asked the merchant if he had a bag to put them in. The merchant scratched his head and looked at him strangely.

"You want a bag for two oranges?"

When Colman nodded his head and proffered two Egyptian pounds, the man suddenly smiled and began looking earnestly around his stall for something to enable this crazy man to carry his two oranges. He reached underneath the stall and found some dirty brown paper.

"Is this all right?"

"It's fine, thank you." He gave the merchant the additional two pounds and wrapped the oranges in the brown paper.

He crossed the street and walked down two alleyways to the apartment building where Fayez lived. He rang the bell and heard the bolt on the door being slid to the side.

"It's all right, Menya, it's for me. I'll get it."

The door opened and Fayez looked at him. "Is this the package? Come on, man I don't have all night." Colman offered the package with his left hand and as the former camel jockey moved forward to grab it, Colman plunged the knife he held in his right hand deep into the man's stomach. He twisted the knife to insure that it cut into other organs then quickly departed.

Fayez's mouth opened as though trying to say something while his hands wrapped themselves around the deeply embedded knife. He staggered backwards into the hall and fell against the railing of the staircase without uttering a sound while the two oranges rolled down the steps into the street.

Colman walked rapidly to the corner and as he turned out of sight, he quickened his pace to the main boulevard and soon was lost in the safety of the milling crowds.

'That's for eliminating one of our contacts, Mr. Fayez,' he muttered to himself as he unlocked his car, still stationed where he had left it, and drove back to the embassy.

His secretary was typing a report as he entered his office. "Excuse me interrupting you, Judy, but would you please send off this message to CIA, Langley immediately: "Mission accomplished. Drew can sleep safely tonight. Colman."

CHAPTER TWENTY-SIX

MINNEAPOLIS, MINNESOTA

Drew was reading Time magazine in his apartment when the 'phone rang. It was McShane.

"How are you feeling? Are you relaxed enough after your last encounter to accept another assignment?"

"I feel fine, Brendon, although I must confess that the Egyptian episode might have colored my previously-held opinion of Cairo. Any word on the camel driver who can identify me?"

"He doesn't exist any more." There was silence for a few seconds before he asked what had happened.

"Colman located him and ended his camel driving career. Let's just leave it at that. Now there is no one who can identify you, so your career as a courier is back on track. Unless you've changed your mind?"

"No, as I said, I'm still in. Strangely, I found the danger exhilarating. Not like one of the rides at the State Fair, but a different kind of exhilaration that disavows negligence and makes you more aware of your responsibilities. I must admit that a lot of the time I was nervously scared, scared and exhilarated simultaneously. Does that make sense?"

"Yes, it makes perfect sense to me because I have been in the same sort of situation many times before. Drew, you told me that your company operates trips to China. Does your company have any trips scheduled there next month? I haven't received next month's Operations Report from you, so am not aware if any such trips are scheduled."

"Yes, I think we do. I know we have one to Hong Kong and Beijing and another to Beijing and Tokyo."

"Are you on either of them?"

Drew asked him to wait a few seconds. As the following month's schedule hadn't yet been released, he told McShane that he would check with the office and call him right back.

Within five minutes, he was back on the 'phone with McShane. "Sorry, Brendon, I'm not on either of the China programs.

"Is it real important?"

"Yes, it is. Is there a chance you could request one of them? It doesn't matter which, just as long as you go to Beijing."

He pointed out that requesting trips was not encouraged in his company, but because of his friendship with the Director of the Travel Staff and his many years with the company, both part-time when he was in College, and full-time since his graduation, putting him in a senior position, it shouldn't be too big a problem to request a China trip. "I'll have to check and then get back to you."

"It would be really helpful if you can get yourself on a Beijing trip. It would help us a great deal. I'll wait for your call."

* * *

"How's your father doing, Drew? One of the account managers asked as he walked past her on his way to the Trip Director department.

"He's making great progress, Carol, and thanks for asking."

It brought back the unpleasantness of the lies he had told to hide what had really brought him back so quickly from Cairo. It was easy to salve his conscience, however, by telling himself that the lies were necessary.

He noticed Tennant in his office. He seemed to be immersed in an angry conversation with one of the junior trip directors. After a few more minutes, Tennant extended his arm and pointed to the door. The young trip director rose and with a sheepish look on his face walked out of the office, nodding to Cummins who was on his way in.

"Talk to you a minute, Cole?"

"Sure, come on in. Give me a minute to cool down. I had to chew out Forsyth's ass, the stupid bastard. I found out that he was screwing one of the female guests on his last trip to Rome. Do you know what he told me? She fell in love with him and nature took its course."

"No matter how many times you tell these guys that they don't screw guests on trips, they still do it. I don't always hear about it, but I know they're doing it."

"Well, it's better than having Forsyth screwing the men on the trips, isn't it?"

Tennant just turned his head and looked Drew straight in the eyes, and with a smirk on his face shook his head as if in disbelief. "Cummins, I don't need any of your smart-ass remarks right now. Come to think of it, maybe I do. I could use a laugh at the moment."

"How's your father doing? As you seem in a jovial mood, I'm assuming that he's doing well. Am I right?"

"Yes, he's doing very well, thanks. The doctor is very pleased with his progress. And, of course, that means my mother has settled down. My sister said mom needed as much attention as my father did. She had to be given a sedative at the time, but she's much more relaxed now." He felt he had to embellish the recovery a little so as to add a little more strength to his story, particularly as leaving a trip in a foreign land is not an easy thing for a trip director to do.

"Well, that's very good news. What's on your mind?"

"Cole, I want to ask a favor of you. I've been with the company, part-time and full-time for almost fourteen years now and I've never asked for a particular assignment because I know how much that irritates you. You know that I've always taken what I've been given and never complained. I would really like to go on one of the Beijing trips next month. Would you mind changing the schedule to accommodate me?"

"Why do you want to go to Beijing? You've been there half-a-dozen times already, haven't you?"

"Yes, I have Cole, but there are parts of the city I haven't seen and China is changing and growing. I think it would be helpful to me if I knew more of the tours. I would be better prepared when accompanying one of our account executives on a client presentation. I would be able to speak about all the tours rather than just the few I've been on."

"That's a crock and you know it. You must have the same thing in mind as Forsyth. Have you got some Chinese pussy over there? Never mind, don't answer that. Okay, I'll take Holm off the Beijing-Hong Kong and put him on the Hawaii trip to replace you. Does that make you happy?"

"It does. Thanks a million, Cole; I really appreciate it."

Drew had a desk in a large room designed for the trip directors. Each 'TD' as they are known, had his own desk but used a common telephone in the room. The call that he wanted to make, however, required privacy, so he slipped downstairs to one of the public telephone booths in the lobby and dialed McShane's special number.

"This is Courier Thirteen," he told the operator. "Good morning, Drew," McShane said, coming on the line almost immediately. Cummins told him that he had been assigned to the Beijing-Hong Kong program and asked him what was the next step.

"Where is the gateway city for that trip? Does the group meet in LA or San Francisco?"

"I'm going to be the lead trip director on the program, so I'll be going in advance. I can pretty much make my own travel arrangements as long as they don't take me on a strange zig-zag pattern."

Drew gave him the dates of the trip and McShane suggested then that he fly out of Los Angeles. "Wait in Northwest's World Club on Thursday afternoon, September 14, at 2:00 p.m. The club receptionist will announce there's a telephone call for you. The person on the other end of the 'phone will give you your instructions. We'll use the same method of contact as in New York. Hopefully, it's a nice, easy and safe way to pass along the article to be carried. Any problem with that?"

"No, Brendon, sounds fine to me. See you."

"Oh, by the way, Drew, Chase Barron spoke very highly of you at our staff meeting a couple of days ago. He said he was very impressed by you and how you handle yourself. He also said he wants to go ahead with recruiting more travel people, so after your next assignment, why don't you plan on coming into Langley and we'll have some fuller discussions on this very important matter, ok?"

'Whenever you say, Brendon."

Drew replaced the receiver and stood for a few minutes in the 'phone booth. He reminisced briefly about New York and his meeting in the Clipper Club with the man with the camel hair coat. He had wondered then about the 'cloak and dagger' antics and whether they were all necessary. He remembered thinking that maybe too much was made of these simple package exchanges. Then he remembered Egypt. He didn't question the CIA's tactics any more. He was convinced that the CIA knew what it was doing and he had no more reservations about their modus operandi.

CHAPTER TWENTY-SEVEN

LOS ANGELES, CALIFORNIA

The World Club was busy, as usual. Drew wondered why Northwest Airlines' clubs were always so busy while most other airlines' club rooms, with the definite exception of Pan Am's Clipper Club at JFK, were normally quiet. Must be the free booze or something, he thought.

He looked at his watch. It was 1:59 p.m. He was relaxing at a table near the window with a cup of coffee and some cookies when he heard his name paged.

He approached the reception desk and was told there was a call for him and to take it in one of the booths.

"Cummins," he said into the receiver.

"Drew, this is a friend of McShane. I believe you were expecting the call?"

"Yes, I was."

"I think we should meet where we can talk privately. I know the World Club is busy at the moment, so why don't you come down to the restaurant on the floor below. Ask the hostess for Ralph Blattner's table and she will show you to my booth."

Replacing the receiver, he left the club and descended the stairs to the restaurant. He asked the hostess if she would show him to Ralph Blattner's booth.

"Certainly,' she said. "He told me you would be asking for him."

Blattner rose to shake his hand while thanking the hostess for bring him over.

"Hi, I'm Ralph Blattner. Would you like a cup of coffee?" he asked Drew as he sat down.

"Yes, please," he answered "black will be fine."

Blattner put his briefcase on the table and opened it so that the top shielded the contents from the other patrons.

"Drew, we've been asked to be extra careful about passing objects to be carried abroad. We had a little trouble with one of our couriers over in the Middle East somewhere. This envelope I am touching is for you to carry to Beijing. I'll give you the details in a moment. I'm going to withdraw something from the case just now and pretend to be discussing it with you."

He took a newspaper and some other documents from his case then put it beside him on the seat. While he talked, he pointed to the newspaper occasionally and opened up the other documents to make it appear these were the items they were discussing.

While he was pointing to the newspaper and opening its pages occasionally, he was giving him the instructions for his next delivery.

"Do you know Beijing well?"

"Yes, fairly well."

"Do you know the Underground City?"

"The what?"

Blattner smiled. "There is an underground city in Beijing. I'm not too surprised by your ignorance of it. It's not too well known by tourists, but since you've got a group going there, it is something you may want to recommend to them. You'll be a hero with your client because it is really well worth seeing and yet few people know of it. And there's no charge for the tour."

'What is it, some kind of bomb shelter?"

"Exactly," Blattner continued. "It was not built as protection against the Americans but rather against the Russians whom the Chinese trust less than they do us. It's a maze of labyrinthine tunnels, high enough for even an American to walk through without having to lower his head. There are shops, cafeterias, a hospital and even a cinema down there. It was designed specifically to protect against atomic explosions."

"Why haven't I heard of it then?" Drew asked, somewhat offended that his comprehensive knowledge of Beijing had just been assaulted.

'It's not a scheduled tour although you can request permission for your group to see it. Ask your contact with the Chinese Travel Service to get the approval for you.

'There's no trouble in arranging it. And your group will enjoy it tremendously, I assure you. It's very different from anything you have ever seen before. Anyway, do you have a morning or afternoon free of scheduled tours during your time in Beijing?"

"Yes, we have one free morning and afternoon."

'What are the dates?" Blattner asked. "Do you think you'll be able to convince the client to make this tour?"

"I know the client very well and I am positive he will be very keen to do it. He relies on me for many such changes and additions to the program. But, of course, he always wants me to ask him first. And the fact that we can offer an exciting tour and at no charge will make him very happy."

Drew gave him the dates of the free segments, then Blattner asked him to pick one for the item to be passed.

They agreed on the afternoon and the time.

"There is one large room where Chinese groups and foreign tourists are always taken. Its purpose is a community food hall if an atomic raid is ever made on Beijing. At the moment, it is used to show slides on how the Underground City was built and to explain the other uses for the many rooms in case of war. By the way, no photos are allowed and while the Chinese officials will answer most questions, they will not reveal where the entrances and exits are located other than the one that you will use to enter it.

"When you are in this room, stay as close to the entrance as possible. As the one in charge of the group, they will understand if you do not sit down with your group, assuming you want to watch your people. Make sure you dress in tan pants and a red shirt. I understand that you have such clothes with you, is that correct?"

"Yes, I do," Drew answered, smiling to himself."

"Good. A Chinese, wearing a red, open-necked shirt and carrying a basket, will brush past you. He will say 'Excuse me, Drew,' just like that and in English. Drop the envelope in his basket as surreptitiously as you are able. That's all. In case you're wondering why would a Chinese be carrying a basket on such a tour, as I pointed out. there are shops down there, selling goods, so it would not be unusual to see someone carrying a basket. How many people are there in your group?"

"One hundred and forty. I don't know if everybody will go as this is an optional activity, but I'm thinking that if I present it properly and do a good job in describing it as you have described it to me, I would guess at least 100 will go on the tour."

"The room will be busy, mostly with Chinese from different parts of the country. The Underground City is something they have heard about and want to see when they make their pilgrimage to Beijing. Just have the envelope ready to drop in the basket, and of course, do it very discreetly. It's a perfect spot for a drop because the officials leading you on the tour will be at the other end of the room showing maps that detail the length and directions of the tunnels. Any questions?"

"Just one. The Chinese has to say the exact words, right? If he says something other than those three simple words, I abort the mission, correct?"

"The answer has to be precise. It has to be exactly as I've given it to you. Remember, it's "Excuse me, Drew."

"Okay, well then, I'm ready."

Blattner brought the case back up on to the table. "When I open it, I'm going to push it over more to you. Reach in while the top is up, retrieve the letter and slip it between the newspaper pages and take the paper with you. You should hide it, of course, so that it would not be easily found on your person. You'll find, however, that the Chinese Customs officials seldom stop an American and look at their bags. Good luck, Drew."

They both left the booth and walked to the cashier's desk where Blattner paid for the coffees. They shook hands and Blattner set off for the exit while Drew climbed the stairs back to the World Club.

CHAPTER TWENTY-EIGHT

BEIJING, CHINA

This was Drew's seventh visit to Beijing. It was not the type of city that stirred deep feelings within him such as Paris or London, but it was interesting in that it was so different from any of the other major metropolises of the world. There were many things about China's capital city that he liked: the friendliness of the people, the historical importance of its landmarks such as the Forbidden City, the Temple of Heaven, the Great Wall and the more modern landmarks like Tiananmen Square.

He enjoyed the beauty of the city's wide, tree-lined boulevards which had once been free of traffic congestion but that he now noted were catching up with the rest of the world. He recalled on his first trip to Beijing and how almost totally devoid of traffic the main boulevards and avenues were. One could cross the Avenue of Heavenly Peace with the Forbidden City on one side and Tiananmen Square on the other and not bother to look right or left because there was no traffic. Once in a while, a truck or a bus would amble along, but so seldom that the chances of being struck by a vehicle were one in a million. But this was a different story now with the streets choked with Rolls Royces, Audis, Mercedes and BMWs.

And he was always amused by the frontage roads used by the cyclists who were not allowed on the main highways. No matter what time of the day one saw the frontage streets, they were clogged with cyclists going off in every direction.

It bothered Drew that he had never heard of the Underground City and wondered why, in six previous trips, the guides with whom he had become friends and the tourist officials whom he had met on numerous occasions, had never mentioned the city beneath the streets.

It was more a matter of his pride being hurt than anything else. He was one of the most traveled people in the incentive industry; he was also the most often sought member in the company when account executives needed a representative of the travel division to accompany them on a presentation. He fully intended to know everything there was to know about the underground city before this trip was over.

As he exited Customs, he immediately spotted Li Tang, one of the officials of the China Travel Service, who had driven out to the airport to meet him and transfer him to the modern and elegant Sheraton Great Wall Hotel. When it opened in 1985, the hotel had astounded those Chinese who were privileged to see inside. They had marveled at the magnificent carpeting, furniture, the opulence of the lay-out and particularly the richness of the décor of its fine restaurants.

Until the Sheraton Great Wall Hotel had opened in 1985, tourists were housed in the city's then showplace, the Peking Hotel, a structure that reflected a combination of Chinese, Russian and French architecture. The French had built the first section of the hotel to which was added, many years later, the Chinese extension. When the Russians had enjoyed smoother relations with the Chinese, they added another wing to the existing buildings which were joined together to resemble one hotel. It was a hodgepodge of different styles, as if of different building blocks that someone had pushed together without any regard for aesthetics or appearance.

The Peking Hotel was a far cry in comfort and elegance from the Great Wall Hotel which had quickly become the forerunner of many other spectacular chain properties built in anticipation of the millions of tourists from around the world who would be flocking to Beijing in the years ahead.

Drew recalled the first time he had visited the city. It was in 1978 and the Harrison Motivation Company had been invited by the Chinese government to send a representative to their capital city in the hope that he or she would like what they saw and persuade clients to visit China.

Cole Tennant had asked Drew to take the trip and write a report on the nine important criteria that the Harrison Motivation Company used in appraising a destination's worth as an area to be visited by groups. These were Hotel, Food, Service, Weather, Sports, Entertainment, Shopping, Sightseeing and Local Attitude.

He smiled when he thought of the Peking Hotel where he had first been housed. A Holiday Inn in any of the small towns in the U.S. would have been luxurious by comparison. The food had been mediocre at best, the service was indifferent, and the public toilets emitted the foulest odors imaginable.

When he had written his report, he had exposed these weaknesses while pointing out the great shopping, sightseeing tours and the incredible friendliness of the people. But he cautioned the salespeople to make their accounts well aware of the poor hotel accommodations.

Shortly after his return to Minneapolis, he learned that several hotel chains were negotiating with the Chinese government to build new and spectacular properties, all incorporating modern technology and western styles and comforts.

'How quickly the Chinese learned,' he now thought. Less than a decade later and their hotels were copies of the gems in Hong Kong. Their food had improved tremendously and their service showed the influence of their Hong Kong teachers who were imported to teach the Chinese the art of the hospitality industry.

He was enjoying the ride into Beijing when the Underground City intruded on his thoughts. He wanted to question Li Tang about it.

"Li, as you know, I have been here in Beijing six times, but I just learned recently that there is an Underground City here. I was attending a trade meeting in Chicago and heard someone say what an interesting tour it is. The person mentioned that he had been taken to see the area and its sights and spoke of the stores and restaurants and other services that exist down there. I wonder why I had never heard of it before?"

'Quite frankly, it is not publicized, but it is certainly not a secret. We take many foreigners down to see it. Perhaps it is because we don't want to turn it into a regular tour, but we never refuse anyone who wants to visit it. I don't know why you have never seen it. I'm sure that it's because we just don't think of it as a tour. Would you like to go down there? I would be happy to arrange it for you."

"I was thinking of something more grand. I would like to offer it to our group as an optional activity on their free afternoon, that would be next Thursday. Would that be possible?"

"Of course, I will be happy to secure the necessary permission for you and arrange the buses for the transfer. As I said, it's not secretive, it's just that it's not promoted as a tour. How many people do you think would like to see it?"

"I would think at least 100. Is the number a problem?"

"No, but the city government will not allow that many people at one time, only because of the limited space. I suggest that we have four groups of 25 each and have them leave the hotel at half-hour intervals. Is that satisfactory?"

Drew assured her that would be a good arrangement and asked her to set it up and to organize the buses.

* * *

Dennis Bigony, president of the Kelmar Building Products Company, was puzzled at first when Drew explained the optional activity that he wanted to offer his people. Bigony had many friends who had visited Beijing but none had mentioned the Underground City. "Is it really worth seeing?" he had asked. "You know, these people will be doing a lot of sightseeing and they'll be tired. Do you really think it's worth offering to them?"

Drew convinced him that it was something they would talk about to their friends when they returned home, and, more importantly, talk about it with people who had been to Beijing and be one up on them because no one else would have been likely to have seen it.

"There's no charge for the tour. And even the buses are complimentary because they are assigned to us for our entire stay in Beijing, meaning that we can use them as we wish."

"Well, Drew, if you think it's worthwhile, go ahead. I just hope that some of my guests won't be so tired that they go on the tour and wish they had gone shopping or spent the afternoon napping."

* * *

Drew wasn't sure whether to be surprised or not. The tour proved to be so popular that 126 members of the group showed up for it.

'Wouldn't want to miss an Underground City. I didn't even know they had one," Dick Walberg, one of the dealers from Omaha, said. The others, talking among themselves, agreed.

The dealers and their spouses were split into five groups and boarded their buses at half-hour intervals. The first bus pulled away from the hotel and headed towards the South Gate of the city that leads towards Tiananmen Square. En route, the Chinese guide told the group that the subterranean city had been built because the Chinese feared an atomic attack. "But we did not fear the attack from the Americans," he said as a smile split his face and revealed two rows of teeth that were sadly in need of dental care. "Oh, no we feared an atomic attack from the Russians. That is why we built our Underground City."

Drew rode the first bus and it stopped near the South Gate allowing everyone to descend and follow the guide as he led them through some narrow streets before stopping in front of a furrier's store.

"This is one of the entrances, and the only one we are permitted to show foreigners,' the guide said, once more revealing a rictus of brown-stained, decaying teeth. "Please enter this shop and stay closely together so that you can see how cleverly the entrance to the Underground City is disguised."

The group moved slowly into the shop and gathered around the guide. He asked them to stand together at one end of the floor. "Now, please watch the floor," he said, then pointed to the area behind the shop's main counter. The clerk pressed a button under the counter and the linoleum-covered floor began to slide under the half where the group had congregated. As it did, there were murmurings from the group, obviously in amazement at the cleverness with which the entry had been concealed.

As the floor moved away, a stairway appeared and slowly descended to the ground, twenty five feet below. The group walked down the stairs and followed the guide as he led them from one room to another, always describing the purpose of each. The dealers and their spouses were surprised to see other Chinese groups walking around the spacious tunnels, nodding and smiling as they passed.

They entered a huge room and noticed that it was filled with items being purchased by other visitors. Moving down another tunnel, the guide pointed out a hospital where, he mentioned, the injured would be cared for in the event of an atomic attack.

An enormous room was next and the group was told it was designed to serve as a cafeteria.

"How many was the City designed to accommodate?" one of the dealers asked. "All questions will be answered at the end of the tour," the guide informed him as he pointed out a theater where live plays would be performed and films would be shown.

All of the people in the Kelmar Building Products group were amazed at the size of the Underground City and the capacious rooms. Many were discussing the enormity of the space among themselves when the guide mentioned that they were now entering a room designed for meetings and that it was here that their questions would be answered.

There was another group in the room, all Chinese, and Drew held back until all his group had entered. He positioned himself at the back near the entrance. He could not see anyone with a red, open-necked shirt, but kept scanning the room to be sure he would be ready when approached. He felt the envelope which he had slipped into his own red sports shirt.

When everyone was seated an elderly man rose. He held a wooden pointer in his hand and was attired in the usual gray tunic uniform that was once the only dress worn by men and women in China. Nowadays, there are choices and the young men wear trousers of various colors, with blue jeans growing rapidly in popularity as well as white and colored shirts, a radical departure from the dullness of the tunics.

The elderly man spoke in Chinese and then switched to English as he welcomed the foreigners. "I hope that all our visitors understand English," he said, "as this is the only other language I know." He smiled as if anticipating some applause from the group, but none was forthcoming.

He told his audience that no photographs were allowed and asked those assembled not to attempt to photograph the huge map on the wall behind him. He pressed a button and the map became illuminated with dozens of small red bulbs. He pointed out that these were the entrances to the Underground City and with his pointer indicated the directions of the tunnels. No streets were named on the map although it would have been impossible to make them out anyway due to the distance of the guests from the board. He gave a commentary on the construction of the city, spewing out facts and figures, and always surveying the assembly to note the expressions on their faces.

There was still no sight of the contact and Drew began to worry that the lecture would end soon and the people move out.

The official ended his talk and asked if there were questions, adding that there was some information he would not be allowed to reveal.

The wife of one of the dealers raised her arm and asked the capacity of the City. "It was planned to hold 250,000," the elderly man answered.

"But Beijing has a population of about 13 million, doesn't it?"

"That is correct," he answered without any further explanation of what would happen to the other 12 million, seven hundred and fifty thousand.

Another asked how many entrances there were to the underground city and inquired if there were any located in the suburbs of the city. The guide provided the answers but in a way that had no specificity.

At this point, the official smiled and thanked them for their attention and hoped that they had found their tour and his commentary interesting. There was generous applause before everyone rose to leave.

There was still no sign of the contact. Drew began to worry as he smiled and said a few words to some of his group as they exited the room. The crowd was becoming intense now and the atmosphere stifling when he spotted his man. A Chinese with a red, open-necked shirt and holding a basket came out of nowhere and was wending his way through the crowd. He was about twenty feet away and maneuvering his way to the far wall where Drew was standing. He bumped into him. 'Excuse me, Drew," he said as Drew quickly dropped the envelope into the basket., The Chinese immediately covered the envelope with a cloth, but he didn't move away.

"I must speak with you; it's imperative," he said as he was jostled by the crowd trying to leave the room. "I must speak with you tonight. Please be at the front door of your hotel at exactly midnight. Wait a moment or two at the front door for me to see you then walk in any direction you choose. I will make contact with you. This is urgent."

He disappeared into the crowd and Drew spotted some members of his group and joined them. 'Wall to wall Chinese," one of the wives said laughingly as they were buffeted on all sides. "There are certainly plenty of them," Drew agreed.

His group had gathered outside the furrier shop, waiting for all 25 to assemble. Another of the Kelmar Building Products groups had just arrived and was waiting to enter.

"How was it," one shouted. "It's unbelievable," a dealer shot back. "You'll be amazed. It really is worth seeing."

CHAPTER TWENTY-NINE

BEIJING, CHINA

It was almost midnight when Drew looked at his watch. He had been doing some paperwork in his room, killing time until the meeting with his red-shirted Chinese contact. He rode the elevator down to the lobby and heading for the front door when Tom Wold, vice president of marketing for Kelmar Building Products, called out his name. Wold had been sitting in the lobby talking to some of his dealers when he spied him.

Drew waved to him, hoping that he could avoid having to talk to him, but Wold signaled for him to come over. 'Where you goin' in such a hurry? Got some Chinese cookie waitin' for you?" He laughed loudly at his remark and the other distributors and their wives joined in.

"I think he's got a hot date," one of them said, grinning from ear to ear.

"No, no, nothing like that. I enjoy going for a walk before going to bed and I thought I would take a spin around the block," Drew explained.

"Would you like some company or would I crowd your style?" Wold asked, still laughing.

No, not at all. I'd love the company," Drew answered, now worried about how he was going to meet his contact. "Let's go."

"Naw, I'm only joshing you,' Wold answered. Drew felt relieved. 'Well, like I said, you're more than welcome to join me."

"You go for your walk but we're gonna time you and if you're not back in 20 minutes or so we're gonna know for sure that you found a fortune cookie."

Everybody laughed even harder as he moved away, adding: "I should be so lucky." Drew muttered.

He pushed his way through the revolving door, stood for a few minutes to let his contact see him, then set off at a brisk pace toward the street that was still busy with pedestrian and vehicular traffic.

He had covered about a hundred yards when he heard a soft female voice say: "Drew, I'm right behind you. Don't turn around. I'll come alongside."

Within seconds, a small dark figure caught up to him. She was petite with long, black hair that flowed down her back. She wore a nondescript dark blue T-shirt over form-fitting blue jeans. It was too dark to distinguish her features but from what he could see and hear, he knew she was very attractive.

"Who are you?" he asked.

"I am Erin. That's the anglicized version of my name. I know you were expecting the man you saw this afternoon in the Underground City. I work with him in the movement. We thought it better if I spoke to you tonight. We have a very important message that you must take back to your agency."

"Wait a minute," Drew said. "I don't know what you're talking about." He was nervous now. Was this a trap? Why was this woman, admittedly better to look at than his contact of this afternoon, here instead of the Chinese man? Why didn't he come when it was he who made the request for the meeting?

The woman anticipated his remark. "You were told to make contact with an open-necked, red-shirted man in the Underground City. He was to accidentally bump into you and say: 'Excuse me, Drew' and you were to slip an envelope into the basket he was carrying. How am I doing thus far? Is this not what occurred?" She was silent as though waiting for confirmation.

"After you had done this, he asked you for a meeting this evening saying it was imperative. He suggested he meet you at midnight, asking you to stand outside the front door of your hotel and then go for a walk, choosing either side of the hotel. Right? Now can we go on? I have something important to tell you. Please listen carefully."

She was silent for a few moments as though collecting her thoughts while trying to maintain the fast pace being set by Drew on the deserted sidewalk. "Tell your sponsor that the students are ready NOW." She emphasized the word 'now'.

"We want to begin the operation November 1. We had planned to have a start date of November 15, but now feel we must begin the revolution earlier. We don't need any more time. We must have the money to buy the weaponry by October 20. Tell your sponsor to assure the taipans that we are confident of success. We feel that this time the army will come with us."

They were approaching a street light and the young woman moved away from him to avoid being caught in its glare. After he passed through the light, the woman returned to his side.

"Did you get all of my message. Do you want me to repeat it?"

Drew shook his head. "No, I think I can remember all of it but let me go over it."

He played back the entire message as she had relayed it to him.

"Good," she said. After a few more paces, she stopped and turned to face him. A light from a nearby apartment building cast an eerie glow on her face. She was beautiful, he thought, but he noted the tenseness of the look on her face. She had a flawless, olive skin, a delicate nose that highlighted full lips and sparkling brown eyes whose shape only hinted of her Asian race. She had full breasts, tightly pressed against her T-shirt and a figure that even a model would envy.

"I must go," she said, yet lingered for a few more seconds as she gazed into Drew's face. 'Good luck and please get our message through safely." She slipped away, then stopped in the darkness for a few seconds more and looked back at Drew without saying anything. He was suddenly suffused with a strange feeling of loneliness. His eyes tried to discern her outline, but her dark clothing only served to blend perfectly with the somber surroundings and there was not a trace of her, only silence . . . a strange silence. Her message sounded so ominous, he thought to himself. It sounds like another revolution is in the making. I'm surprised there isn't another way they could communicate their message to the U.S. Maybe they're afraid someone will pick up any telegraphed message and that would undoubtedly spoil all their plans.

Drew was mesmerized by her beauty. He had been with many gorgeous women and that included Maria in Rio, but Erin was the complete package . . . the beautiful face, the lissome figure, the melodious, sing-song voice, the way she walked and carried herself. And, of course, her obvious bravery. He was thunderstruck.

As he retraced his steps back to the hotel, he couldn't get her face out of his mind. She had been so intense, so serious yet so beautiful. 'Why shouldn't she be serious?' he thought. 'It's a dangerous business she's in.'

He recalled her soft, attractive voice and the message she gave him to take to his 'sponsor.' He was deep in thought as he entered the front door of the Great Wall.

"Well, you were only gone about 20 minutes, so I guess your little fortune cookie didn't turn up, right?" It was Tom Wold who was still talking to the same guests. They all began to razz him, telling him now they knew why he was always so tired during the day.

"You've got to get some more sleep," one said., "You gotta give up this wild night life," another suggested as they all laughed uproariously.

Drew didn't feel like bantering with them or even listening to their good-natured kidding, but he had to put on a pleasant face and make a few clever remarks to offset their friendly jabs.

"Well, it takes a lot of energy walking around looking for a fortune cookie, so I think I'll say goodnight to all of you and see you in the morning. As I didn't see any while out walking maybe there's one waiting for me in my room.'

"I don't think you could do her any good anyway," Wold shouted after him as he entered the elevator. "You look awfully tired."

Drew popped his head out of the elevator and retorted: "Wanna bet?"

CHAPTER THIRTY

BRITISH CROWN COLONY OF HONG KONG

The Kelmar Building Products Company's group was enjoying its last night in Hong Kong after four fascinating days in Beijing. The people had stayed at the Excelsior Hotel for four nights and were in their rooms getting ready for the farewell cocktail party which was to be held in the hotel's ballroom foyer.

Following the cocktail reception, a great evening had been planned with a sumptuous banquet in the ballroom then a special performance by the Hong Kong Police Band. This was always a successful climax to any trip and the band's performance resembled that of the Coldstream Guards in London, after which it had been modeled.

The guests were unaware of the special entertainment that had been arranged for them. They only knew that something unusual had been planned and the anticipation was mounting. As guests passed the hospitality desk, they read a note on the blackboard reminding them to bring their movie and still photographic equipment to tonight's function.

But Drew Cummins' mind was elsewhere. He had difficulty thinking of anything other than Erin. How beautiful she was, he thought to himself, and she's got courage to match her looks. He had little trouble figuring out what her message meant. There was going to be another revolt like the one in Tiananmen Square in June of 1989 that had gained the young Chinese men and women great admiration around the world, but had cost the lives of many of their fellow students.

There was no doubt in his mind what Erin was asking, no she wasn't asking, she was telling the taipans that she and her fellow students were ready and now needed only money to purchase weaponry. But who were the taipans? He knew that it was a name for extremely wealthy and powerful people and had common usage in Asia.

'For a humble courier, I have a feeling I am in the middle of one of the biggest incidents of this century," Drew thought to himself.

He was scheduled to return with the group the next day and on arrival in San Francisco, he would call McShane immediately and relay the message. He had thought of calling from Hong Kong but decided against it. He wasn't sure if a call from Asia would be secure. 'They can do wonders securing 'phone conversations in the U.S., Drew thought, but can they do the same thing overseas?"

The last night function was the great success that he knew it would be. He remembered that as everyone finished dessert and enjoyed coffee and after-dinner liqueurs, a distinguished looking Caucasian stepped up to the platform which had been erected at the end of the ballroom. Although no signal was made to command silence, everyone stopped talking and concentrated their gaze on the platform where the man, resplendent in a police uniform of obvious high rank, spoke into the microphone.

"Ladies and gentlemen, I am Major John Duhamel of the Hong Kong Police Band and it is now my distinct pleasure to introduce the band to you for your entertainment."

With that, the doors of the ballroom swung open and 22 diminutive Chinese, banging drums, blowing into trumpets, clarinets and saxophones, and squeezing bagpipes, marched in perfect synchronization, around the room while cameras whirred and flashes popped.

The band played for 20 minutes before members of the group were invited to accept the baton from the conductor, ascend the platform and lead the musicians in several numbers which they did with great alacrity, but little skill. It was a memorable evening and the client was ecstatically happy.

Another successful program. Drew should have been pleased that the trip had operated so well, but his thoughts were still in Beijing, thinking of Erin and fearful of what lay ahead for her and her fellow students.

CHAPTER THIRTY-ONE

SAN FRANCISCO, CALIFORNIA

The United Airlines jet's wheels touched the ground so smoothly at San Francisco's International Airport that many of the passengers didn't know they had landed. They collected their hand luggage and prepared to pass through immigration then Customs.

Drew watched the Watkins, one of the couples whom he had gotten to know well on the trip, struggle with their carry-ons. Tim Watkins had two bags in his hands, his video camera over his right shoulder and a flight bag over his left. Sarah, his wife, carried two bulging shopping bags; her purse, which more closely resembled a good-size overnight bag, was slung over her shoulder.

It was difficult not to laugh, and he wasn't able to suppress a smile as he watched them trying to negotiate their way down the aisle towards the exit door.

He recalled seeing three signs, including one on the check-in counter in Hong Kong, reminding passengers that it was an airline regulation that only one piece of hand-carried and a purse or briefcase, were allowed in the airplane cabin. No matter how many signs were posted or how many times it was announced over the public address system, passengers still waddled on to the aircraft and along the aisles burdened down with packages, bags and other obvious signs of joyous shopping.

The great shopping opportunities in Hong Kong, known affectionately as the world's Bargain Basement, were so enticing and so omnipresent that airline employees turned a blind eye to the passengers struggling with all sorts of packages.

After the last members of the group had cleared customs and hurried to the various airlines to catch connecting flights to their home cities, Drew presented his Customs Declaration Form. He had claimed $58. The official gave it only a perfunctory glance, stamped it and passed him through.

A United Airlines representative stood at the door outside Customs and directed him to the conveyor belt where he could put his already tagged luggage for the flight to Minneapolis.

Almost impatiently, he headed for United's Red Carpet Club, presented his membership card to the hostess, and sought a 'phone where he could have some privacy. The other 'phones nearby were not being used. It was probably because of the early hour, he thought.

He dialed 222-555-1000. It rang once and an Operator asked for his access code.

"Courier Thirteen," replied. There was silence for almost a minute before McShane came on the line. "Brendon, it's Drew Cummins. I've got a very sensitive message that I think is very important to pass along to you. Is it safe to mention anything sensitive on this line?"

"Go ahead. As long as no one can overhear you at your end, then it's OK."

'The message actually was given to me by a young lady, a cohort of the Chinese gentleman to whom I gave the envelope." He explained everything that had taken place, the meeting with Erin and the message she had given him. "She asked me to tell the taipans, her very words, that the students are ready now. She emphasized the word now. They want to begin the operation on the first of November. She said they don't need any more time, but desperately need the money to buy the weaponry by October 20. She told me to tell my sponsor—again her word—to assure the taipans that they are confident of success. They feel that this time, the army will come with them.

That's it, Brendon, exactly as she gave it to me. I wondered if she was getting a little mixed up when she said taipans. Do you know what she meant?"

The 'phone went dead for a few seconds. "Hello, are you there, Brendon?"

"Yes, Drew. I want you to forget everything you've just told me. Expunge it completely from your mind. It never happened. I don't want you to recall anything of what you've told me. If your mind drifts to it, think of something else. Do I make myself clear?"

McShane was very stern, almost as if he was displeased with the message Drew had given. He was not his usual pleasant self and did not speak in his laid-back style.

"Perfectly, Brendon. It's forgotten. Did I do or say something wrong?"

"No, Drew, you have done well, extremely well, it's just that the information you have relayed is most sensitive and I want to stress how important it is that you forget it."

"Fine, Brendon. Well, you know where to reach me if you need me. By the way, that Erin was gorgeous, and I mean gorgeous. If you need another job done in Beijing, just let me know and I'll do everything I can to get on a China program."

"Well, I noted in the Operation Outlook you sent me that you do have another Beijing program coming up soon. I believe it's a Tokyo-Beijing combination and the dates are October 8-15."

Drew rummaged through his briefcase and found the Operation Outlook. "Yes, it's a Tokyo-Beijing program and it operates in about two weeks."

"Drew, go back to Minneapolis and enjoy a well-earned rest. If I need you, I'll get a hold of you. OK? And remember what I said: Beijing never happened."

After McShane hung up the 'phone, he called Chase Barron. "Chase something big just happened. I need to talk to you right away. Highest urgency."

They met in Barron's office and McShane relayed the entire conversation with Drew. "I had better send this message to our brothers upstairs. It's obvious that they have to transmit the message immediately to the taipans in Hong Kong.

"Yes, I agree," said Barron, "and do it right away."

CHAPTER THIRTY-TWO

BRITISH CROWN COLONY OF HONG KONG

The silver gray Rolls Royce passed through the tall iron gates of the private estate overlooking the magnificent Hong Kong harbor, rated among the best havens in the world, and slipped into the light traffic. The chauffeur guided the luxury automobile in its descent from the mid-level district on Victoria Peak with its million-dollar plus homes, to the congested parts of the island with their endless apartment buildings and burgeoning population.

Some five and a half million people live in the British Crown Colony's 403.7 square miles, earning it the dubious distinction of having the densest population per square mile of any city in the world.

The chauffeur looked in the mirror to make sure that his employer was comfortably settled in the back seat. Comfort came easily to Lee Xoping. He was one of the richest men in Hong Kong with a personal wealth estimated at more than seven billion dollars. His income was derived from several businesses, the most important being hotels, shipping, office buildings and three shopping malls.

Kevin Wong, who had been employed by the taipan for almost fifteen years, was more than a chauffeur. He had earned a black belt in karate and was expert in kung-fu as well as other martial arts. He had been hired not just for his considerable driving skills, but also for his ability to defend Mr. Xoping from any unwelcome visitors.

The Rolls Royce moved effortlessly through Aberdeen Tunnel and headed into the mainstream of traffic in Kowloon. Although it was almost seven o'clock in the evening and a time when the traffic should have been lighter, there were many cars and vans speeding towards the main tunnel connecting the island to the mainland.

Emerging at the other end in Kowloon, Wong gunned the automobile through several streets before stopping at the rear of a 40-story skyscraper. Wong smartly opened the car door for his boss who wrestled his portly frame from the Rolls and walked to a little-used door. Closely followed by his bodyguard, Xoping inserted a key and entered the building, then used the same key to open an elevator right behind the door. Once again, the key was inserted in a lock, the doors closed and the elevator silently and swiftly ascended to the top floor.

When the elevator door opened on the 40th floor, a receptionist, seated at a desk, smiled pleasantly. 'Good evening, Mr. Xoping. Everyone has arrived and they are waiting for you,' she said.

The receptionist pressed a button under her desk, and one of the walls disappeared behind another designed in a pocket style. The taipan and his chauffeur entered the spacious and elegantly furnished room. There was a heavy odor of cigar smoke in the air. Ten men, all exuding an air of wealth and importance, sat in comfortable easy chairs around a highly polished table. The room had two walls of windows that ran from floor to ceiling, affording unparalleled views of Hong Kong's exciting and always busy harbor. A third wall had a bar occupying one half, and shelves of books taking up the remainder of the space. The fourth wall housed the hidden entrance to the room.

A few words of welcome were exchanged before Xoping, the chairman of the group, suggested that the taipans convene and start the meeting. Wong, the chauffeur, returned to the receptionist's area, took a seat opposite the elevator and lifted a magazine from a nearby table to read.

A notepad, pencil, customized pens with the name of the skyscraper etched in each, and an empty glass lay at each place. Large decanters of iced water occupied the center of the table. The men took their seats with Xoping occupying one at the head of the table.

'As I am sure you have all guessed, I had a very important reason for hastily convening this meeting," he began. "I have received word that the students want to start the new revolution in just a few weeks. To be precise, on November 1. I know that we had planned on it taking place later in the month, but the students say they are ready now and are confident of success. They feel that a delay might compromise the plan and that this time the army will come over to their side. They want the money and weapons we promised them by October 20.

"Gentlemen, I view any change in a schedule as dangerous," he said, gazing intently at his colleagues around the table. 'I can't dispute the students' belief that they are ready and want to begin the revolution, but, but it means that we have to alter our plans. We have to speed up everything. We thought we had ample time to go over the details. Now we must expedite everything. I hope that this is not a case of 'haste makes waste'. October 20 is only a little more than two weeks away, but I'm sure we can move that soon."

"We have to," one of the other taipans answered him. "If the students say they are ready, then I have to believe they are ready. They are the ones who are going to do the fighting. They are the ones who are going to suffer the agonies and the deaths. I think they have the right to tell us when they want to start. We shouldn't have a problem arranging the delivery of the money so they can buy the weaponry, should we? How long does it take for us to arrange the money?"

"I don't think that it's a matter of the date or arranging the money or the deliveries that is the problem," Kam Wu spoke up. 'I think we are a little nervous about the venture on which we are about to embark and we want to be assured that it will succeed. Perhaps we feel that the students are overly enthusiastic, but they are obviously chomping at the bit to get started."

"Let's face it, if they feel they are ready, I don't think we have the right to tell them they must stick to the original schedule. They may have reasons of which we are unaware that cause them to make this change. Maybe they are concerned about leaks. They are putting their lives on the line; we're only putting up money. I agree that they will suffer a lot more than we if the plot fails. We don't have a choice. We have to go with them."

"Nobody will dispute what you say, Wu," another taipan said, "but I think we have a lot more to lose than money. If this plot fails, how many more can we expect to conceive before the change-over in 1997? Time is running out. The Communists are bound to know where the money and the weapons are coming from. They might suspect the Americans of being surreptitiously involved, but they know the U.S. won't do anything overt and not too much covert either because of America's desire to maintain good relations with China.

"No, my friends, the Chinese will know who are at the bottom of this plot. If it fails, any plans we have to remain in Hong Kong when China takes over the colony will be blown away. I can tell you that I am already making contingency plans to leave. I have established an office in Bermuda, as I know many of you have, too, and it's there I will head well in advance of the British leaving Hong Kong."

All of the taipans at the table were billionaires, powerful men who controlled the business world of Hong Kong. Nothing happened without one of these taipans ordering it. They feared for their empires when the Chinese entered Hong Kong in 1997. Despite the protestations from the Communists that nothing would change in Hong Kong for 50 years, the taipans knew that one very important area would change, and that was the one that worried them more than any other—the administration.

The Communists would install their people in all the key positions. For a time, the opulent shopping malls would be filled with the latest products, the hotels would continue to lure tourists from countries around the world, and the restaurants and the race track and all the other wonderful attractions of Hong Kong would be jammed with tourists pouring hard currencies into it.

But how long would the glitter last before it faded and turned into dust? The power and the decision-making would be in the hands of Communist officials with no knowledge of a market economy. Just as surely as all of the newer Chinese-managed hotels that had been built in Beijing were falling into disrepair because of inexperienced management, so would the glitter and glamour of Hong Kong soon be effaced and its charm as the 'Pearl of the Orient' quickly eradicated.

It was more than the loss of their businesses that worried the taipans, although that was a primary concern. Some had been born in Hong Kong, others had escaped from China and landed penniless in the Colony. They had made their fortunes through acute business senses, cunning, hard work and learning how to make money quickly. All of them loved Hong Kong with an unquenchable passion and were proud of what it had become. They were proud of their contributions that had helped it achieve its pre-eminence in the Orient, and a very special place in the world.

They loved their island enclave with a passion that even exceeded personal greed or wealth. It was their home; it was a tiny piece of land that had given them a chance to succeed and carve out empires that were among the most economically powerful in Asia.

They had visions of a Hong Kong even more exciting and more glamorous and more powerful than the one that now existed. The taipans saw their Hong Kong as a paragon for other countries in the Orient and the rest of the world. They saw it as a model for other societies to emulate, but always their vision saw it as a leader that would some day be far ahead of any other in the world.

"I don't think we need to ask for more discussion, gentlemen," Xoping said. 'We have no choice. The students say they are ready, so be it. We must now do our part as we pledged. I will ask each of you to bring $10 million in U.S. currency to our next meeting which we will schedule for this Friday evening. This is the sum that each of us agreed to contribute to finance the operation. Does anyone have a problem with the money or the date?"

The heads around the table moved from side to side indicating there was no dissension.

"Right, then, Friday night, gentlemen, will be the start of an operation that we hope will allow us to keep what we have worked hard to build and what we want to continue to build in the future. I, personally, become very bitter when I think of what will happen to our beautiful Hong Kong if those rascals from the mainland take it over. To me, twenty million, 50 million dollars is a small price to pay to wipe them out. Remember, if the students succeed, then we and our overseas brothers and sisters will also have a golden opportunity to help grow our mother country into a glorious empire that will continue to be a paragon for the rest of the world to emulate.

"Until Friday, gentlemen."

CHAPTER THIRTY-THREE

MINNEAPOLIS, MINNESOTA

Drew was fumbling with a bunch of keys, trying to locate the one for his apartment when he heard the 'phone ringing. He quickly found the right one, inserted it in the lock and dashed inside to try to lift the receiver before the caller hung up.

"Hello," he almost shouted into the apparatus.

"Drew, this is Brendon McShane. How are you?"

"Oh, I'm fine, Brendon. What's happening?"

"I've been trying to reach you for the last few days and surmised that you were on a trip."

"Yes, I've been on a program to Tobago, 'way down deep in the Caribbean."

"That's just off Trinidad, right?

"You get the prize. It's about 60 miles off the northeast coast of Trinidad and, of course, they, Trinidad and Tobago, form one country. Anyway, I have a feeling that I'm about to be pressed into service."

"Yes, Drew, hopefully. Your Operation Outlook shows that you have a trip to Beijing coming up."

Why did his heart suddenly start to pound, he wondered. Just the mention of Beijing and the palpitations increased. Was it Erin . . . or was it the excitement of another job?

He knew very well what it was. He had been thinking of Erin frequently, several times each day, in fact, and finding it more and more difficult to concentrate on other things.

"Yes, you're right, Brendon. We do have one coming up. Let me see . . ."

He opened his briefcase and sought his Operations Report which listed all upcoming trips for the next three months as well as pertinent details concerning them.

"As a matter of fact, it operates in another ten days. What can I do to help?"

"Drew, I remember you said you have enough seniority that you can pretty much request the trips you want. Well, I want you to get yourself assigned to that Beijing trip."

"I'm sure that can be arranged. I'll speak to my boss about it tomorrow. I'm supposed to be off tomorrow, but I can go in and see him and twist his arm. So, what's the next step?"

"Call me with confirmation and let me know when you're leaving and the city from which you'll be flying out. It will probably be L.A. or San Fran, right?"

"You choose because I can leave from either city."

"OK, let's make it L.A. again.

* * *

"What're you doin' in today? You're off 'til Thursday, aren't you?"

Cole Tennant was writing on a pad when he heard the knock on his door and looked up, disbelievingly, to see his senior trip director.

"Yes, Cole I am off until Thursday, but I thought I would come in to ask something special of you once again."

"Shoot," Tennant said, putting down his pencil and leaning back in his chair.

"Cole, I would like to go on the Simpson Enterprises' trip to Tokyo and Beijing that leaves October 4."

"Now, Drew, you know the rules. You're not supposed to ask for a trip; you're supposed to take what I assign."

"Yeah, I realize that, Cole, but I know that you respect seniority in the travel staff and as I am the most senior of the trip directors, I didn't think you'd mind if I asked."

"Say, what's with China? Are you having a love affair with some Chinese babe?"

"Yeah, I've fallen madly in love with a Chinese. In fact, she's the daughter of the President of China and I can hardly wait to get back to her so I can help cement American-Chinese relationships. Kidding aside, will you okay it, please?"

"Look, Drew, the trip directors have been assigned, but I'll tell you what I'll do. You are scheduled on the Western Industries cruise which leaves

October 8. I had assigned Ralph Schmidt on the Beijing program. I thought I was doing you a favor putting you on a cruise and giving you a few extra days before having to go out again. I am sure that Ralph will be delighted to swap with you, so I'll say it's okay. Happy now?"

"Ecstatically, Cole, ecstatically. Seriously, I do appreciate it. Thanks."

"Get the hell out of here, I'm busy."

He smiled as Drew closed his office door behind him. 'He's got something going in China,' he thought to himself. 'Probably one of those girls who work in the hotel. That's just great. I've got Forsyth screwing the guests and Cummins screwing the suppliers. What kind of an organization am I running here?'

* * *

When he returned to his apartment, Drew lifted the 'phone and dialed the special number in Washington.

The voice came on the line and asked for his code access.

'Courier Thirteen," he replied.

There was silence for a minute before McShane came on the line.

"Hi, Brendon, it's Drew Cummins. Well, I'm all set for Beijing, so it's your move."

'Great. When are you leaving and where are you leaving from?"

"I am scheduled to leave a week from Thursday, that's the first of October, and I will fly to San Francisco to connect with a flight to Tokyo. This program has four days in Tokyo before continuing to Beijing."

"Are you meeting your group or are you flying out alone/"

"I'm the trip director, so I'll be going in advance of the group."

"Good, Drew. Can you go in the night before to San Francisco, say October 3?"

"Yes, that won't be a problem. I was planning to leave the morning of October 1 for the coast, but I can easily change my itinerary."

"Then, I'll book a room for you at the San Francisco Airport Hilton. Let's plan to meet in the hotel's dining room at 8 o'clock for dinner. You'll have to schedule a flight that will get you into San Fran around 7 p.m."

"I'll be there, Brendon, but it's better if my account manager makes the reservation in San Francisco. This must be big when you plan to meet me yourself. Other times, I have had to put up with the hired help."

McShane laughed. Well, let's just say that it's another important job. Look forward to seeing you on October 3. 'Bye, Drew."

CHAPTER THIRTY-FOUR

SAN FRANCISCO, CALIFORNIA

The bellman opened the door of the hotel's courtesy bus and carried the bags of the three occupants to the lobby. Drew quickly registered at the reception desk and obtained his room key. He thrust two dollars into the bellman's hands and asked him to take his bags up to his room.

The flight from Minneapolis was scheduled to arrive in San Francisco at 6:50 p.m. but had been almost an hour late in departing and the pilot had only been able to make up a little of the time. Consequently, Drew had arrived at the hotel a few minutes after eight o'clock. He did not have time to go up to his room and freshen up. Instead, he went straight into the dining room to see McShane sitting at a secluded table with a beer in front of him.

"Sorry I'm late," he said as he shook hands. "My flight was delayed. I didn't even take time to go up to my room."

"I figured that your flight might be delayed and called the airline, so I knew you were running a bit behind. Do you want to relax and order a drink then we can order off the menu."

The waiter asked if he wanted a drink and he shook his head. "No, I'll just have a black coffee, please."

He gave the menu a quick glance and ordered Chicken Kiev. McShane ordered the grilled salmon.

"So, what's so hot that you were so keen for me to go back to China?"

McShane took a swig of his beer. "When you've finished dinner, I'll bring a suitcase up to your room. I want you to transfer your clothes from the case you brought with you into the one I'll give you. I'll take your empty suitcase with me and mail it to your apartment. Your new case contains money, lots of money.

"When you get to Beijing, your contact will give you instructions on when and where to deliver the money. You will have an initial meeting with her at the Beijing zoo. You do like zoos, don't you?"

"Sounds wonderful," Drew smiled. "I particularly like the Beijing zoo because of its family of pandas."

"I assume you will be in Tokyo for three or four days with your group and then on to Beijing. So, if we set up the meeting for about a week from now, say October 12, that will be a safe time. Do you agree?"

"Yes, that will work out ideally."

"Then, I will make the arrangements.

'Yes, that should be fine."

"I'm glad that you like pandas so much because that's where you'll meet your contact. Just be at the panda enclosure at 1:00 p.m. and you will be approached."

"What, no code word, no particular apparel to wear?"

"Yes, you are to wear your uniform, but the contact indicated she knows you well enough to identify you. It's Erin."

Drew's heart missed a beat. He felt a sudden rush of elation.

"Erin? Hey, that's great because I won't have trouble at all recognizing her. I don't know if I mentioned it to you but she is an absolutely gorgeous looking woman. You know, we had only ten minutes together with some of that time in a dark light and I would have no trouble picking her out in a crowd."

"Funny, we, too, were told that it would not be necessary for you to wear any particular outfit because she remembered you very well. I think you two have something going," McShane smiled as he spoke.

"Are the contents of the case cumbersome?"

"No, you'll see them later. There is also an ordinary white business envelope with a letter inside. Carry the letter with you to the zoo. Instructions for the subsequent transfer of the package will be determined by her. As you will see, it would be difficult to transfer the package to her at the zoo. She will tell you where and when you are to make the delivery. Any questions?"

The waiter interrupted their conversation when he brought Drew his coffee. They both ordered their meals and the waiter departed.

Drew sipped coffee slowly. He gazed pensively at the cup for a few seconds, obviously trying to formulate his thoughts.

"Okay, what is it, Drew? You look as though you have something big on your mind. Spit it out."

"Brendon, I've never asked you anything about what I'm doing, have I?"

"No, you haven't. So, now you have some questions, right? Well, ask them, but I can't promise you that I will answer all of them."

Drew looked carefully around him and noted that the closest table was sufficiently distant for the occupants not to hear what he and McShane were discussing.

"I have a very good idea of what is happening. I think I'm carrying some of the funds to help the Chinese students start another revolution, right?"

McShane was silent for a few seconds. He lifted his beer and took a few swallows.

"Drew, you've done a great job for us. You even got the credit for pulling the Cairo mess out of the fire and delivered a bonus, so I'll level with you. You've earned it, but what I'm telling you is dangerous for you to know. Do you still want me to spell it out?"

"Yes, Brendon, I do. I want to know what is going to happen. You don't need to tell me dates although I think I know the big one, but I would like to know if what I am carrying is of the highest importance. I won't back out no matter how dangerous. That's not why I'm asking.

"When I was walking with Erin outside the Great Wall Hotel in Beijing, I could tell she was very intense. I saw her face and it was filled with determination. She has a cause and I think she would give her life for it. I know there's going to be another revolution."

McShane fidgeted with his beer. "Yes, there's going to be a revolution. One of the reasons we're using you to carry the messages is that the Chinese government knows something is about to happen. They are being very watchful of our diplomats and journalists and other functionaries. They don't suspect the U.S. of being involved and trying to foment a revolution, but they do suspect—and rightly—the Hong Kong taipans. The taipans have everything to lose and they don't want to lose anything.

"They are extremely wealthy and powerful people. They asked our government for help and we've side-stepped the issue. Help is being given them, but it's not official. It's being done clandestinely, even without the quote knowledge unquote of our government. The white envelope you carry is in a code which would be very difficult to decipher without the proper equipment. The students have the equipment. The false bottom conceals large sums of money; they're in Hong Kong dollars and U.S. dollars, and in large denominations.

"So, yes, Drew, there's going to be a revolution, but you and your group will be long gone from Beijing before it erupts. Have no fear on that point. You already know the date. You got that from Erin and it has been approved.

"There have not been any changes. I must be honest and say that I would not have told you anything except you already knew most of it. You learned it from Erin and there's no way she could have done otherwise. She didn't want to entrust the dates and information to a letter for you to carry back to the U.S. or even for an attempt at electronic communication. She made the decision that it was better to give you the details verbally. Like all the students, she is concerned about being watched by the authorities. That's why she thought it better to tell you the date and other information so that if someone was watching, it would look like a harmless tryst."

The waiter brought their meals and McShane skillfully changed the topic of conversation to sports, asking if the Vikings were going to win the Super Bowl this time around.

Drew caught on. "Don't worry, Brendon, I'll deliver your envelope and the money. I won't ask any questions of Erin and I'll forget dates and everything else about Beijing."

"You know, Drew, I have the highest confidence in you. I thought that when I first met you and I haven't changed my opinion. I'm a very good judge of character and I formed that assessment of you within two minutes of our first meeting in Minneapolis."

"Yes, I remember that meeting very well. You wanted to give me a huge automotive account."

They both laughed and enjoyed an animated conversation on the topics of the day as Drew devoured his Chicken Kiev and McShane his grilled salmon.

When McShane paid the bill, they rose and walked to the lobby.

"What's your room number, Drew?"

"Three twenty-two."

"'I'll bring the case up to your room in five minutes."

* * *

Drew had emptied his own case when there was a knock on the door. He opened it and McShane entered, carrying a Samsonite that had obviously made a few trips.

"Heck, I thought I was gonna get a brand new piece of luggage on the government."

"No, we wanted you to have something that didn't say you were a novice traveler, but also something that would not draw any particular attention or admiring glances from the customs officials. This should do nicely."

McShane put the case on the bed and opened it. "Looks like any other case, doesn't it?"

"It does to my eyes."

"I've already told you that it has a false bottom. Try to open it."

Drew was unable to find a way to open it. "I give up," he said. Show me how it's done."

McShane pressed two points on the inside of the case and the bottom sprang loose. Piles of U.S. and Hong Kong dollars lay neatly folded. Drew looked at them for a few seconds but didn't touch them. A white envelope rested on top of the money. McShane gently pressed the side back on to the case. There was a click and it looked like an ordinary piece of luggage once again.

"Let me show you how it's done," McShane said, "as you would have a long and difficult time trying to locate it." He opened and closed the case three times asking Drew to watch closely.

"You must press here on the letter 'N' of the word 'Samsonite' printed on the lining. You must also press 'E' of the word 'luggage' and they must be pressed simultaneously.

The magnitude of the whole thing was now beginning to hit him. "What if the Customs officials find the money and the letter? I'm not afraid of being the courier, I'm afraid of all that money falling into their hands. All airports have x-ray machines that accurately reveal the contents of a case, so why won't they easily see the money?"

"You've been to Beijing many times before. The Customs officials have never looked at your bags, have they?"

":No, but I guess there's always a first time, isn't there?"

"True, but they would never think of a false bottom unless they had been tipped in advance and knew where to look, and this project has been given the tightest possible security. They could open up your bag, search diligently and never find anything suspicious. Guaranteed. You see, that false bottom will have this thin, very fine sheet covering the money. This sheet is of a material that is exclusively used by the CIA. Even our airport TSA organizations don't know of its existence, so I assure you, the Chinese officials at Beijing airport won't be aware of anything out of the ordinary if they search your bags."

"They have no knowledge of who you are or what you are doing, and if they question you and learn that you are in the travel business and are bringing in a large group, they'll treat you very well, I assure you. They know that the group will be responsible for depositing large sums of money into their economy. That sounds kinda funny, doesn't it? You will indeed be depositing large sums of money into their economy but perhaps not quite in the way they think."

"You're not just an ordinary tourist, you are an important person in that you bring groups into their country. They will be polite, but if they do go into opening your bags and questioning you and then learn who you are, they'll roll out the red carpet for you.

"Although it was a few years ago, the Chinese are still putting out the fires of the Tiananmen disaster and they are not anxious to create any more problems that will make the front pages of newspapers around the world. They want to show their best side to the tourists and do everything possible to make them have a great time so that they will speak glowingly of China when they return home and spread the word of how well they treat tourists and how wonderful the people were to them."

"Don't be concerned, Drew, you won't be a failure. Of that I am certain. I'll take your case with me and have it sent to your apartment. It will be waiting for you when you return home."

"I have a flight to Los Angeles tonight, so I had better get going. Good luck, Drew. If it means anything to you, I think you've done an outstanding job for us and I have no qualms that you'll deliver the goods on this one, too. Call me when you get back, as usual."

They shook hands and he was gone.

CHAPTER THIRTY-FIVE

BEIJING, CHINA

The CAAC 747 landed smoothly at Beijing's international airport and the Chinese flight attendant welcomed the passengers to the capital city of her country. The flight from Tokyo had been surprisingly good and the meals were tasty. Even the movies were recent-issue American films and the flight service was all that one could ask. This was the first time he had flown the Chinese airline and he approved. It was a very satisfying introduction to the most important trip that Drew had ever or would ever make.

'Now on to the more important segment of the trip,' he thought to himself. The Tokyo part had gone very well, and Drew had left before it had concluded so that he could advance the Beijing segment and make sure that everything was ready for the group's arrival two days hence.

As he left the front door of the aircraft, his thoughts were of the suitcase he would soon pick up and take through Customs. He left the ramp and turned into the long hallway which would take him to the Immigration booth. He would present his passport and the other documents he had been given and had completed on the 'plane to the Immigration official.

He was confident that Customs would not be a problem. He had passed through them six, or was it now seven, times? The Customs officers had always been polite and friendly and seemed glad that Americans were returning to their city. He hoped that they would be as friendly as they had been on all his previous visits, and that they would not ask him to open his case.

The Immigration Officer scrutinized his documents, then looked carefully at his passport and his visa before stamping them and authorizing his entry.

He walked slowly to the baggage claim area and stared somberly at the inactive carousel belt. 'What if they do ask to see my bag' he thought. 'What if they find the false bottom?' He could feel small beads of perspiration trickling down his back. He was working himself into a panic at a time when he should be calm and confident.

'Just because they have never looked at my bags before is no guarantee that they will not want to see them this time,' he thought. 'There is no way that these friendly but naïve young officers will find that false bottom. They have probably never even heard of such things. No, I am worrying myself for no reason at all. I'll just be cool and wear a smile and . . . .

The belt abruptly began to move. After a minute or so, the first of the bags tumbled out of the huge maw as though being regurgitated from an unseen stomach.

Suddenly, a thought occurred to Drew. What if his case got lost? He had lost luggage in the past but it always turned up. His mind was so full of all possibilities that his suitcase passed him twice. He was looking for his own bag and had forgotten the substitute when he suddenly saw it with his business card attached to it. He relaxed and withdrew it from the carousel.

What a stupid thing to do, he thought. I hope that nobody noticed I've been standing here waiting for my bag when it has been going around on the carousel.

He walked slowly to the Customs area. He passed through the green channel, the one for those who have nothing to declare, mustering all the strength he could to affect an air of nonchalance. With just a few more steps to go, he saw one of the officers smile at him and crook his finger in the accustomed sign for 'come here.'

He smiled back and walked over to the officer while putting his case up on the table to be examined. The officer, still smiling, nodded his head in a friendly way. "Hello, nice to see you again. You must like China; you come often. I hope you have a good vacation."

He waved him through. "Thank you. It's nice to be recognized and it's nice to be back in China. You don't want to see my case?"

"No, not necessary. You go through. Goodbye."

"Goodbye and thank you."

Drew felt sure that the sweat on his forehead would have given him away. He was perspiring profusely now, much more than the mild temperature should have induced. But he had made it.

"Ah, Drew, it's nice to see you back." It was Li Tang with the China Travel Service, who knew Drew well from previous trips.

"I'm pleased to see you again, too, Li. Thank you for meeting me."

Tang waved her hand and a black limousine moved toward them. She put Drew's bag and briefcase in the trunk and they set off for the Sheraton Great Wall Hotel.

It was a beautiful afternoon with a pale blue sky and a warm sun, but Drew could see the usual brown haze hanging over the city as they approached it.

"Has the weather been good, Li" he asked.

"Very good, Drew, very good. No rain for long time, so good for tourists but bad for farmers."

Although he had seen the scenery en route to the hotel many times, Drew still enjoyed looking at the hotels, used only by Chinese tourists, and the other buildings they passed. He was equally fascinated by the primitive methods of transportation still employed by the Chinese, like the horse-drawn carts that were slowly moving along the highway, some filled with hay and some with bricks.

Even the more modern mechanized vehicles they passed were peculiarly Chinese, such as the tractor-like trucks that Drew could remember seeing only in China. These machines resembled a small tractor, where the driver sat, and was attached by the flimsiest of steel rods to two wheels with a good three or four feet separating the units. Drew thought that they must do the job as he saw scores of them.

The drive in from the airport was pretty with straight, tree-lined roads and lots of undeveloped land on either side. Old and young people toiled in some patches of gardens, stooping to pick vegetables or till the soil for new plantings. They were peaceful, bucolic scenes that would soon give way to the bustling, people-congested streets of Beijing. Old buildings soon melted away to newer ones and the narrow highway from the airport suddenly expanded to wide boulevards with trucks and buses, some belching foul-smelling, black smoke, and all jostling for space.

"It's amazing, Li, each time I return to Beijing, I see more and more traffic. Is that the symptom of prosperity, do you think?"

"Yes, it's true. It seems traffic becomes more dense each day. We get more and more cars on road, too. Pretty soon our streets look like New York."

"Fortunately, you're still a little ways away from that kind of congestion. I hope you never have to experience the traffic jams that are daily occurrences in most American cities. One thing for sure, we don't have a fraction of the bicycles that you have here. You know, I think bicycling to work is a good idea; it reduces smog and keeps everyone fit and healthy."

The main boulevards of Beijing are flanked by smaller streets on which the bicyclists must travel. He noticed that nothing had changed. Bicyclists were still not permitted on the boulevards so as not to impede traffic or endanger their lives by competing with the mechanized vehicles.

They were nearing the hotel when Li asked him if he was very tired and wanted to go to sleep. "Yes, Li, I think that would be a good idea. Actually, as you know, I've only come from Tokyo, not the U.S. so I'm not as wiped out as I would be otherwise, but I have had a rough few days in Tokyo with the group, up early in the morning and late to bed at night, so a nap right now seems really appealing to me. Perhaps we could meet in the morning and go over the details of the program. Is that okay with you?"

"Yes, fine with me. I have arranged a meeting for 1 p.m. with the Director of Sales of hotel for tomorrow for lunch. Okay?

"Yes, that's a perfect time."

The black limousine pulled up to the front door of the Sheraton and the doorman rushed forward to open the car door.

Tang asked the driver to unlock the trunk and take Drew's bag to the lobby.

"It is good to see you back, sir," the front desk clerk said as Drew stepped forward to register. "There is a letter here for you from Mr. Chang. As most of the front desk and sales people were from Hong Kong, they spoke excellent English and so were easy to understand."

He tore open the envelope and read that the Director of Sales would be pleased to see him for lunch the next day and to meet in the restaurant at 1:00 p.m. during which they could discuss all the requirements of the group.

"I'll see you in the morning then, Li. Thanks for coming out to the airport to meet me."

The bellboy, carrying his bags, accompanied him on the elevator to the seventh floor. He opened the door of the room and placed the suitcase on the rack.

He thanked the bellman and placed a dollar bill in his hand. "I don't yet have any Chinese money, so I hope you won't mind American money."

Official Chinese propaganda claims that there is no tipping in China, but Drew was always amazed how quickly the people accepted tips, particularly if they were in U.S. dollars. They could change the dollars for 10 times the official rate of exchange, but the penalties were stiff if they were caught.

He unlocked his case and hung up his uniform and other clothes. He wanted to empty the case and check that the money and the envelope had not been removed. He touched the sides and the bottom of the case sprang up. He looked intently at the money and the envelope then snapped it shut.

Showering quickly, he tumbled into bed and was sound asleep almost immediately.

* * *

China is so huge that it should encompass many time zones, but, surprisingly, it doesn't. All of China has the same time. There is only one time zone in the more than 3,000 miles that separate its westernmost and easternmost borders. When it is noon in Kashgar in Western China, it is the same in Shanghai in the east. China is 14 hours ahead of Central Standard time in the U.S. meaning that when one is asleep in Chicago, the Chinese are hard at work.

It is not easy to adjust to the difference and it usually takes two to three days to be able to stay awake when the sun is shining and not have cobwebs clouding your thoughts.

Drew was glad that McShane had made the zoo visit for the Sunday and not the Saturday. He had kept his appointments with Li Tang and Mr. Chang on his first full day in Beijing, but he had problems staying awake during the meetings and concentrating on what they had to say. Even though there is only a one-hour time difference between Tokyo and Beijing, it was enough to induce a soporific feeling. Or he thought it might be a delayed effect from the big time change between Minneapolis and Beijing.

He had soaked in a warm bath early Saturday night and gone to bed at nine o'clock. He knew he would wake up in the middle of the night, and he did. He read, did some paperwork in connection with the trip, read some more and finally managed to drift off to sleep again.

He had set his travel alarm for 11:15 a.m. because he wanted as long as he could to build up some strength. When he opened his eyes, it was almost 11 o'clock. He canceled his alarm, rose and pulled back the drapes. The sun streamed in. It was another beautiful morning with not a cloud to be seen anywhere.

He showered, dressed and went downstairs to the restaurant for something to eat. He knew he wouldn't be able to have breakfast at this hour, not even in a property like the Sheraton, but he was able to enjoy an American hamburger in the hotel's Orient Express restaurant.

His wristwatch told him it was now 12:20 p.m. It was only a 15 to 20 minute cab ride to the zoo, so he had plenty of time, but he was anxious to get going and to see Erin again. She had occupied his mind almost from the moment he awoke. Taking the elevator to the seventh floor, he made for his room. He had an important letter to pick up and take with him.

He unlocked his suitcase, pressed the buttons and the false bottom sprang open. Collecting the envelope, he carefully stuffed it inside his trousers, half way below the belt, and covered it with his loose-fitting sports shirt.

There were some American tourists waiting for the elevator as he approached. "Goo mawnin'," one of them, an elderly man with a baseball cap, said. "Y'all American?"

"Yes, sir, from Beautiful Minneapolis."

"Nevah bin theah mahself, but ah sure have heard it's a nice place. Enjoyin' yoh vacation?"

"I'm enjoying myself, but I'm here on business," he replied, and I've been here about half-a-dozen times before, but it's still nice to come back to Beijing. You're all on vacation, I would guess?"

"Yessuh, we sure are. On one o' them package tours, you know the type, six countries in two days and another four countries seen from a low-flyin' airplane."

Everyone laughed and the man's wife said: "Oh, David, it's not such a bad tour. You make it out like it's an army exercise."

She turned to Drew and explained. "We've been to Bangkok, that's in Thailand, you know, and then to Singapore and Manila and Hong Kong. We're goin' from here to Tokyo, in Japan, you know, and then home. We've been gone almost three weeks."

The elevator door opened and the seven tourists and Drew got in.

"Well, it certainly sounds like you're seeing the world . . . and enjoying it, too," Drew said.

"Oh, yes, we're havin' a wonderful time, aren't we?"

All other members of the group nodded their heads in agreement and mentioned that they were meeting their fellow-travelers in the lobby to go on a tour of Beihai Park.

"Say, ah'm Dave Turner and this is my wife, Colleen. We hail from Jackson, Mississippi."

"And I'm Drew Cummins. Nice to meet you."

The others introduced themselves in turn and the hand-shaking was continuing when the elevator reached the lobby.

There were about 20 people already gathered there for the tour and they waved to the late-comers.

"I hope you have a great day and maybe we'll bump into each other later on," Drew said as he headed for the front door.

"Yeah, look forward to it, Drew, and don't you work too hard now, yuh heah?"

"Taxi, sir?" the doorman asked him as he walked to the front of the sidewalk.

"Yes, please."

The doorman waved his arm and a taxi appeared instantly.

"Where do you want to go, sir?" the doorman inquired.

"Oh, I think I would like to go to your zoo and see the pandas."

"You will like those pandas, sir. Everybody likes our pandas."

The doorman muttered to the driver in Mandarin then opened the door for Drew who slipped a small paper note into his hand. He tipped his hat and closed the door after he was seated.

The taxi took off and he smiled to himself. 'This is a classless society,' he mused, 'and I have yet to find a Chinese who has refused a tip. They really are a smart people.'

Surprisingly, there was little traffic and the driver made good time. It took only 15 minutes to reach the zoo. He paid the driver and included a tip which evoked a wide, gap-toothed smile from the driver who constantly nodded his head as he muttered 'Tse tse, tse tse," which means 'thank you' in Mandarin.

The panda exhibit was near the front of the zoo, just to the right of the entrance. Already a large crowd had gathered to watch the antics of a baby panda as it climbed in and out of tires which had been placed in the compound to keep it and the tourists amused.

His heart was pounding with excitement, and not from watching the pandas. His watch read 12:50 p.m. He was early. Most of the onlookers were tourists and he could pick out German, Scandinavian, French and, of course, various accents from the U.S. There were other languages being spoken, but he couldn't determine just what they were.

The panda rolled on its back, then stood up on its hind legs to nibble at a small pile of bamboo shoots. It picked up one shoot and began to chew slowly, alternately looking at the crowd then back over its shoulder at its mother.

Drew was completely absorbed in its antics when he felt someone brushing against him. "Don't look at me just listen. First, hello, Drew, and welcome back to Beijing. I'm going to move away in a few seconds. Count ten and then follow me. I'm wearing a bright red blouse."

He counted ten after she left him and followed her at a respectable pace. His heart was still pounding. He hadn't even seen her face yet, just heard her voice and now he was looking at her walking away.

His eyes were moving up and down her slim body. She was clad in a pair of blue jeans that did full credit to her lissome figure, and a loose-fitting red blouse. He found he couldn't take his eyes off her rear end. The blue jeans clung to her buttocks in a really tight fit and as she walked, there was just enough movement to get his juices flowing.

They walked for about a half-mile when she turned off the main road and strode down a side street which led to a crowded marketplace. When she reached the perimeter of the crowded booths, she turned left, down another street and was lost to his view. He knew she would be watching and would lead him to the meeting place, so he just kept walking following the general direction she had taken.

He had just squeezed into the crowd when he felt someone take his hand. He turned and saw her face. She was even more beautiful than he remembered and her smile revealed perfect, gleaming white teeth, something of a rarity in China.

She turned still holding his hand and led him away. They jostled the crowds for a short while before she let go his hand and moved ahead of him and away from the marketplace. She walked down a narrow alley that was devoid of people. He followed her at a respectable distance, passing only two dogs lying listlessly on the ground that seemed unaware of his presence.

They came to an old battered wooden door and Erin pushed it vigorously. It gave way and they entered, passing through the door which led into a small covered courtyard.

She was standing in the middle of the courtyard, waiting for him. They stood looking at each other; neither said anything. She didn't pull her eyes away as most Chinese would have done. She stared at him, almost longingly. He gave way to impulse, walked up to her, pulled her close to him and kissed her passionately. She didn't resist. When their lips parted, he looked straight into her eyes. Slowly, she put her hand behind his head and pulled him forward to enter another embrace.

'Do I need to tell you that I'm glad to see you?" he asked. She dropped her face slightly and said, "Maybe I am even more pleased to see you."

"I don't think that's possible." He pulled her forward and their lips pressed hard. He slipped his tongue forward into her mouth and she accepted it, rolling her own around his and now beginning to moan. He was stunned at his untypical aggressiveness.

Abruptly, she pulled.away "Drew, we must keep a clear head. We are going to have a very important meeting upstairs. We will find time later." She turned around and moved through another door. He followed her as she climbed a stairway. She was looking carefully around her and listening for any noise. When they reached the second floor, she looked around once more then turned the handle on a door and moved inside, waving to him to follow.

A short and dingy hallway led to a large room where eleven young men were sitting around a table and six more lounging on worn chairs against the wall. They were drinking tea and talking animatedly but their conversation suddenly stopped when the visitors arrived.

They did not rise but peered curiously at him. He didn't look like an American, they thought. He was wearing a pair of faded blue jeans and a dark shirt. If he had almond eyes and was a foot shorter, he could have been Chinese, they thought. There were no introductions. Erin spoke in Mandarin then turned to Drew and told him to sit at the table. She asked someone to bring him a bowl of tea.

"Now," she said, "to business."

One of the men rose and motioned to him to take a seat. He nodded to the man and sat in a spindly-legged chair which didn't look as though it could support his 170 pounds. The others watched him intently.

"Do you have the envelope?" a man asked.

'Yes, I do." Drew raised his t-shirt, pulled it from his trousers and gave it to him.

The man took the white envelope then handed it to another committee member who tore it open. He took a small book from his pocket, quickly deciphered the code and read the letter without any expression on his face. He then leaned over to Erin and whispered in her ear. Her face crinkled slightly then broke into a smile.

The one who had spoken and was obviously the leader, spoke in Mandarin and the others emitted what amounted to soft cheers, slapping each other on the back and nodding in unison. There was excited conversation among them before the leader slapped his hand on the table and muttered more Mandarin, obviously letting everyone know that it was time for business.

He turned to Drew and in perfect British-accented English said: "We thank you for your courage and for your help in bringing the envelope and the money to us. Please inform your people that we are most appreciative of what has been done for us. I would like to ask you to stand outside your hotel tonight at 10 o'clock and have the money with you. It should be placed in an inconspicuous bag. Do you have something like that?"

"Yes, I do," Drew replied. "I have a Northwest Airlines flight bag which would be ideal for that purpose."

"Good. A motorcyclist will pick you up. He will use the code word 'Panda.'

You will say your name in reply. When you have been taken to a spot where it is safe, the cyclist will take the money from you. Are you clear on the instructions?"

"Yes, they're perfectly clear."

"Then you may now leave, and again, take with you our sincere thanks."

"I'd like to ask something," Drew said. "I know I've brought a huge amount of money, but that can only buy so much weaponry. You're going to need a great deal more to take on the whole Chinese army. Why are you so confident that you can win?"

The leader smiled as he fidgeted with some papers on the table. 'The money you have brought us will be used to purchase a highly sophisticated arsenal from a foreign source, right here in Beijing. This is to arm the students. We know that hundreds of thousands of members of our military are with us. There is a real and deep hatred of our government. The soldiers have their own weapons, and they will use them. Does that answer your question? "I should also mention that there are many more such donations from Overseas Chinese and many other sources. We are now well financed and we will win. I promise you, we will win."

"I sure hope that you will succeed. I pray that you do."

At first Drew was hurt by the quick dismissal and had anticipated being a part of the meeting, perhaps assisting where he could be helpful. The leader's explanation soothed his feelings and made him realize that his job was over. He had performed it well.

"Isn't there anything else I can do to help? Maybe I should wait and if there are any messages to take back, I would be happy to do so."

"No, thank you. This is our problem now. What foreigners could do to assist us, they have very generously done."

He got up to leave and this time, everyone in the room rose, too. The leader shook his hand and the others, in turn, did likewise.

Suddenly, Drew froze. One of the hands thrust at him had a small snake tattooed between the thumb and the index finger. He tried to keep his composure as he raised his eyes to see the face of the man. He was Chinese like the others, and there was nothing particularly different about him. He smiled broadly and nodded his head in a form of friendship.

He had to make a quick appraisal of the man so he could identify him later, but he was no different from the others. It was as though all of them bought their poorly-made clothing from the same store. But then he did notice something.

The man had a jagged scar on the right side of his neck. It was an old scar that had not been sewn properly, if at all, and had healed leaving tell-tale raised tissue.

After the man had shaken hands with him, they returned to the table and Drew took his leave. Erin preceded him out the door as they walked down the stairs to the courtyard.

When he felt they were far enough to talk safely, he quickly turned her around.

"Erin I can't believe what I just saw. You've got a traitor in your group."

"What?" she stared at him incredulously. "A traitor? Never. What makes you think that?"

He related the incident in Pan Am's Clipper Club at JFK Airport when he saw the small snake on the man's hand and the same tattoo on the hand of the camel handler in Cairo.

"I saw the same tattoo on the hand of one of the men in that room."

She was confused. Her face wrinkled in puzzlement as she listed to him.

"Are you sure? Maybe it was dirt or oil or something like that?"

"Erin, it was a snake. I am very familiar with that tattoo."

"I know all these men and I don't remember ever seeing one with a snake on his hand?"

"Shaking hands is not a Chinese custom. I noticed it because he offered me his hand and when you are about to shake hands, the thumb is extended from the other fingers and this made the tattoo much more visible. Or maybe you just haven't bothered to look closely, but it's there, I assure you. You've got to do something about it, and now. If he belongs to the same sect as those I saw in Egypt, you've got a traitor in your midst and all your plans may already be known to the government. My God, I just thought of something. Suppose they're watching your meeting place. Suppose they've already seen me."

He suddenly felt ashamed of his cowardice. In the midst of danger, his first thought was of himself.

"I didn't mean that the way it sounded, as though I was only concerned for my own safety. I want to be sure that you and your compatriots are safe, too. Please believe that."

'Of course I believe that," she said. "You've already taken chances just to help and we're very grateful. What do you think I should do?"

"I would start by asking your leader to step out of the meeting for a moment. Say that I had forgotten something I wanted to tell him and ask if he could come down to the courtyard for a moment."

She climbed the stairs and returned a few minutes later with the man who had taken control of the meeting.

"Yes, what is it you wish to tell me?" he asked.

Drew repeated the story he had told Erin. The man's face went pale. He was visibly shaken and remained silent for several seconds.

'Which one was it? Can you describe him because I can't remember seeing a tattoo on a hand of any of our people"

"He also had a crooked scar on he right side of his neck."

The leader's face was impassive. He just stood there, saying nothing and making no movement. Beads of sweat formed on his forehead. After what seemed an eternity, he turned to go back to the meeting.

"We shall take measures to insure the safety of the operation. Our revolution will begin as scheduled and we'll be successful this time. Thank you for your information.'

He climbed the stairs and was gone.

'Drew, you had better go to your hotel now. I will have to return to the meeting. What you have told us is devastating. Will you be able to find your own way back to the hotel?"

"Yes, I've been finding my way around the world for much too long ever to get lost. Good luck, Erin. I wish I were wrong in what I have told you, but I know I am right.

He opened the door leading from the courtyard into the street and turned to look at her once more. "When will I see you again? I want to see you."

"I'll be in touch with you. I don't know when or how, but I'll be in touch. That was something I had planned to do."

CHAPTER THIRTY-SIX

BEIJING, CHINA

Promptly at 10 o'clock that evening, Drew stood outside the front door of the hotel, holding the flight bag with the money inside. He had been there only a couple of minutes when a motorcycle drew up to the front door. The driver motioned to him and safely said: 'Panda.' Drew gave his first name in reply and the 'cyclist pointed to the rear seat of his machine. They drove off and sped down darkened side streets for about five minutes before the driver stopped.

Drew gave him the flight bag. The 'cyclist said 'thank you' in English and sped away, leaving Drew to find his own way back to the Sheraton hotel.

* * *

It was difficult for him to rid his mind of Erin, the students, the traitor and the impending revolution. They kept intruding on his thoughts when he should have been concentrating on his travel program.

That evening, as he read his travel kit to refresh his memory of what the group would be doing over the next few days and his responsibilities, his mind strayed frequently to what changes his revelation of the traitor would cause among the students.

He wondered how they would verify what he had told them. Would they beat it out of the man with the tattoo? Would they torture him until he revealed the truth? What would this do to their plans and the confirmed dates for the revolution?

He didn't sleep well that night. There were too many unresolved problems and they would not leave him alone or give him the peace of mind he needed to relax and fall into a deep sleep.

* * *

The sun was streaming in his bedroom window when his travel alarm woke him. He felt drained because of too many nightmares and too many times waking up in the middle of the night.

In one dream, the man with the tattoo pulled a knife from inside his jacket, slashed the leader then grabbed Erin as a hostage. Soldiers and police were waiting outside the apartment, rifles raised and aimed at the courtyard door.

As the traitor and Erin emerged, a volley of shots pierced the silence . . . and he awoke in a sweat, his heart beating wildly.

He showered, put on his uniform and went downstairs to the hospitality desk to print 'Welcome' on the flipchart as well as the activities in which the group would participate that evening. He placed the Simpson Construction Company's banner on the desk, then spoke to Reception about having the room keys ready for the group when it arrived.

It was now beyond the hours for breakfast, but he couldn't care less. He had no appetite. The unsatisfying sleep and the students' dangerous situation robbed him of any desire for food.

He looked at his watch. It was almost noon. He was to be picked up by Li Tang at one o'clock before departing for the airport and meeting the group. 'Maybe a walk will help,' he thought and decided to take a stroll. I'll go along the same street where I first met Erin; how nostalgic, how romantic.' He began to smile. It was the first light moment he had enjoyed in some time.

It was warming up to be a beautiful day, so he removed his tie and left it and his coat over the back of the chair at the hospitality desk. No one would touch it. If there was any theft in China, he certainly had never experienced it.

He walked out the front door, turned left and came to the main street where he turned left again to walk along the tree-shaded boulevard. Everything had a dry, baked look to it, evidence of the need for rain in the city. Occasionally, a wind would spring up and little swirls of dust would dance in front of him, then disappear as the wind died down.

"Don't turn around," a voice commanded him. It was Erin. "I'm walking behind you and will overtake you. Just follow me."

In a matter of seconds, she had passed him. He maintained his same pace but kept her in view. She turned into an alley and he followed her. The alley was deserted but he kept walking knowing that she would let him know where she was.

"Drew, over here," she cried. She was standing in a corner with an overhang shading her from the sun. He quickly strode towards her and grasped her in his arms. He kissed her and her response indicated that this was what she wanted him to do. His hand slipped to her breast. It was firm and surprisingly larger than he expected. Her blouse never indicated that she had anything more than the typical small breasts of the Chinese.

She was moaning now and encouraging him to go further.

"I wish we could go some place," he said. 'I want to make love to you. I've wanted to make love to you ever since I first saw you.'

"Why can't we go back to your room?" she asked.

"How I would love that," he said, "but I am being picked up by someone from the China Travel Service in about half-an-hour then going out to the airport to meet my group coming in."

'Then, let's keep more pleasant thoughts until we have the time to enjoy them," she said. "Drew I want to tell you what has happened. I was walking to your hotel and planned to call your room from the lobby.

"When we returned to the meeting, our leader, Zhang Yuiyao, told the committee what you had said. There was almost pandemonium for about five minutes. Someone asked who was the traitor. Another suggested that everyone in the room was a loyal Chinese who wanted to see democracy come to our country, and that there must be some mistake.

"Then our leader revealed to them what you had revealed to him. He told them about the snake tattoo and your problems in Egypt. That's when Shao Quiang, the infidel stood up and shouted loudly, 'I have a tattoo, but I am not a traitor. Are you referring to me'?

"We questioned him for over an hour, but he would not yield. Then one of our committee remembered something very important that laid the guilt at his door. He remembered that when we had the disturbance in Tiananmen Square in May, Wu Feng, the student leader of the revolution, who was later executed, told him and Quiang that the Third Army would be called in to quell the disturbances. This was good news because many members of the Third Army had already told the students that they were reluctant to fight against a cause that they believed was just. They didn't want to break the heads of their brothers and perhaps have to kill them.

"But instead of the Third Army being called up, the government brought the First Army into Beijing despite the fact that it was almost 100 kilometers away while the Third Army was in the suburbs, only seven kilometers from Tiananmen."

"Our leader suddenly got furious and rushed at the throat of the miserable wretch. 'You told them, didn't you, you told them.' He shouted at him. 'You betrayed us.' He was pummeling him when the other students pulled him off.

We held a court right there in the room and two other students relayed incidents that pointed the finger at Qiang. After three hours, he finally cracked and pleaded for mercy. He said if we would spare his life, he would tell us everything and could even assist us in feeding wrong information to the government. He also said that he had been doubting the Communist tenets for some time now and was hoping that the army would join the students in the pro-democracy riots.

"Zhang Yuyao agreed to spare his life and to meet the conditions he had set. The infidel poured it all out. The snake is the symbol of an international cartel of terrorists known as 'The Vipers' and is made up of members of the Bad Meinhof, the Shining Path and numerous Middle East and Communist organizations. It's actually a very new organization. Each gang has a certain number of representative members in 'The Vipers' and Quiang was one of those representing China. It is a small new and exclusive group which may be one reason we have never heard of it."

"Did he say how much the government knows about the impending revolution?"

"Yes. He said they know a revolution is coming, but nothing more. We know he was telling the truth because only our leader, one other student and I knew the original date and now the new date."

"'I wouldn't trust him. Do you really think he will feed lies to the government? If he is a member of The Vipers and this is a very secret organization, he must be a die-hard Communist and terrorist to belong and to have been assigned to it by the Chinese government officials."

"It makes no difference, Drew. Our leader ordered him executed. He was shot with a bullet in the back of the head. What I have come to tell you is that we're bringing the date of the revolution forward once again. If the government does know our date, they have November 15 which was the original date. They don't know that their man is dead and so will be looking to that date as the start of the demonstrations. We are taking no chances. The committee told me to tell you that because of what you have done for us, we will delay the revolution until three days after your group leaves, that's October 15. We know that you have to stay two days after the group's departure to clear the bills. The new date then is October 15. This will give your group and then you time to be clear of Beijing and back in America before our war begins."

"Are you ready now?" he asked her. "I mean, do you have weapons and ammunition?"

"We already have a lot of weaponry and have had it for almost a month now. We have much of the arsenal we will need and will now secure as much more as we can with the dollars you have brought us. Much of your money was used to pay off those who trusted us with the weapons without making payment. Yes, we're ready, as ready as we will ever be, and this time we're going to succeed. I think the government is going to be very surprised when they see how well armed and organized we are. We have hundreds of thousands under arms. With that many people, the government was bound to suspect something, but they couldn't break any of us to find out the exact dates or just how strong we are because no one person had all the answers."

"Aren't you nervous that Qiang has communicated more to the government than he said? What if they are watching you? What if they know who you and the others are and will pounce if he doesn't report to them?"

"He said that he only made contact with his superiors when he had something concrete to give them, and he really wouldn't have known much until our meeting, and fortunately, he didn't last long beyond that. They are not going to tip their hands by arresting us because they still don't have all the details nor all the members of our committee who are the key players. Until that meeting you attended yesterday morning, the other members had never met each other. Even I didn't know all of the committee until yesterday. No, we think the government is relying on their spy to keep feeding them information and to let them know when the revolution is set to begin so they can strike before it starts. They won't move until they have the names of all members of the committee. Only Yuyao knew all the names and he told no one. Qiang's contacts wouldn't expect to hear from him for days and perhaps weeks yet. Time is on our side."

'Erin, it's about ten minutes to one. I have to go. I love you very much and I want to see you before I return to the States. When can we meet?"

"You pick the time and place. I will make every effort to be with you; just tell me where and when."

"Let's see," he said, "the group will be leaving next Monday. As you know, I will be staying two more days to complete the billing. Do you want to come up my room on Monday when we will have some privacy? There's so much I want to say to you.'

"I'll be there. What time and what is your room number?"

"The group leaves on a flight at 10:30 a.m. I'll be back in my room about noon. Can you watch for my return and then come right up afterwards? It's difficult to meet when the group is here. I can never say I can do something because so many things can happen that cause me to change my plans. I think it's best to wait until the group departs and then my time is my own."

"Fine, but you still haven't given me your room number."

"It's 713. Do I need to tell you that I have never been so anxious for a program to be over as I am this one. One more thing. It makes me feel almost cowardly to think that I'll be running off home and leaving you here to face so many dangers."

"You mustn't think that way, she said. "This is not your war, and besides, you've already done a great deal for us. You, too, have been facing danger, so you mustn't think you are cowardly. I think you're very brave."

He looked at her beautiful face then kissed her. "Goodbye, Erin, I must run. I love you."

"And I love you," she whispered as he quickly walked away.

CHAPTER THIRTY-SEVEN

BEIJING, CHINA

It was going to be a long and arduous program and Drew could never remember feeling this way before one was about to begin. He enjoyed the incentive programs and his job and found most of the people a real pleasure to be with. It was a genuine delight to make sure that the trip participants had a great time, and he never considered it a chore when he could do something that would enhance a particular activity or someone's enjoyment.

But this trip dragged. Of course, it was the thought of seeing Erin again and he frequently conjured up in his mind unrestrained images of making love to her.

There was another image, however, that was superimposed on his lustful reveries. He was sitting on a powder keg, and he knew it. A revolution that might change the whole of China and that could have a profound impact on the entire world was about to happen, was about to explode. The only reason that the match was being kept away from the fuse was in deference to Drew who had done so much to make it all possible.

Every evening before retiring, he would say to himself: 'Well, that's one less day.' It was so unlike him, but the conditions were so unusual.

On the morning of the fourth day, the group was scheduled to visit the Great Wall, the highlight of the visit to Beijing and the tour to which they had most looked forward. Drew was at the hospitality desk at 7:00 a.m. Shortly afterwards, Lois Friederich, a member of the travel staff showed up. She had taken breakfast in her room and asked if he would like to go to the restaurant and have something to eat while she manned the desk. The group was scheduled to leave at 9:00 a.m., so he thought the idea a sound one.

He entered the Orient Express restaurant and saw several members of the group. There were four at a table for six.

"Are you fussy about the people you eat with, or may I join you? he asked.

"Well, normally we are, but in your case we'll make an exception," one of them joked.

It was a buffet breakfast, so he moved through the line quickly and returned to the table with a full tray.

"Aren't you eating lunch today?" one asked.

Drew laughed. 'With all this running around after you nice people that I have to do, I must eat enormous meals to keep up my energy level," he retorted.

As he spooned the corn flakes into his mouth, Ramona Kelly, one of the participants, asked if he had been to the Ming Tombs and the Great Wall before.

"Oh, yes, many times. I think today will be my seventh visit."

"I'm really looking forward to the tour, to seeing the tombs, but I'm especially excited about seeing the Great Wall and walking on it."

"Everyone who comes over here rates the Wall as their number one sight to see. And it certainly is worth seeing. We'll be stopping at the Ming Tombs first to see where one of the Emperors of China is buried, then we'll have lunch at the Ming Tombs restaurant and afterwards move up into the mountains to see the Wall. You'll see remnants of the Wall before we actually come to the part that has been restored so that tourists may walk on it. As many times as I have seen it, I still enjoy gazing at it, and I always manage a walk along it."

One of the guests asked about the Ming Tombs. 'The guides do an excellent job of describing the tombs, and as I have heard them describe them so many times, I know something about them.

"There were thirteen Emperors of China and all of them are buried in the foothills of the mountain range along which the Great Wall stretches. Only one of the tombs has been unearthed. The remaining twelve are still buried, so their tombs are intact.

"One thing in particular that you will find very interesting is the explanation of how the archaeologists had to destroy a magnificent door to enter the tomb. All the achievements of modern science and technology at that time notwithstanding, they couldn't find a way to open the main door to the tomb after they had dug down and discovered it. They surmised, incorrectly as it turned out, that several of the Emperor's slaves had interred themselves with their master's sarcophagus; you know, die for the glory of the Emperor and all that sort of stuff. But that's not what happened.

"Joan," he said, directing his attention to one of the wives, "have you heard of the Chinese lock? It's on Asian jewelry boxes and on items of Chinese furniture such as dressers."

"Yes, sure I have," she replied.

"Well, there was no lock on the door and no conceivable way of opening it other than smashing it in. So, the archaeologists pounded and smashed their way through the magnificent door of marble and wood, but they did not find the skeletons of any slaves inside. Instead, what they found was the origin of the Chinese lock. Just on the other side of the door, they found a huge hole in the earthen floor. It was about six feet deep, six feet long and three feet wide.

"After the Emperor's sarcophagus and the two sarcophagi of his wives, the Empresses, who had preceded him in death, had been placed inside with precious objects to help them pay their way in the after-world, his subjects on the outside pulled the door forward to lock it. This released a huge chunk of granite which hit another piece of granite and so on, much like the domino effect, until the last enormous block of stone plunged into the hole in the ground and solidly locked the door.

'The reason I tell you this is that I don't want you to miss the tomb. Listen carefully to what your guide says and you will be told a fascinating story. And remember, there are still 12 tombs beneath the ground that have not yet been touched., no one knows if they contain more of the same amount of precious jewelry, gold and silver objects as the first."

Drew noticed that the guests were glued to his every word. He thought to himself that Americans really do make great tourists. 'They are anxious to know about other countries and are genuinely interested in speaking to the local people,' he thought to himself.

The group departed on their great odyssey and after an hour, the buses pulled into a parking lot for what the guide said would be an opportunity to stretch their legs for fifteen minutes. As they descended from the motorcoaches, they were besieged by hawkers urging them to buy their wares, while others directed them to their nearby stalls where they sold everything from Chinese army hats to astrakhans to cloisonné vases and embroidered silk panels.

Drew walked around the area, watching the people buying as much as their arms could carry. Some even made quick trips back to the bus to drop off their purchases, so laden down were their arms, so they could return to the stalls.

Several young men were standing near the parking lot. They were not hustling the tourists, just standing as though waiting for someone. It turned out they were.

Three soldiers came out of nowhere and approached the men. They exchanged only a few words before one of the men handed the soldiers what looked like a bundle of money.

The soldiers held open the briefcases they were carrying and the men plunged their arms inside and withdrew objects which they, in turn, put in a large box that was lying next o them on the ground.

'They are buying guns and ammunition,' Drew thought, and they're doing it so openly anyone can see them. They are not even making any attempt to be secretive. While he was thinking about this, one of the guests tapped him on the shoulder.

"Are those soldiers selling guns. It sure looks like it."

"No, that's a common sight, Bill," Drew told him. "They are ancient guns and even some modern ones, but their barrels are blocked so that they can't fire. They are sold mostly as souvenirs for tourists to put on the walls of their dens at home."

"Hey, that sounds interesting. If I don't see any while we're on tour and you do, would you point them out to me? "Sure will," Drew replied while saying softly under his breath, 'but don't count on it.'

The coaches were re-boarded and soon drove through an archway on their approach to the Ming Tombs. The road was lined with the statuary of animals, some popular, some mythical and some grotesque. The tourists asked the guide to stop the bus so they could have their pictures taken on the back of a camel, standing next to an elephant, or beside a creature with dragon-like features and numerous feet.

The guides told everyone that 10 minutes would be allowed for picture-taking and the buses were emptied very quickly.

Drew saw more young men talking to soldiers. Again what looked like money was exchanged for the right of the young men to put their hands inside the soldiers' briefcases or plastic bags and withdraw weaponry. Was he mistaken?

All sorts of ideas came into his head. Were the young men buying weapons and ammunition from the soldiers? Was this a prelude to the revolution? 'Maybe my imagination is more active than usual,' he thought. 'I know a revolution is about to happen so I'll be attributing every incident I see to the impending uprising.'

The coaches moved on along the avenue of the animals and soon arrived at the parking lot of the Ming Tombs. It took an hour for the group to descend into the tomb and witness the remnants of the once-magnificent door and the Emperor's and Empresses' sarcophagi.

Lunch in the restaurant was the next stop, and after everyone was seated, Drew noticed the people with whom he had breakfast waving to him. He moved over to their table and they asked him to join them.

"Hey, Drew," one of them said, "you were right. Because of what you said, I listened more attentively than usual and I was absolutely fascinated by our guide's description of the door as well as her dissertation on the tomb."

"Yes," another piped up, "but you didn't tell us about the odor in the toilets."

Everyone laughed uproariously. 'That odor in there would stun an elephant at 50 feet," one said, and they all laughed loudly again. Guests at the next table asked what was so funny and when it was explained, they agreed and joined them in their hilarity.

Soon, it had spread to all the other tables and the Chinese waitresses admired the Americans who found so much to laugh about and seemed to be enjoying themselves tremendously.

The Great Wall proved to be the highlight of the tour. The guests oohed and aahed when they caught their first sight of the huge structure that snakes across China for almost 4,000 miles and was begun 500 years before the birth of Christ.

The guide pointed out that when American astronauts were circling the earth, they said the only landmarks they could recognize were the Great Wall of China and the Grand Canyon.

Just before the steps leading up to the Wall are reached, there is a cluster of small stores that sells most of the souvenir-type items to be found all over Beijing. But there are also stores that sell paintings by local artists and one where the artist himself does superb brush works and will execute a painting with the purchaser's name in Chinese characters. This shop became especially popular.

'It's funny,' Drew thought. 'They get so excited about the wall but as soon as they see anything resembling a store, they'll stop in there first.' He laughed to himself thinking about the members of his group and their acute shopping propensities as he climbed the steps to walk along the wall once again.

For some inexplicable reason, most tourists, when they reach the Wall at the end of the steps, turn to the right. And this is what Drew had always done before. This time, he decided he would walk to the left. It is a little steeper, and he thought that maybe this is what deters tourists from choosing the left walkway.

There was only one other couple ahead of him and he noticed that they had stopped in one of the turrets, obviously to rest. It was somewhat quiet with only the cacophonous sounds of the vendors in their stalls below trying to sell the tourists their goods. He had a good vantage point from which to look down over the area with the small stores that had attracted so many of his group.

He leaned against the parapet and looked up to his left to survey the beautiful undulating scenery. He could see the Wall stretch like a serpent for a couple of miles before disappearing beyond a hill. The Chinese had done a very good job restoring this part of the Wall. Returning his gaze to the shopping area below, he noticed several young Chinese men standing behind one of the stores, out of the view of visitors. There were about seven or eight of then, each holding what looked like an empty bag.

A dozen soldiers suddenly turned a corner and confronted the young men. They conversed with each other for a while before one of the soldiers turned and waved his arm. Two more soldiers came into view, holding two large boxes. They looked all around them as if to be sure there were no onlookers. The soldiers placed the boxes at the feet of the civilians and turned away to come back minutes later with two more.

Something was given to the soldiers then they and the men embraced each other, turned and walked away.

The young men tore open the boxes. The distance was too far for him to see what was inside, but it looked like they were transferring grenades into their bags. Was his imagination playing tricks again? But what else would soldiers be selling civilians? It had to be weaponry or ammunition.

He reminded himself that the revolution was nearing. It reinforced in his mind that soon there might be a new and very different China.

CHAPTER THIRTY-EIGHT

BEIJING, CHINA

"Hey, theah, Drew, howya doin' boy?" It was Dave Turner, the tourist he had met in the hotel. He was sitting with a few members of his tour group in the lounge of the Great Wall Hotel.

"Well, Dave, it's nice to see you and Colleen again. Have you been enjoying your sightseeing?"

"Why, we surely have. We've been seein' the Great Wall. Great history. Not this heap of concrete and glass," he said, sweeping his arm around the room. I mean the great big heap of stones out theah in the country," he said giggling to himself.

"We've been havin' the time of our lives, ain't we folks?" Turner asked as he turned to his fellow travelers, inviting their acquiescence.

All of them nodded their heads and made comments about how wonderful the Ming Tombs and the Great Wall had been and how it was an even more dramatic sight than they had anticipated.

"Sit down heah, boy, for a minute and let me buy you a drink."

"No thanks, but can I take a raincheck on it? Maybe I can have one with you later. I'm working on something just now and have to get it done.

"You know, son, we've been havin' a good ol' chin-waggin' heah and we've been talkin' for the last half-hour or so about some of the strange goings-on we've seen over the last couple of days or so.

"Jeff ovah theah was just sayin' that he saw soldiers sellin' grenades and guns to some young men not two blocks from heah.

"And Bill ovah yonder sweahs he saw the same thing at the Ming Tombs today. Have you seen anythin' like that?"

"No, I can't say that I have. Are you sure they were guns? It might just have been surplus army items the soldiers were selling to make money, much like the army caps you can buy in the stores or those huge military fur hats that are sold at the stalls near the Ming Tombs. Maybe that's what they saw."

"It could be," said Jeff, "but it looked to me like these guys were selling the kids the real McCoy. Maybe they were old rifles or other such relics that the soldiers had pinched from the barracks, but I'll tell you this, they sure as hell looked real."

Everybody started laughing and making fun of Jeff's eyesight.

"You know, Jeff, you ain't getting' any younger," Dave laughed. "Maybe you need glasses."

"Hell, I have glasses, and I was wearin' them today when I saw the exchange goin' on."

"Ah'm just glad that me and Colleen are headin' for somewhere else tomorrow anyway, that's all I want to say. Don't want to get mixed up in no shootin' war, no sirree."

"Ah guess that ah'm glad, too," Jeff's wife said, almost whining. "All this talk of guns and bombs and what have you doesn't do mah mind any good. Well, Drew, we're going to Tokyo tomorrow. That's in Japan, you know."

"It certainly is," Drew smiled. "Knowing she had just been gently ribbed, Colleen added "Well, maybe we'll see you later."

My group leaves tomorrow, too, but I'll be staying for a day or two to finalize the billings then I'll be heading back to Beautiful Minneapolis myself."

"Well, good luck to you and don't be a-buyin' any of them guns or grenades, yuh heah?" Dave said, holding out his hand to Drew.

There was more laughter as he took his leave and headed for the elevator.

'Things are moving fast,' he thought to himself as he rode up to the seventh floor. What the tour group people had seen and what he had personally witnessed this afternoon were all the proof he needed that the atmosphere was heating up. The students were obviously getting all the armament they needed and they were getting it from soldiers who seemed more than willing to take great risks stealing guns and ammunition from their barracks and stores and handing them to the students in exchange for U.S. and Hong Kong dollars. And Drew knew where those dollars had come from.

CHAPTER THIRTY-NINE

BEIJING, CHINA

The last bags were being picked up from the group's rooms and brought down to the front of the hotel to be loaded on a luggage truck.

It was the final day of the trip and Drew was experiencing such a feeling of euphoria as he could never remember enjoying on any previous trip. It was as though he had taken an elixir and was reveling in its comforting, soothing effects.

The luggage had been tagged to San Francisco, thanks to the efficiency of Pan American which had provided the trip coordinator back in Minneapolis with the tags in advance. Drew's staff had merely to attach one to each piece of luggage, an action that would save much time at the airport.

The last suitcase had been loaded and the truck grunted and groaned as it slowly departed. Drew watched it move away, then turned back to the lobby to check with the cashier that all members of his group had paid their incidental accounts.

'There are only four still to pay," the cute little cashier said as she patted a sheaf of papers on her desk.

"They are probably still eating breakfast in the restaurant," he said. "I'm sure they'll be here soon."

The hospitality desk banner was removed and Drew gave it to Sandi Wallace, another travel staffer, and asked that she pack it in her carry-on case and take it back to the office. It would be mailed to the client along with the final billing.

Some of the guests stopped at the hospitality desk to ask a few questions. "Is there duty-free shopping at the airport? "Do you happen to know what movies they will be showing en route to San Francisco?" "This is a non-stop flight to San Francisco, isn't it? I mean we won't be stopping in Tokyo on the way home, will we?"

"Yes, there is a duty-free shop at the airport," and "No, we don't know the titles of the movies to be shown on the return flight, but we'll ask for this information at the airport and let you know before the flight is boarded, and yes, it is a non-stop flight to San Francisco."

Drew asked Lois Friederich to check with the cashier and ask if the four remaining guests had paid their incidental charges yet. As Lois walked over to the cashier, Dick MacBean, one of the hosts of the Simpson Construction Company, stopped at the hospitality desk to congratulate Drew on his handling of a superb trip. He said, "your company has done it again with the planning and execution of a wonderful program.

"Funny, I had some reservations about coming to China. Even though it's a Communist country and their way of doing things is sure different from ours, I must say I really felt perfectly safe. In some respects, I felt safer than if I were in some of our big cities. After the disorder in Tiananmen Square, I was always wondering if another eruption would take place. Heck, this place is as quiet and peaceful as you could wish for . . . . except for the traffic, that is. In fact, now that I'm here, I would have liked to stay on for a few days more and visit some of the other areas of China. Have you ever been to Xian where they have the terra-cotta figures, Drew?"

"Yes, I've been there once. I thought it was very interesting. You certainly don't see anything like it anywhere else in the world. Another city you might enjoy is Guilin. It's in the Chinese lake district and is known as the 'Garden City'. It has beautiful waterways with huge monolithic rocks that look as if they had been missiles that had been shot out of a submarine and didn't quite get out of the water. It's a beautiful area.

"Shanghai is a fascinating place, too. You have the western area called the bund which fronts the harbor and right behind it is Old China. You see western structures of steel and concrete juxtaposed dilapidated wooden homes and buildings. The contrasts are what make it so worthwhile to visit. And the city is growing so fast that everywhere you look, you see cranes and all other signs of construction. The joke in Shanghai is that the crane is the national bird of China."

"Wow, you certainly have done a lot of traveling, Drew. I envy you that. Just wish I could have stayed over in China for a few days. I should've arranged some vacation time and extended my visit. The only reason I didn't is because I wasn't sure if China was safe. Well, that's another big mistake I made."

As he walked away, Drew knew that Dick MacBean would soon know that he had made the right decision and that he would have had diarrhea if he had been aware of what Drew knew. If Dick had stayed just three more days in China, he would very definitely change his opinion of the "quiet and peaceful" place he was visiting.

The group began to gather in the lobby. The departure time from the hotel was set for 8:00 a.m. and everybody was anxious to get started on the long journey home.

Lois returned to the desk to tell Drew that all the incidentals had been paid. "As a matter of fact, Drew," Lois told him, 'the cashier said she wished all groups were as disciplined as incentive groups. She told me that most of the time, the bellmen have to board other groups' buses and call out the names of those who 'forgot' to pay for their telephone calls, drinks in the bar, laundry or items they had purchased in the gift shop and signed to their rooms."

Drew was waiting for a call from Jerry Blatz, the fourth member of the travel staff, who was already at the airport. He had gone out earlier in the morning to secure all the boarding passes which he would distribute to the group as they disembarked the buses on their arrival.

As he was thinking about this, the telephone at the desk rang. Drew answered it and heard Jerry's voice on the other end.

"Drew everything's on time. I spoke with the Pan Am supervisor who said the 'plane is on the ground and is now being provisioned. They're anticipating an on-time departure and I have all the boarding passes and all the luggage is lined up for our people to check that all their luggage is here and allow Customs to see them. The Pan Am rep told me that Customs will probably pick one or two bags and ask the owners to open them. I'll see you at the airport."

Let's get started," Drew told Lois and Sandi. They made an announcement for everyone to board the motorcoaches for the airport and those who had been seated in the lobby rose and gathered up their hand-carried bags.

"One of these days, an airline is going to get so fed up with the amount of carry-on bags that tourists take on the 'plane that they really will enforce the one carry-on per person regulation that they continually talk about," Drew said to Lois who was laughing at the struggles some of the guests were having carrying their extra flight bags, paper bags, carefully wrapped vases marked "Fragile" and framed paintings.

The guides were instructed to tell the people that when they arrived at the airport, they would find their bags lined up. He mentioned that Customs may ask one or two couples what they were taking out the country. They were informed that a few bags would undoubtedly be opened and examined by the Customs officials, but not to worry as it is a fairly simple function and almost never is a fine imposed. The bags would then be put on carts and taken out to the Pan Am jet.

The guides were also asked to mention that Jerry had already secured their boarding passes which would preclude the need to line up at the check-in counter, a laborious and time-consuming procedure. This announcement was greeted with loud cheers and applause.

Drew had been dreading that something would go wrong and that the flight would be delayed or worse, have a mechanical that might cause the flight to be canceled. But luck was smiling on him. Everything went so smoothly, he wondered if his own departure in a couple of days would be the opposite.

As the people cleared their bags with Customs and passed through Passport Control, he said goodbye to them and wished them a good flight home.

Jerry Blatz had already gone through and Lois and Sandi waited until all the guests had cleared Immigration and Customs. Drew turned to them and thanked them for the great job they had done and said he would see them in the office in a few days.

'Oh, if you girls only knew what's about to happen here in quiet and peaceful Beijing in a few days, you would be running like hell to get on board that PanAm aircraft,' he thought to himself.

He watched them pass through into the Departure Lounge. He planned to wait until the aircraft lifted off, then enjoy the great weight that would be lifted from his shoulders.

At 10:45 a.m., he saw the Boeing 747 lumber away from the gate. It turned on to the active runway, stopped and roared its engines as though defying gravity to try and hold it back. The pilot released the brakes and the jumbo slowly gathered speed as it raced down the tarmac then climbed effortlessly into the blue sky.

* * *

Drew felt a stirring in his loins. He was starting to achieve an erection. Maybe it was the rhythm of the bus, a common culprit, or perhaps it was the anticipation of being alone with Erin without having to worry about the Simpson Construction Company or anybody else.

One of the bus drivers who had taken the group to the airport had been instructed to wait and take Drew back to the Great Wall hotel. The ride gave Drew time to think pleasant thoughts which soon gave way to somber ones about the explosion that was about to erupt in another couple of days.

He thought about the students and their determination to bring democracy to their country, no matter what the cost. And the cost would be considerable. There would be hundreds of thousands and maybe millions of deaths. And despite the students' confidence, no one could predict the outcome. Would most of the army join them? Everything depended on that. Or would the soldiers once more be loyal to a government that most did not respect and all feared? Whichever way it went, one thing was sure: there would be much suffering and pain, and there would be blood spilled. China's history was full of terror, its pages were etched with the blood of its heroes and villains. And there were certainly plenty of both.

The scenery rushing past the windows of the bus was that of a tranquil landscape. A few people were in the fields harvesting vegetables, a few others were walking to business and social obligations. The ubiquitous tractor-like device could be seen every so many hundred yards with the driver lazily sprawled out on the metal chair, resting his legs on the spindly connecting rod.

Over to the west, a huge plume of black smoke smudged the pale blue sky. A fire, perhaps, or maybe it was someone burning a lot of garbage.

They passed an apartment building and some children were laughing and chasing a dog that was much too agile to be caught.

Suddenly, short staccato noises rent the air. They sounded like firecrackers. Drew mindlessly surmised that it must be some sort of celebration. He was watching a thin, emaciated little man with a wispy beard and wearing a knitted skull cap pull a two-wheeled cart full of scrap metal. The man looked as though he would have trouble just walking never mind pulling a cart whose piled contents looked very heavy.

The bus stopped at a light, the first they had encountered since leaving the airport. Some people were running down a street, shouting loudly. Others were rushing after them as though hurrying to join the crowd. Maybe it was an automobile accident, he thought. Strange how people love to watch crumpled autos or smashed bikes to see if there has been any blood splashed on the ground.

Blood spilled! 'My God,' he stiffened as a thought occurred to him. 'Has the revolution begun? No, surely not. The committee said it would be deferred until I had left Beijing. Surely it must be something else.'

The light turned green and the bus moved forward. The driver, suddenly wild-eyed, shouted something in Mandarin at him. 'What is he saying?' Drew wondered. The driver made some gesticulations with one hand as the other held on to the wheel of the bus.

He was not making any sense, but it was obvious that something had disturbed him. Without warning, he pulled the bus to the side of the road and shouted once more at Drew while waving his arm in a sweeping motion. He opened the bus door and ran off, leaving the engine running.

'It's true,' Drew murmured to himself. 'It's the revolution; it's started.'

He had driven often enough to and from the airport that he had a good sense of the direction to the Great Wall Hotel, and he decided to run towards it. He figured it was about a mile or maybe a little more.

Turning a corner, he saw four policemen beating a young man with their sticks. The man fell to the ground, blood spurting from a severe gash on his forehead while they continued to swing their sticks with abandon. One of the police shouted something and all four took after another man who had come upon them accidentally. The man quickly stopped, turned and tried to run away. Just as the police caught him, a crowd of about 30 others appeared and surrounded them. The people were armed, not with sticks, but with guns.

Several shots rang out and the four policemen crumpled to the ground.

Drew took a detour. He had no desire to stop and discuss the situation with the assailants, not that he could anyway, having no knowledge of Mandarin. As he ran, bystanders shouted to him. Drew surmised that they must be friendly gestures because there would be no reason for them to be mad at him, a Caucasian. He was not a government official, something that would be easy for them to see. He was a foreigner and this was an internal problem.

He was panting. He slowed down and walked for a short distance before resuming a trot. Two men shouted at him and waved their sticks threateningly. For a moment, it appeared that they would run after him, but decided against it.

'Why should they be so upset at me?' he wondered. He was determined now to keep his head down and avoid any direct visual contact with anyone.

He saw the huge tower of the Great Wall hotel. He was now out of breath. He stopped and held his side for a few moments because of a sharp pain, but there were people all around. He had to keep moving forward until he reached the safety of the hotel.

About a hundred yards to go. He was reduced to a labored walk, still holding his side to relieve the sharp pain. Fifty yards to go. It looked as though he had made it.

He turned the corner and his heart almost stopped. There was a barrier set up and about a hundred young men and women were manning it, preventing anyone from entering or leaving.

He walked towards them. Surely one of them could speak English or have some understanding of the language. Perhaps he could tell them he was a guest in the hotel and they would let him through.

He walked slowly to the barrier, reaching for his room key. One of the men stopped him. 'I am a guest in the hotel," Drew said softly because the pain in his side was still hurting him. He brandished his room key and asked that he be permitted entry to the hotel."

"Nationality?" the man asked.

"I'm American," he answered. "Let me show you my passport." He reached his hand inside his coat and another man lunged at him, pulling Drew's hands behind his back.

"What's going on here?" he asked. "What are you doing?"

"We have revolution has stated. You in very dangerous area," the man holding his arms said.

"Then, please let me pass to the hotel. I have nothing to do with your revolution."

"You American you say? Did you help us in last revolution? No, your president wants to resume relations with those pigs who have suppressed our people and ruined our country with their idiotic schemes and stupid ideology."

Drew was thinking how well this young Chinese man spoke English when a female voice, angry and excited, intruded. Drew heaved a sigh of relief when he saw that it was Erin. She spoke Mandarin to the young man. There was animated conversation back and forth for almost three minutes when the man holding Drew's arms released them.

"Come with me," Erin said as the man opened the barricade to let them through.

"What was that all about? What did you say to them?"

"There is still a strong feeling among the students that the Americans have sided with the government and that the U.S. doesn't care what happens to the students or democracy or China. I told them that I was a member of the Revolutionary Committee and threw a few names at them. I also told them that you had played a major part in assisting our committee. I also passed along some secret code words."

"Erin, what the hell happened? I thought the revolution was being delayed until the day after tomorrow."

"I don't know what started it. Nobody knows. It suddenly erupted and there are fights going on all over Beijing. The students are very well armed so perhaps somebody shot a bullying policeman and the anger spread. We've been distributing weapons all around the city and the students are anxious and ready for the fight. Maybe one of them could not stand the cruel behavior of an official and shot him. Who knows?"

"Drew, you have to get to the U.S. embassy now. Don't go to your room to pack'; you must come with me now. The fight has only begun. It's going to get much worse. We have dynamite, grenades, bazookas and the latest rifles and machine guns. It's going to get rough."

"What about you, Erin? Am I just supposed to run for cover while you shoulder your rifle and go off to kill the enemy? How do you think that makes me feel?"

"Stop trying to be a damned, stupid hero, Drew. This is my fight, it's not yours. The people don't really know what role America has played in all this. You saw those students at the barricade. They would just as soon have beaten you as let you go through. If I hadn't been here to explain to them what you have done for us, you might very well be lying over in that field with a bullet in the back of your head. I love you. I want to see us both live, but it won't happen if you continue to be pig-headed. Please have faith in me and do as I say."

They ran around the side of the hotel, through a field and on to a road. A black car was parked at the corner. "Do you know how to start a car without a key?" Erin asked.

"Sure, every American kid knows how to do that," he replied. The doors of the car were not locked, so they got inside and Drew located the necessary wires. He touched one with the other and the car coughed several times before it caught.

"If I were a car doctor, I'd say this auto had a very bad asthmatic condition," Drew joked as he walked to the driver's side.

"No, let me drive," Erin said as she slid behind the wheel. I know the way and it's much easier than shouting directions to you. Keep your eyes open for anything that looks like trouble."

The car had no real power. It moved slowly down the street at about 25 miles an hour, gradually gathering speed until it was covering ground at the rate of 35. The streets were filling with people and it was becoming increasingly difficult to weave around them.

A shot rang out and the car became uncontrollable. The clunk, clunk noise told him that a tire had blown, probably the result of the gunfire they had heard.

Abandoning the car, Erin grabbed his hand and ran down a narrow side street. Ping, ping, ping. Pieces of concrete from the buildings were falling as bullets whacked the apartments on both sides of them.

'Dammit," Erin shouted. 'We're caught in the middle of a gun fight. The army is on one side of the street and the students on the other."

They jumped out of the car and she pulled him into an alley and they ran for their lives, not stopping until they had reached the end.

"You said 'army'," he shouted between breaths. "Didn't the army join your cause?"

"It's too early to say. These are probably soldiers based in Beijing. The army we're relying on is based outside the city. I don't know what is happening. This has all caught me by surprise. We had a carefully thought-out plan but it's obviously been disregarded due to the early start to the fight. I don't know if our committee is directing the revolution or if they are, like me, still trying to get organized."

As they turned the corner, a group of several hundred students was approaching. They saw Erin and Drew and shouted to them to stand still. As they neared, Erin spoke to them in Mandarin, but this time she withdrew an armband from her inside pocket and showed it to the students.

They talked back and forth before Erin said: "I explained again who I am and what you have done for our cause. They are assigning a dozen students to help us get to the embassy. It will be safer with a guard in case we encounter police or renegade soldiers."

Drew's heart was palpitating. He had never been in a situation like this before in all his travels. Once, in Puerto Rico, he was caught in the middle of a very nasty strike that turned to violence. Some shots had been directed at the group's hospitality desk and damaged a marble wall behind it. The shots were obviously not meant to harm him but to warn him that he should vacate the premises immediately. He took the hint and moved his group out of the hotel. But this was different, much different. He was in the middle of history in the making. He should have been afraid, but instead, he was hyper from the tension.

Moving at a fast trot, the students led them down two blocks before turning right into a secluded area. It was an unusually quiet street with no movement and no noise other than distant, muffled gunfire.

"The people are afraid and are staying in their homes," Erin said. "It's better this way. We can make greater progress."

She had no sooner finished the sentence, when a shot rang out and one of the students fell. His white shirt bore a huge crimson stain. The nearest cover was the entrance to an apartment building, about 50 yards away. As they ran for the opening, three more students fell from the gunfire.

"Bastards," Erin shouted. "There are soldiers in the building across the street."

As they entered the apartment building, the students regrouped. 'Give me a gun," Drew demanded. "I don't like feeling naked, and certainly not this way."

He was handed an AK-47 assault rifle capable of firing 600 rounds a minute. "I have a feeling those soldiers are going to come after us. They will probably assume that we'll be running as fast as we can. If we do, they'll catch us. Let's spread out and take them as they rush after us through the back door."

The students saw the wisdom of his thinking and quickly agreed. A small hut stood in the middle of the common area at the back of the building. Four students ran to it and hid themselves inside the hut but positioned themselves behind two windows where they could clearly see anyone rushing through the doorway.

Several others ran into the grass that, fortunately, had not been cut in quite some time. Drew and Erin climbed one flight of stairs inside the building and positioned themselves at a window where they could watch the soldiers exit the back door.

'Why are you so sure they'll run into the back area? Don't you think they may assume we've run up the stairs and come after us?"

"No, they'll think that they've frightened us and that we'll run as far and as fast as we can from here."

He was right. A loud roar of voices mixed with thudding boots on the stone floor told them the soldiers were dashing through the back. When the noise abated and Drew was sure that they were all in the backyard, he opened fire from the window above them.

Six or seven fell immediately. Then the other students opened fire and the soldiers began falling like nine pins. Drew silently walked down to the first floor, his head against the wall to conceal himself and waited for any retreating soldiers. He heard the door slam shut then dashed into the open and sprayed bullets from side to side. In seconds, there was not one soldier left standing.

Erin was right beside him. He told her to let the students know that all the soldiers are dead and to hold their fire. She went to a window and gave the students the 'all clear'. Then they ran down the stairs, climbed over the dead bodies and into the backyard.

They regrouped and decided to move on to another street at the far side of the apartment complex. The street was tranquil, more tranquil, in fact, than any they had seen so far.

"How far, Erin?" he asked. "It's not that I'm anxious for us to get there, it's just that I don't want to see any more of your compatriots shot down in my behalf."

"We're close now. If we don't encounter any more opposition, we will be there in five minutes."

A loud roar could be heard from a nearby street. "It's tanks," said one of the students and they all took cover. "Oh, how I wish we had one of those bazookas," another commented. "We could immobilize them with little trouble."

"Erin was translating so that Drew could keep apprised of what they were saying. 'With kids like this fighting for you, Erin, I don't think you have too much to worry about. They've got guts."

"And so do you, Drew. I haven't seen you running away and hiding in some safe spot."

'Strange,' 'he thought to himself, 'I would have thought that I would have run away. It's amazing how you react when trouble hits. I guess no one really knows what they will do until the moment occurs.'

The tanks roared along the cross-street en route to action somewhere else. There were six of them.

One of the students jumped up and said: "I am going to get that last tank and that will be one less for our brothers to worry about wherever they're going."

Two other students tried to stop him, but he was too quick for them and ran after the tank. He caught up with it, grabbed something at the back of it and hauled himself up on to the iron monster. He steadied himself then pulled a grenade from his pocket. He pulled open the hatch, withdrew the pin and threw the grenade inside. He clanked shut the hatch but didn't have time to get clear. There was a loud explosion and the tank shook violently. When the smoke cleared, the student was lying on the ground, mortally wounded and the tank lay silent and crippled, incapable of joining the rest of the convoy.

Two of the students began to cry. 'A very human emotion,' Drew thought. He had an impulse to pull Erin close to him and wrap his arms around her when tears began to run down his own cheeks. She freed an arm and wiped away his tears with the sleeve of her shirt.

"Those are his brothers," she said. They have a right to cry.

"They are my brothers, too, now," said Drew, and I have a right to cry with them."

The student leader whispered a command and the students rose to follow him. The sun was low in the horizon and the light was fast disappearing. They walked past empty shops, occasionally seeing fellow students, also armed, on the other side of the street. They brandished their rifles in the air and waved frantically to each other, but seldom exchanged words.

"We are here," said Erin. She pointed across the street to a high, brick wall with several buildings enclosed. An American flag was dormant; there was no wind to let it proclaim that this compound was U.S. territory.

"We must say goodbye here, Drew. My war has begun and I must return to it."

"Erin, I thought you were coming with me. No combatant will enter the embassy grounds. You'll be safe there. What difference can one woman make in the millions of people who are going to be fighting?"

"You don't mean that, Drew. You know that I have to go. You know that if it means my life, I must go back into the streets and fight with my people. I want you to know that I love you. I have loved you from that moment when I first saw you on that darkened street near the Great Wall Hotel, brief though our meeting was. I have never been in love before and I didn't think there was such a thing as love at first sight, but I knew then and I know now that there is."

"If we succeed and our revolution brings the democracy we seek, please come back to China and find me. I'll be here and I'll wait for you."

Drew knew it was impossible to try to convince her to join him. She had a cause and there was no doubt of the fierce loyalty she had to it, highly dangerous though it may be.

Drew kissed her again and again as the students looked on. As far as he was concerned, he and Erin were alone. The war was thousands of miles away. There were only the two of them, embracing fiercely in a last farewell.

She stepped back and looked at him. The tears were rolling down her cheeks. "Goodbye, Drew. I do love you."

He watched as she and the students swiftly retraced their steps. When they reached the corner, she turned and stood there for a few seconds, then slowly raised her hand, waved it twice and was gone.

CHAPTER FORTY

SAN FRANCISCO, CALIFORNIA

The chartered United Airlines aircraft coasted up to the jetway at San Francisco's international airport. The front door opened and swung to the side as the gate agent lifted the microphone from its cradle inside the cabin.

"Ladies and gentlemen, United Airlines welcomes you home from your unpleasant ordeal in China. I have to tell you that there are scores of newspapermen and television reporters gathered in the waiting area. They are looking for willing passengers to give them accounts of your personal tribulations. If you do not wish to be interviewed, may I suggest that you ignore their pleas and push ahead until you are clear of them."

The passengers quickly moved out of the aircraft and strode up the ramp to the terminal. Drew had been seated at the back of the 'plane and when he reached the end of the ramp, it appeared that each of the press had found someone eager to relate the horrors they had experienced. People were being questioned on live television and strobe flashes indicated that many of his fellow passengers would be on tomorrow's front pages.

He walked smartly to United's private club, the Red Carpet Room, and pressed the button for entry. A buzzer sounded unlocking the door and he proceeded to the desk inside to show his membership card.

His next stop was to a bank of telephones. He wanted to call his office and inform Cole Tennant that he was safely home. Drew knew, of course, that Tennant was well aware of the success of the program as Sandi Wallace and Lois Friederich would have already given him a complete report. But, of course, Tennant would be more anxious to hear from him and to know that he was safely on American soil.

Drew's office had been in touch with both of Minnesota's U.S. Senators to ask their help in ascertaining whether he was safe and to do everything possible to get him out of China.

His company had been quickly notified that he was safe in the U.S. embassy and that he and hundreds of other citizens would be flown out of Beijing in a specially-chartered United Airlines flight.

"Cole, it's Drew. Just thought I'd call and tell you that the trip went well and . . ."

"Don't be a smart-ass, Cummins. We were worried shitless about you. We've been on the 'phone to Senators Carlson and Jensen, to the State Department and just about everybody else we could think of to find you and get you back safely. "Seriously, we're glad you're home. We got word from a State Department official that you had made it to the embassy safely."

They talked for half-an-hour with Drew assuring Tennant that he had hitched a ride from the hotel to the embassy and that the diplomats had done a superb job of arranging a hasty exit from Beijing.

"Drew, take a couple of days off, hell, take a week off. You deserve it. Relax at home and when you feel like it, come in and we'll talk some more. By the way, you're a real hero. All the girls were wettin' their pants when they heard you were still inside China after the revolution broke out."

"Well, tell them not to get too excited. Nothing spectacular happened. Hell, I didn't even hear a shot. The embassy officials took very good care of me and all the others who made it to their compound. They kept us wrapped up safely inside a cocoon for almost three weeks until they felt it was safe to transfer us to the airport. Well, got to go, Cole. I'll call you in a couple of days or so. 'Bye."

His heart raced. Now he could put through the call he was anxious to make. He dialed the number in Washington D.C. and gave his access code. Less than a minute later, McShane was on the line.

'Welcome back, Drew. It's great to hear your voice. I learned almost immediately from the CIA Beijing that you were safe in the embassy. I put out a top priority call to them to locate you, but the message had not been out more than three hours when they notified me of your safety.

'You did a superb job, Drew. I regret that you got caught in the revolution. I didn't think it was scheduled to start for three or four days after you were supposed to leave. Do you know what happened?"

He relayed what had occurred from the contact at the zoo to seeing the snake tattoo and the resulting need to bring the date of the revolution forward.

"Looks like you're due some special recognition, young man. We've been unaware of any real details and were surprised that the fighting broke out as soon as it did. What you've just told me explains a lot of things. I'll send your information through to those agencies that need this report.

'Drew, I think it would be a good idea if we had a meeting so that I can debrief you personally. There may be more details I can get from you in a vis-à-vis meeting and it's imperative that we do it as soon as possible. When are you planning to be back in Minneapolis?"

"I'll be home tonight, but I'm exhausted, as you can well imagine. If you want to come in tomorrow, I'll be happy to meet with you, but Brendon, there's one big favor I have to ask of you."

"Ask it. If it's humanly possible, it will be done."

"I would be grateful if your people in Beijing can keep tabs on the young woman who was my contact in Beijing. Her name, you may remember, is Erin. That's her Anglo name. I haven't any idea what her real name is. She's very special to me, Brendon, and I think a lot of her. She has incredible courage and she saved my life. If it hadn't been for her, I would never have made it to the embassy. If there's any way you could keep me informed of how she's doing, I would sure appreciate it. I can tell you that she's a member of the Student Committee that planned the revolution and the one who met me at the zoo. I hope it's not too difficult for you to track her down. Is that too much to ask?"

"No, it isn't too much to ask, Drew. Rest assured I'll do everything I possibly can to meet your request. You've earned it. As you probably know, the fighting is still in progress and no one knows which side is winning. China has refused entry to the press, so news is difficult to obtain. Our embassy people have been monitoring radio and TV newscasts so we have a little information. But, of course, those communications are slanted to the government's advantage. Anyway, I suggest we meet at the same restaurant as we did last time, Murray's Restaurant, say about noon?"

"Brendon, I'll pick you up at the airport if you give me your airline and flight number. It's not a problem for me."

"OK, Brendon, it'll be Northwest flight 326 and I'll arrive at 10:10 a.m. See you then."

CHAPTER FORTY-ONE

MINNEAPOLIS, MINNESOTA

It had been twenty-four days since that painful moment when he had seen Erin disappear around a corner with the armed students in Beijing. It hadn't been two minutes since he last thought of her. He had dated many women before, even a few in his office, but he had never felt this longing before. All of his past affairs had been 'une affaire du lit', never 'une affaire du coeur.' But this time, a slim, dark-haired beauty of a Chinese girl had captured his heart. He was in love, deeply in love and the cause of his condition was on the other side of the world enmeshed in a war whose resolution was still undecided.

He showered and dressed in dark brown slacks and a white wool polo sweater. He wore a heavy car coat then set off for the 20-minute drive to the airport. He parked in a nearby 'cell-park' lot to await McShane's call when he arrived.

He was immersed in the Minneapolis Star Tribune newspaper when his cell 'phone rang. It was McShane, ready to be picked up, and three minutes later they were headed for Murray's restaurant in downtown Minneapolis.

Susan, McShane's secretary, had made a reservation for them and they were seated immediately on entering the restaurant.

The waiter took drink orders. Drew ordered a coffee but added that what he really needed was a good stiff drink. McShane laughed, said he deserved one, then he, too, ordered a coffee.

They both ordered the steaks for which Murray's is famous. 'It's so tender you can cut it with a butter knife,' it said in the menu.

"Normally, I'd say let's eat and socialize and we'll get down to business after we've eaten, but this is too important and too urgent for that kind of luxury," McShane blurted out, almost impatiently.

"You know, you really can cut this steak with a butter knife," Drew said. "I've heard Murray's advertising before, but never really thought that you could have a steak that could be devoured using only a knife."

"With all you've gone through, you're marveling at cutting a steak with a butter knife?" McShane asked incredulously.

They were on their coffee when he finished relaying all the incidents that had occurred in Beijing.

'That's quite a story. For someone who isn't even a hunter and who hasn't handled a rifle before, as you once told me, it's remarkable that you were able to shoot and kill soldiers so easily. Most people get sick the first time. You didn't feel anything then?"

"No, I didn't, Brendon, and it's strange to me, too. I guess I was so keyed up and was so conscious of Erin beside me and wanting to protect her that I didn't think anything of it. By the way, have you heard anything of her?"

McShane looked down at his coffee and stared at it for a few seconds, fidgeting with the spoon on the saucer.

"You have heard something, I can tell. What is it?"

"Drew, this is the moment I've been dreading. Erin's dead."

Neither man spoke. Drew's face turned an ashen color. He was looking straight at McShane who was still observing his empty coffee cup. He hadn't raised his eyes.

It was a minute before Drew broke the silence. "How did it happen?"

McShane continued to fidget with his spoon. 'After I spoke to you yesterday, I sent a coded message through to CIA Beijing. I asked them to check on her, giving them the information you gave me. I was surprised when they sent me a reply only two hours later.

"They said that the government radio reported that one of the quote principal architects of the student Committee, a woman unquote had been captured with a group of students armed with rifles and grenades. You left on the Tuesday; she was captured and executed about a week later.

The government soldiers who captured them found an armband in her pocket identifying her as a member of the organizing Committee. She had a student membership card in her pocket with her name on it. Her name was printed in the Beijing newspapers. The newspaper story reported that she and the students were . . . ." He didn't finish the sentence, finding it difficult to say the word.

"I'm sorry, Drew. I'm really sorry. You deserved a better ending than this one. I would have gone to any lengths to be able to tell you anything but that.

"Our office in Beijing heard on the radio that the Chinese authorities said that she was apparently known by the name of Erin, obviously a code name given to her by the western powers that had financed and fomented the revolution, and, as a result, the slaughter of Chinese civilians and soldiers alike. Typical propaganda.

"I really am sorry, Drew. I lost a brother in Viet Nam, so I know what you're going through. I only wish I could shoulder some of your grief."

"Thanks, Brendon. Let's get out of here."

McShane left money on the table to cover the bill and a tip and followed Drew out the door. "When is your return flight to Washington?"

"There are two or three available, so just drop me at the airport and I'll be able to get one without too much waiting. Or would you like some company for a while?"

"No, thanks. I have to take this ride alone."

He dropped him at the airport. McShane reached over to Drew behind the wheel and gave him a hug. "Goodbye, buddy. I'll be in touch."

* * *

He thought he would just drive around a while, and perhaps stop at Minnehaha Falls where he could have some solitude with only the cascading falls to punctuate the tranquility. It was his favorite spot when he needed some quiet to reflect or ponder a difficult situation. But he knew he was about to crumble and that he had better get back quickly to his apartment.

The tears were streaming down his face, almost obscuring his vision. Unconsciously, he wiped them away as he stared ahead at the fast-moving traffic, his mind filled with the vision of Erin as she waved that last goodbye to him. Pulling into the parking lot of his apartment building, he switched off the engine and sat in his car for several minutes, trying to collect his thoughts.

He swung the car door open and walked as though in a daze to the building. He opened the front door, almost as a reflexive action, and checked his mailbox. He could see there was quite a bit of mail inside. He turned the key in the lock and withdrew nine letters and three magazines.

Drew prayed that he would not meet anyone in the elevator; he didn't feel much like talking. He felt so drained that every step took a lot of effort. He closed the door of his apartment, threw his coat on a chair and dropped the mail on a table. One of the letters dropped to the floor.

He spotted Hong Kong stamps on the envelope and a jolt of energy revitalized him when he saw it bore Erin's handwriting.

He stopped to grab the envelope and feverishly tore it open to withdraw the letter.

His legs and hands were shaking as he sank into an easy chair and began to read:

> *My darling Drew:*
>
> *I don't know if this letter will reach you. One of our committee members is leaving for the coast to board a power boat and head for Hong Kong. We desperately need more help and he plans to meet with the taipans to ask for more money and weapons. It's a very difficult journey and few have made it before him.*
>
> *I have asked him to mail this letter to you from Hong Kong. If anything happens to him, he will have to destroy the letter and you won't be able to read it. Even if it doesn't reach you, however, writing it eases my pain. I feel I have to bare my soul and pour out my heart to you; my loneliness has become so heavy since you left only two days ago.*
>
> *"Drew, when we first met on that shadowy street near the Sheraton Great Wall Hotel, I must confess that I fell in love with you the minute I saw your beautiful face. Does that sound silly? Is there such a thing as love at first sight as I have heard it said? Your voice sounded so strong and self-assured and I could only catch glimpses of you in the darkness when you passed under the street lights, but I loved you even then. And when we approached an area illuminated by an overhead light, do you remember how I stepped to the side to remain unseen? You boldly walked through it and I caught my first real look at you. Oh how wildly my heart beat. We were together only a few minutes and I was hopelessly in love with you.*
>
> *"I thought of you endlessly until the joyous news came that you were coming back to Beijing and bringing money to help our cause. We were asked to have one of our people meet you at the zoo.*
>
> *"I volunteered immediately to be the one to bring you to the committee. I told the other committee members that I had met you before, so could easily recognize you. And when I saw you at the zoo*

that day, enraptured by the antics of the pandas, I watched you for several minutes before approaching you. I didn't think I could make my legs move to walk over to you, I was shaking so much.

"I had actually arrived at the zoo a full half-hour before our meeting. Just waiting to catch sight of you.

"You didn't realize how I felt at our first meeting, did you? Or did you? Is that why you kissed me so unexpectedly in the courtyard? When I first heard you say you loved me, I think it was the first time I wished I were not in my beloved China, but somewhere else in the world where we could be alone together and enjoy some time in each other's arms without the ugly specter of communism hovering over us.

"There is so much more I could say, but I must finish this letter and give it to my compatriot. He will be leaving on his own perilous journey in just a few moments.

"Drew, darling, more than I have ever wished for anything before, I pray that we are successful in our struggle to overthrow these tyrants who have destroyed our wonderful country. Then I will ask you to return to Beijing, to come back to me. Promise me that you will.

"You are so handsome. I try not to think that there must be many beautiful American women who feel the same way about you as I do. I was not just something to occupy your time in China, was I? You really do love me, don't you?

"Until the moment we are together again, I will keep saying to myself: 'Yes, Drew really does care for me as much as I care for him.'

"I must have these thoughts to help sustain me in the battles that lie ahead.

"Something just occurred to me. After all we have been through together and falling in love, I have just realized that you don't even know my real name. I want you to know it. I am called Xiao Shiying.

"I love you dearly, Drew. I love you deeply and passionately.

"All my love,
"Erin"

The letter slipped from his fingers and fell to the floor.

"Yes, Erin, I loved you. I loved you more than you will now ever know."

He fell back into the chair, covered his face with his hands and wept uncontrollably.

Breinigsville, PA USA
14 July 2010
241829BV00003B/74/P